Secrets of a Kept Chick Saga:

Renaissance Collection

Secrets of a Kept Chick Saga:

Renaissance Collection

Ambria Davis

www.urbanbooks.net

Urban Books, LLC
300 Farmingdale Road, NY-Route 109
Farmingdale, NY 11735

Secrets of a Kept Chick Saga: Renaissance Collection
Copyright © 2017 Ambria Davis

ISBN 13: 978-1-62286-554-3
ISBN 10: 1-62286-554-5

First Trade Paperback Printing February 2017
Printed in the United States of America

10 9 8 7 6 5 4 3 2 1

This is a work of fiction. Any references or similarities to actual events, real people, living or dead, or to real locales are intended to give the novel a sense of reality. Any similarity in other names, characters, places, and incidents is entirely coincidental.

Distributed by Kensington Publishing Corp.
Submit Orders to:
Customer Service
400 Hahn Road
Westminster, MD 21157-4627
Phone: 1-800-733-3000
Fax: 1-800-659-2436

Secrets of a
Kept Chick Saga:

Renaissance Collection

by

Ambria Davis

Mimi

I swear I was getting tired of Kay and all these late nights he pulling. If it ain't one thing, it's another. I was especially tired of him not being able to keep his dick in his pants. The shit was getting real fucking old to me. My man was a so-called ladies' man: twenty-seven years old, six foot two, with a light complexion, a well-built body, tight braids, and a face you'd only see on a magazine. My man was every bit of fine, and he knew it. There was not a place that we'd been where bitches weren't hanging all over him. That nigga was the shit, and he acted like it, but what my man failed to realize was that I didn't need his ass.

I had my own shit. I was the owner of several successful business ventures. When I say I had my own, I had my own. I could most definitely take care of me and my three on my own, without any help. I was twenty-six years old, five foot four, with smooth, dark chocolate skin, long jet-black hair, and a body to die for. People often said that I resembled the actress Stacey Dash, only prettier.

This nigga thought he was fooling me when he really wasn't. I might have pretended like I was quiet, but I was far from it. He actually thought I don't know about them little bitches he be playing with. Shit, I knew because a side piece would never stay in her place. They always had to make themselves known and shit, like they had to prove a point. I didn't do nothing but laugh at them. What they failed to realize was that they were the main reason why I was always knee-deep in his pockets. I got my hair done every Monday and sometimes on Fridays, and I rocked the baddest clothes and shoes. My whip was one of the sickest in Atlanta, not to mention the fact that I lived in a house with five bedrooms, three-and-a-half bathrooms, and a two-car garage. So, yes, I was living that life, the one those scheming heffas could only dream of. I could easily see why they were so envious. Thanks to Kay, I had it all, but like I said before, I had my own damn money.

So why was I in my bedroom, pacing the floor like a crazy woman at 2:35 a.m.? I'll tell you why—because I was up waiting on my fiancé to come home yet again. But this nigga really had me fucked up, though. I had no idea why I kept putting up with his shit. He was constantly out and about, like I wouldn't catch on. This nigga thought I was slow, or I didn't have a clue as to what was going on, but I actually did have a clue—a few of them, in fact—and I was tired of his ass.

You see, a man only does what his woman allows his ass to do, and I knew that I'd allowed him to do enough. I put up with a lot of his shit because I loved his ass. He was also a great provider and a great father. But enough was enough. I'd had just about all I could take. I had to put my fucking foot down.

"I swear, I've been calling his ass all night, girl," I said, talking on the phone with my friend Troy.

"I know, fuck all that, though. Shit, we're about to go looking for this nigga," she replied.

Troy was my down-ass chick, unlike most of the people we grew up with. We were like two peas in a pod; whenever you saw her, you saw me, and wherever one went, the other was sure to follow. We both came to Atlanta from New Orleans a couple of years ago, and all we had to lean on was each other. Troy knew me, and I knew her. That's why I called her. I knew she would be down for whatever.

"Well, bitch, where are you? Because I was going to do that anyway," I replied while changing into a pair of gray sweats and my white Air Nikes. I combed my long jet-black hair into a ponytail, just in case shit got real. I've had it with Kaylin and these simple bitches thinking they could continue to play with me. They obviously don't know who they're messing with.

I'll admit that I don't say too much, because I don't have the time to play with these hoes. After all, I'm already wifey.

This nigga wanted to play with me when I was the one that was there when he ain't had shit. I was the one going to school and working to support us when he went to jail, and to make matters worse, I was pregnant with our oldest daughter, Kailay. All that time, I held us down, but, nah, niggas like him don't be hearing or remembering all of that. They think that they can do whatever they want, but not in this day and age. I've fucking had enough, and this nigga gonna see just how much. I'm about to show him that you can't always have your cake and eat it too.

"I'm outside already, ma. Shit, once you started talking all that noise about some chick named Jade calling ya phone, saying Kay just left her house, I jumped in my car and came straight over," she stated.

I smiled. That's why she's my girl. I swear, my bitch was always down to roll, whenever I needed her.

"All right, let me grab my purse and keys right quick. Give me five while I lock up."

I walked out of my bedroom and down the stairs into the kitchen to get my keys and purse. Once I made sure that I locked everything up, I headed out the door to meet my friend. It was a good thing that my kids were with the babysitter, or I wouldn't have been able to leave.

I removed the spare from underneath the plant by the door, and then I headed toward Troy's car. Getting in the car, I looked over to see my friend was dressed almost like me. She was in a pair of black sweats with black Air Nikes.

"I swear we should've been sisters, because we're forever thinking alike and shit," I said laughing.

For a minute, I was actually happy, because I hadn't smiled all day.

"Shit, I know and you know what they say . . . Great minds think alike," she replied while backing out of the driveway onto the streets.

We were both quiet for a minute, lost in our thoughts.

"So, Mimi, what you want to do?" she asked while stopping at a red light.

"Hmm, first we're going to stop at this gas station right quick, so I can get me some Phillies. Then we're going to smoke a nice, big, fat-ass blunt. After that, I'm going to go and find my nigga, and then put my foot up his ass. Who knows, I might even have to put my foot up a bitch's ass in the process too," I replied, as she pulled into the gas station parking lot.

"You need some gas or something while I'm in there?" I asked while getting out of the car.

"No, I don't need any gas, but you could catch me some Kools, a fruit punch, and some Skittles," she replied while reaching for her cell phone. I swear she stayed with a hotline.

"All right, girl, I got you."

As I got out of the car to go into the store, I pulled out my iPhone and tried to call Kaylin's dawg ass again. But just like earlier, his phone went straight to voice mail. I was really pissed, and this time I decided to leave him a message.

"Say, bitch, I promise if you don't answer this muthafucking phone before I find you, you and whatever bitch you with will regret it. The fuck wrong with you, nigga? You trying to play me for some bird, bitch? Like I'm supposed to sit back and watch you do you and not say anything? Humph, well, I got some news for your bitch ass, though. When, and if, I catch you, I'm going to fuck both of you muthafuckas up, and that's on everything that I love," I said, ending the call.

As I was walking, I bumped into this sexy chocolate stallion. I mean, this nigga was fine as all outdoors and shit. That nigga looked every bit like Daniel Gibson, the basketball player, but he was way better looking, and he was thicker too.

"Umm, excuse me, my bad," I said, as I dropped my phone, cracking the screen.

"No, it was my fault, sexy. Let me get that for you," he replied, showing off his perfectly clean white teeth while handing me my cracked up iPhone.

"Damn! My fucking phone," I said, getting mad at Kaylin all over again.

This nigga really don't know how he's on my shit list. If he was anywhere in sight, I swear I was going to jail for murder.

"My fault, li'l mama. Take my number so we can get you a new phone tomorrow," he stated while looking down at me.

One thing I loved was a tall, well-toned chocolate man. The fact that he had dreads made me wet, and I forgot about Kaylin's ass completely.

"Umm . . . That's okay. You really don't have to buy me a new phone. I could get my own device, partner. I needed a new one anyway," I responded, shifting my weight from one foot to the next.

"I insist. Besides, I don't want you fucking me up if I don't replace what I broke," he joked, but I was embarrassed because he'd overheard my phone conversation.

"Oh, I take it that ya overheard my phone conversation earlier, huh?" I asked while walking into the store. He followed right behind me.

"Yeah, what's a pretty woman like you doing with a mouth like that?" he asked me. I looked at him without saying a word as I got two Arizonas out of the cooler. If only he knew what I knew, I thought to myself.

I turned toward him. "I'm not always like this. I'm the nicest person that you'll ever meet. It's just that my nigga think I got time to fuck around with his cheating ass, but I don't. I'm getting too old for all of that shit," I said while walking to the counter to get some Phillies, a pack of Kools, and some Skittles.

"Let me know what kind of nigga would want to cheat on you," he said. Then he said, "Let me pay for that," he insisted while retrieving a wad of cash from his pocket.

I stood there, looking stunned . . . not because of the money, but because he didn't know me from a can of paint, and yet he was being a complete gentleman.

"Obviously, my nigga wants to cheat on me, and thanks," I replied, signaling for him to follow me out of the store.

We walked over to Troy's car. I handed the bag over to her and then turned to face the dark, sexy stallion.

"We've talked for damn near twenty minutes, and I still don't know your name, sir," I stated, as I folded my arms across my chest, looking up at him.

"Sorry, gorgeous. My name is Jayden, but you can call me Jay," he replied, extending his hand out for me to shake it.

"Amina, but you can call me Mimi," I stated, shaking his hand. "Let me see ya phone, Jayden," I asked.

He handed it to me. I programed my number in it and then handed it back to him.

"I'm about to call, so you can have my number too," he said, as my phone began to ring, showing his number. I saved it and turned to say thanks, but the sound of Li'l Boosie stopped me dead in my tracks. The sight of a white-on-white Camaro halted my words before they could come out.

"I can't believe this nigga. He got a lot of fucking nerves," I huffed while getting Troy's attention.

"Bitch, do you see this shit? This one stupid, bold-ass, fucking nigga here," I said to her, as she walked over to me.

"Girl, he too damn bold for me. Let's go fuck him up," she replied quickly.

"Wait! Hold on right quick, Troy, let me see something first," I said, pulling her behind me.

The nigga didn't realize that I was even out there. *Sad-ass nigga don't ever be on point,* I thought to myself. In the midst of everything that was going on, I had quickly forgotten about Jayden. That's how bad my fucking nerves were.

"What's going on, Mimi, who's that nigga?" he asked with a confused look plastered on his face.

"Shit, that's my no-good-ass nigga, and you can obviously see that he has some bitch in the car with him. So what do you think?" I said, looking at him.

He didn't even have enough time to reply as I walked off and approached my nigga's car with Troy following closely behind me. I went over to the driver's side and got in. As I stared at this high-yellow bitch that was seated on the passenger's side, all I could do was shake my head. I proceeded to take my house keys off Kay's key ring.

"Ummm, who the fuck is you?" this bitch had the nerve to ask.

"Oh, bitch, you ain't know? I'm Mimi. Shit, before this very moment I was Kaylin's fiancée, but since he fucking with a bird bitch like you, you can have him, darling."

Her dumb ass just sat there, looking like a fucking fool.

"Bitch, who do you think you're talking to like that?" she asked, pointing her finger and rolling her neck.

The bitch wasn't on point either, because if she was, she would've seen Troy outside her door ready to stomp her, but before she could turn around, Troy dragged that ass out of the car, and I got out.

"What? Y'all bitches are going to jump me?" she asked, looking from me to Troy.

"Bitch, do I look like the jumping type? First, I'm going to let Mimi whoop that ass, and then I'm going to whoop that ass," Troy said angrily.

"Bitch, pl—" Before she could finish her sentence, I was on that ass like white on rice. The bitch had a loud-ass mouth, but her hand game was way off. I gave her one of them old-fashioned ass whoopings; you know, like the kind when your mama be talking to you while beating you at the same time.

"Bitch, don't fucking play wit' me," I said, as I pounded her face with my fist.

"Bitch, first, you go fuck my man, then you wanna talk reckless to me?" I yelled while giving that ho a two-piece combo to her face. I was so mad that I didn't see the crowd that had formed around us.

"Bitch, bitch, bitch, bitch, bitch," was all that kept coming out of my mouth as I gave that ho a good ol' Louisiana ass whooping.

Every ounce of negative emotion and built-up frustration that I had in me, I took it out on her. I was so into it that I didn't notice Kay until he grabbed me up off of the bitch.

"What the fuck, Mimi?" he asked, looking mad as hell.

"Don't 'what the fuck, Mimi' me, nigga. You should've answered your fucking phone when I called ya dog ass. I told you that I was going to fuck y'all up—you and whatever ho you had with you. What, nigga, you thought I was playing?" I asked as I started swinging on his bitch ass.

I couldn't stand his stupid ass. For every bitch that he cheated on me with and every night that he stayed out, I gave him a lick. I was so wrapped up in trying to whoop this nigga's ass, I was oblivious to the fact that Troy was over there whooping ol' girl's ass. I had completely blacked out, and then all of a sudden, I looked around, and I was on the ground. I couldn't believe this nigga had just pushed me.

"Nigga, I know you ain't just put your fucking hands on me," I said through gritted teeth.

"The fuck was I supposed to do? You shouldn't have put your damn hands on me," he replied.

"Pussy-ass nigga," I yelled, getting ready to charge his ass, but I was stopped in midair.

"Say, Mimi, don't do this out here no more, ma. I'm pretty sure them Chinese people done called the police already," Jayden said. Just as he said that, I could hear police sirens in the distance.

"Who the fuck is this nigga here?" Kay asked, pointing to Jayden.

"Fuck you trying to check me for, nigga! Don't try to act like I didn't catch your doggish ass red-handed. Kiss my ass, you lame-ass bitch," I hollered, trying to go at his ass again. I couldn't get at his ass like I wanted to because Jayden had a firm grip around my waist.

"Come on, Mimi, get ya girl and be out. I'm riding dirty so I got to go, but I'm not leaving until y'all leave first," he stated.

I looked at Kaylin and rolled my eyes at his punk ass. I didn't care if that nigga got arrested. Fuck him. I looked back at Jayden and nodded my head.

"Okay," I said and walked toward Troy.

"Mimi," Kaylin called out to me, but I straight ignored his ass and kept on walking.

"Troy, come on. Them people coming, and I ain't trying to get us put in jail," I said to her.

"Okay, coming," she replied, giving Kaylin's bitch one last kick.

As we walked to the car, I spotted Jayden and some cute light-skinned dude I didn't see earlier getting in an all-black Audi R8. I waved at him, and then we pulled off. Soon as we exited the parking lot, the police were turning down the street. Thank God we were leaving, because I wasn't trying to go to jail over Kaylin's dog ass. Fuck Kay, and I meant that shit. That nigga was dead to me.

Kaylin

Call me crazy, but I love the fuck out of Mimi. My girl is my heart. Without her, there's no me. I just can't seem to control the urge to fuck other bitches. Now, don't get me wrong. I knew I was fucking up, especially when I've got a good girl on my side, but I'm a man, and I'm going to do what niggas do—period. Every time I cheat on my girl, though, that shit eats away at me. I love her li'l short ass to death, and I'd kill her before I let her leave me.

You see, Mimi's the type of chick you'd wife. She got her own money, two degrees in business, she knows how to cook, and she's the perfect mother to my seeds. My girl is classy and beautiful, with the body of a goddess. So, yeah, I got a winner, but I also like to have my cake and eat it too. It doesn't help that there's countless chicks out there who be throwing themselves at me. Now, how could I deny all that?

I'm a great looking dude, and I keep a neat and trimmed goatee. My girl makes sure my braids get done every week. I also got a gym in my house, so I keep my body in shape. Yeah, my life is good, and yet, I'm the one who's fucking it up. Mimi and I got three kids together . . . my oldest daughter Kailay Janaé and my twin boys, Kaylon and Kayson. Kailay's eight and super smart, with a head full of jet-black hair that stops in the middle of her back, and chocolate skin. She's every bit of her mother, but she's a daddy's girl to the fullest. My twins, Kaylon and Kayson, are four years old and bad as hell, with light complexions and braids. My sons are every bit of me, but they're hooked to their mother. That don't mean that my kids are soft, though, because Mimi don't play that that shit. Whatever Louisiana installed in her, she installed in our kids. She rarely shows her ugly side, and I'm glad, because she's a force to be reckoned with.

***

Back in my hustling days, my best friend, Tyreek, and I got knocked, and we went to jail. When I was in the joint doing them three years, my girl went to school and worked, all while having a baby on her hip. She took care of me, made sure that I always had money on my books, and she visited regularly with my seed. Shit, by the time I was ready to come home, my girl was 'bout to walk across the stage to earn her associate's degree in business. She didn't stop there, though. She later went back to get her master's.

My woman's smart and good. Truth be told, sometimes I think she's too good for me, and I don't deserve her love. I do what I do so I can feel better about myself. One thing, though, the bitches that I fuck with know that I could never be their man, but that doesn't stop them from trying me. At times, all I could do was laugh to myself, because can't none of them compete with Mimi. That's why I have no idea how I got caught slipping. Her ass was supposed to be at the club that night. Oh, yeah, my girl owns a club called K3 and two hair salons. My bitch got her own paper. She ain't just sitting around trying to spend my shit, and I love that about her. I've tried to get her to fall back, but once a chick goes independent, she ain't turning back.

Anyway, back to the issue at hand. I'd been busy all day, and I was tired. Since I was on the other side of town, I stopped to lay down by this chick named Jade's house. I've been messing with Jade for about three months now, and she's been the one cooking up my work. She's just too damn needy for me, though. The broad forever got her hand out, and I sensed she was catching feelings. That's why I really didn't want to go over there. Besides being needy, she doesn't know how to stay in her place. A side piece should stay a side piece and play their role. Now, she knew from the beginning that I had a woman, so I have no idea why she let herself catch feelings for me.

I called her number as I drove down the street, and, as usual, the bitch answered on the first ring.

"What's up, Daddy?" she answered the phone in a sexy voice.

"What you got going on over there, ma?"

"Nothing, really, I just got back home. What's up?"

"I'm about to pass through, I'm tired as hell. I need to get a li'l nap in. Been on the road all day yesterday and this morning," I replied, as I pulled into her apartment complex.

"How far are you? Because I ain't cook nothing, but I could order takeout," she asked, as I exited the car and walked up to her door.

"Shit, I'm outside right now. Open up the door," I said and hung the phone up.

"Damn, I swear you took forever to open the door. What, you ain't want to see me?" I asked, smiling at her.

As I made my way into the living room, I noticed one of my young workers sitting on the sofa. I took a seat across from him, wondering all along what he was doing there.

"What up, homie? What you doing over here?" I asked, looking at him.

"'Sup, Kay? Shit, ain't nothing. Just chilling with Jade," he mumbled, looking from me to Jade.

I couldn't do nothing but shake my head at that ho. I couldn't believe she had the nerve to wonder why she could never be my wifey.

"Shit, I'm about to catch me some Zs. I'm dog tired and shit," I said, stretching and yawning at the same time.

"Oh, word? I'm about to leave," he said, standing up and heading toward the door.

"Don't leave on my account. Y'all have fun," I said, making my way to the guest room to get me some much-needed rest. I left they asses looking like two fools, right where they stood.

You could never turn a ho into a housewife, and Jade was a prime example, I thought as I drifted off to sleep.

I was so tired, but I woke up with half my dick down Jade's throat. I looked around to see that it was dark outside. A quick glance at the clock let me know that it was 9:15 p.m. Damn, I was really tired, but that head that I was getting gave me some kind of energy. This nasty bitch surely knew how to give some good-ass head. My dick was deep down her throat, and it was feeling too damn good.

"Oh, shit," I moaned.

I grabbed the back of her head and started fucking her mouth. All those slurping sounds were making me extra hot. I started pumping her face fast, because we'd already been at this shit for a good twenty minutes, and I needed to find my release fast.

"Get up," I told her as I stood up.

She immediately put her face down and ass up, just like I liked it. That bitch was a freak, and she had some good pussy. I slid into her and started off slow. Her pussy was sloppy wet, and it made my dick extra hard.

"Yes, Kay, give it to me like that," she squealed as I started to roll my hips.

"Fuck me, fuck meeeee," she kept repeating.

"Umm . . . Daddy, fuck me, fuck me," she begged, and I did just that. I fucked that bitch like there was no tomorrow.

She screamed out as she backed her ass up, which only made me fuck her harder. I reached rock-bottom in that pussy and fucked her like she stole something from me.

"You like that, bitch?" I asked, as I long stroked her.

"Yes, Kaaaaaaaaaaaaaaay!" she screamed.

I love the way she called my name. It excited the fuck out of me.

"You like this too? Take this dick, bitch," I growled, slapping her on her ass.

"Yes, Kaylin, I love it. Ohhhhhhhh, Daddy, I fucking love it. Give it to me, Daddy, fuck me oooooooh, just like that," she groaned, throwing that shit back hard.

"Ummm," I moaned, feeling my nut coming along.

"Yes, Daddy. Fuck me hard, just like that. Owww, don't stop. I'm about to come, Daddy," she moaned.

"Me too," I grunted, as I started pumping faster and faster. With each thrust, she forcefully threw that ass back. Soon after, I started releasing my seeds deep in her gut as she coated my dick like a glazed donut.

"Shit, I'm tired," she replied. I remained silent as I left to go put the shower on. When I came back, she was still lying there, stuck.

"Yo, I'm about to go take a shower," I said, walking back into the room to retrieve my small overnight bag.

"All right, you want something to eat?"

"Nah, I'm going to get something on my way home," I replied, and she sucked her teeth.

I swear I hate when them bitches get like that. I just gave her some grade-A dick. What more did she want? I had to tend to wifey. She came first before all these hoes. I couldn't leave my home lonely, or else I was going to find myself without a home. Period.

I took a quick shower and got out. When I walked in the room, this bitch had my phone in her hand.

"Yo, what the fuck?" I asked as I grabbed my phone out of her hand.

"Who the fuck is Star?"

"Why the fuck you looking through my phone, Jade?"

I was so mad that I ain't notice how fast I was putting my shit on. By the time I was finished, this bitch was sitting there looking stupid.

"Nigga, who the fuck is Star? You going to see that bitch later on, huh?" she asked, putting her hand in my face.

"Look, bitch, I ain't going see no-fucking-body, and get your fucking hand outta my face," I said through gritted teeth.

"It's bad enough that I got to share you with the black bitch. Now I got to share you with some bitch name Star too?" she said, as she backed up.

"Bitch! What the fuck I told you about disrespecting my fucking woman, huh?" I asked, jumping in this ho's face.

"Nigga, fuck you and her. You think I give a fuck about her, because I'm telling you now that I sure fucking don't. Talking 'bout disrespecting her—what you think you be doing when you fucking me, nigga, while she's at home spending ya money and taking care of y'all bastards?"

I looked at that bitch like she was crazy. I had to laugh to keep from hurting that crazy bitch. Did this ho just call my kids bastards? I could hurt her heart if I told her that my woman was her own boss and that she didn't need my money, but this crazy bitch didn't need to know everything.

"Bitch, don't worry about what the fuck I be doing to my woman. While you down here living like this, my woman lives in an upscale neighborhood. You live in an apartment, and she lives in a house. You roll around driving a Honda, while she's pushing a Benz and an Aston Martin. She birthed three beautiful kids, while me and every other nigga made ya bitch ass have an abortion. My woman has two college degrees, and you're a high school dropout. You're right. I'm disrespecting her by fucking you, because all you are is a good fuck. I make love to my woman, the mother of my children, and my soon-to-be wife," I spat at that bitch with venom.

If looks could kill, that bitch would be dead right now. Yeah, I know I was a li'l harsh, but I had to let that ho know. Don't anybody come before Mimi and my kids.

I guess I caught her off guard because the bitch ain't had shit to say.

"Stop stepping on my fucking woman, bitch. You over there wishing that you were half the woman she is," I continued, leaving her standing right where she was.

I started to finish her off and say, "You gonna regret you said that, bitch," but I didn't have time for all of this shit right now. I walked out and hopped in my car and headed to my side of town.

Before I could make it off of her block, she called me. I pressed the IGNORE button on that bitch. My phone was about to go dead, so I sent her a text and told her ass never to call or text me anymore. After that, I threw my phone in the seat next to me and turned up my music.

As I headed home, I got a call from Star, a chick I met a couple of weeks ago. Like most of the chicks I messed with, she was cute, but in no form, shape, or fashion could she hold a candle to Mimi. I met her at the mall one day, and I've been kicking it with her ever since.

"Hello," I answered.

"What's up, pimping? You still coming to see me tonight?" she asked.

"Star, I don't know if I'm going to be able to come through tonight. I just got back in town," I said.

My other line ended up beeping, indicating that a call was trying to come through. I took the phone away from my ear, to see that it was Mimi calling me. I let the call go to voice mail, thinking I was going to call her back once I was through with Star.

"No, Papi, you said that you were going to come see me tonight. I ain't seen you in two whole weeks. Don't do me like that," she whined, sounding like a big baby.

"All right, but if I come, I can't stay long," I said, looking at my phone to see that it was almost 1:00 a.m.

"All right, Papi," she replied, sounding disappointed.

Shit, I didn't care if I didn't get home soon. Mimi was gonna kill my ass anyway. Lately, I'd been giving these bitches too damn much of my time. That's the reason why I was always going home in the wee hours of the morning.

We hung up the phone, and I made my way to Star's apartment. When I pulled up, she was waiting outside. Star was a five-foot-seven chick with a high-yellow complexion, a skinny body with a li'l booty, and some C-cups. Like I said, she couldn't hold a candle to Mimi.

"What's up, ma?" I asked while giving her a hug.

"Shit, I'm chilling. I been waiting on you," she replied while hugging me back. "Come inside, I won't bite ya."

Unlike Jade's ass, Star had a real job, and her li'l crib was kinda laid out. Wasn't all that, but it was enough for her, I guess.

"You want to smoke this blunt with me?" she asked.

She didn't get to smoke often because of her job. So I joined in with her whenever she could.

"Yeah, put a movie on too," I replied, while she started to light the blunt. She ended up putting on *Boyz n the Hood*. I swear that's my favorite fucking movie.

Halfway through the movie, she tried to make a move, but I had to shut that shit down right quick. I had to go home to Mimi, and I was most definitely getting me some of her sweet nectar.

"Well, let's run to the gas station, so we could get us some Phillies and something to drink. My throat done got dry." She stood up and waited for me to answer.

"All right, come on let's go," I said and stood up.

We walked to my car and got in. I know I'm from the A, but that dude Li'l Boosie be off the meter with his mix tapes. Mimi got me listening to him, but I was cool with it.

I decided to take her to the gas station around my way. As I was driving, I noticed that my phone was almost dead. Shit, I knew Mimi had been calling me, but I'd forgotten my car charger in my truck. When I pulled up to the gas station, I noticed a bunch of people outside as I made my way into the store. I headed down the aisle to get a few things for Mimi, Star, and me.

As I got to the counter, I heard a bunch of loud noises, but I didn't pay it no mind. I was putting my things on the counter when the cashier pointed outside, which made me look. I saw some chicks out there fighting. I paid for my things and grabbed my bag.

I walked outside, and I couldn't believe my fucking eyes. I was shocked. Instead of some random chicks fighting, it was my girl and my side piece. I dropped everything I had in my hand and ran over to them. I swear Star looked a mess as I picked Mimi up.

"What the fuck, Mimi?" I asked. I was mad as fuck to see my woman out here clowning like that.

She totally went off on me about me not picking up my phone. She then charged at me, and the blows started raining all over me. I ain't gon' lie, my girl got a nice set of hands on her, and the shit was hurting. I had no choice but to defend myself.

"Nigga, I know you ain't just put your hands on me," she said.

"The fuck was I supposed to do? You shouldn't have put your hands on me then," I yelled, without thinking.

"Pussy-ass nigga," she said, trying to charge at me again, only to be stopped by some fuck boy.

The two of them had some words until I asked, "Who the fuck is this nigga?"

"The fuck you tryin'a check me for, and I just caught ya doggish ass red-handed. Kiss my ass, ya lame-ass bitch," she retorted, still trying to charge at me.

Dude stopped her again, and then he said something to her. She looked at me and rolled her eyes, then looked back and him and nodded. After that, she walked off.

I called out to her, but she kept on walking. That's when I noticed Troy beating on Star. Shit, I should've known her ass would be here. They rarely went anywhere without each other.

I watched my girl and her friend hop in the car. I thought it was safe, so I went to pick Star up off the ground. I looked back and noticed Mimi waving to somebody driving an all-black Audi R8. I looked closer; it was the same nigga who stopped her from attacking me.

Who the fuck is this nigga? I thought as I pulled off just in time to go unnoticed by the police. Making my way toward Star's house, we rode in silence. Being that I hated that silent shit, I turned my music up. Halfway through the ride, Star decided that she had something to say.

"Really, Kay, *that's* how you do?" she asked, staring at me.

"What?" I asked, catching major attitude.

"Man, you know what I'm talking about. How you just gon' let your bitch and her friend jump me?" she asked, screaming and shit.

I hated when a bitch can't take her lick, and they start playing the "I got jumped" card. She knew that my woman ain't jumped her ass.

"What the fuck you want me to say?" I asked, pulling in front of her building.

"I don't know—sorry, I guess. You let that black bitch and her friend jump me and you ain't going to say shit?" she spat, getting out of my car and slamming the door.

I really didn't give a fuck about her slamming the door. I hated when my pieces went to disrespecting wifey. I got out behind her to check that ass real quick.

"Look, I admit that she was wrong, but you know they didn't jump you. Everyone out there seen that shit, but check it out. You gon' have to watch your mouth when speaking about my lady," I warned as I walked behind her.

"Watch my mouth, huh? Have you forgotten that I never did shit to her? She came at me with it. I didn't go to her ass, now you gon' sit here and tell me to watch *my* mouth when I talk about *your* lady? Nigga, please," she said, as she tried to turn around to go inside. I reached out and grabbed her arm, stopping her in her tracks.

"Like I said, she was wrong for that, but don't you ever in your life talk about my lady like that in front of me again, ya hear?" I asked, before letting her go.

"Whatever, nigga, go home to your lady then."

"I plan to do just that," I spat back while walking back to my car.

I thought about everything that had just gone down. Mimi's crazy ass done went loco. I swear this shit ain't going to be nothing good. I grabbed my phone but then put it back down. Calling her was out of the question. Once you were on Mimi's shit list, nine times out of ten, you weren't coming up off of there. I pulled off, shaking my head as I realized what I had just done.

Mimi

I sat quietly in the car, thinking about what just went down, and I became lost in my own thoughts. As I thought of all the good times Kay and I shared, I began to tear up a little. Shit like that rarely happened. I was never the one to wear my emotions on my sleeve. I learned a long time ago, never show a man how you really feel, because he could use that against you. I was stuck in my own zone. Troy was rubbing my back, and the tears I'd tried so hard to hold back were actually falling. Once I realized that, I couldn't stop. They continued to flow like a damn river. I hated crying. To me, it showed a definite sign of weakness. The last time I cried was when I had to whoop Stacy's ass.

"Mimi, baby, it's going to be all right," she said, as she continued rubbing my back.

"Girl, you just don't know how tired I am," I sobbed.

True, I was indeed tired . . . of Kay, but that wasn't the only thing that had me tired.

"Shit, you need to kick his ass to the curb. You and I both know damn well that you'd be able to take care of you and the kids—without Kaylin's dog ass," she said.

"Girl, I will," I replied, not believing myself because I've been saying that shit for a good six months. The truth is that I never had a father figure. It was just me and my mommy. My father had left before I was born, and I never asked about him. What man in they right mind would leave before his child was born? Shit, I guess my daddy wasn't shit because that nigga left my mommy without batting an eyelash. All the shit that I've gone through in my life was because he wasn't man enough to take care of his responsibilities, and sometimes, I think my mother blamed me for him leaving her. The shit I went through in life, no one should ever have to go through, especially at the hands of their own mother.

My thoughts were interrupted by the ringing of my cell phone. I let it go to voice mail because I didn't want to be bothered. Whoever that was must really have wanted to talk, because they called right back. I had a feeling it was Kay. If it was him, I was not about to answer it. I looked at my screen and noticed that it was Jayden, the dude that I'd met earlier. A small smile crept across my face as I sat there thinking about him, and I decided to call him back.

"Hello," I said as soon as he picked up.

"Yo, ma, you all right?" he asked in a low baritone voice. I swear this man was making me forget about my problems at hand.

"I'd be much better if I could see you right now," I answered.

I swear I had no idea what made me say that, but the words left my mouth before I could think about what I was actually saying.

"Oh, yeah? Tell ya girl to pull over by the park over there," he replied, catching me off guard. I looked around to check out my surroundings.

"How do you know where I am?" I asked, feeling a little creeped out and curious at the same time.

"I followed y'all to make sure y'all were good," he replied.

I was about to ask if he was stalking me, but I decided against it.

"Okay," I replied, hanging up. I then told Troy to pull over by the park.

"What the fuck you mean pull over at the park? What you doing going to the park this late anyway?" she fussed while pulling over. I swear my girl was very overprotective at times.

"Girl, I'm about to meet Jayden. He's behind us in that all-black Audi right there," I replied, looking in the rearview mirror.

I pulled down her visor to make sure that I didn't have any tearstains on my face.

"Jayden? Bitch, who the fuck is Jayden?" she asked, getting all loud and shit.

This bitch had been so into fighting earlier, that she never really noticed Jayden.

"Girl, the dude that I met at the gas station earlier," I said, looking over at her.

"Oh, girl, that cute li'l dude who looked like Daniel Gibson, only better?"

"Yeah, girl, that's him."

I grabbed my purse to get some lotion and rubbed some on my face. Then I got out to meet Jay, but before I walked off, I bent down and said, "Bitch, he got a cute little light-skinned friend. You might want to jump on that."

"A'ight, but you know I don't normally meet people like this. Send him over here once you get over there," she giggled.

"Okay," I laughed and then walked over to Jayden, who was already waiting outside his car. Once I got over there, he introduced me to his friend.

"Mimi, this Mark, Mark, this Mimi." Mark was a cutie too. He had to be about five foot nine, light-skinned, with some dreads, and a cut-up body. Dude had it going on. He resembled a much lighter version of Trey Songz.

"Hey, what's up?" I spoke to Mark.

"Shit, ain't nothing up, Mike Tyson," he said laughing, throwing jabs at the air.

I laughed too, because he was obviously talking about what happened at the gas station.

"Shit, I ain't Mike, but I can definitely pack a mean punch," I said.

"Oh, I know that. Who that is over there?" he asked, nodding toward Troy's car.

"That's my friend, Troy. You should go say hi to her," I smiled at him.

"I was trying to get her attention at the gas station, but y'all wanted to box and shit," he replied laughing, revealing two dimples in his cheeks also.

Damn, these niggas are fine, I thought.

"Anyway, let me go see what's up with ya girl," he said before walking off.

I watched as he headed over to Troy's car and knocked on the window. He said something to her, and she spoke back, then he got in the car. I was happy to see my girl at least giving a nigga some attention, because I couldn't recall the last time I'd actually seen her with a damn man.

I turned around and stared at Jayden. Dude was really fine. He had me thinking all kinds of things, things I shouldn't have been thinking at the moment.

"See something you like?" he asked, flashing his million-dollar smile.

I started to say that I see someone I like, but I stayed quiet. I didn't want my mouth saying anything else I didn't want it to say.

"So what, you don't have anything to say?" he asked, shaking his head.

I kind of felt embarrassed and shit. There wasn't a nigga on this earth beside Kay, who could knock me off my square like that. Shit, I was speechless.

"Yeah, I was checking you out. So what?" I asked, suddenly becoming bold.

"Shit, I don't have a problem with all of that. Just as long as I can return the favor," he replied smiling. He was making me blush, like a schoolgirl meeting her crush. Here we were, two strangers openly flirting in the park at 2:30 a.m.

"I don't have a problem with that either," I said.

"So, Ms. Mimi, are you okay?" he asked.

"Actually, I'm all right. Could've been better, but I'm straight," I said and folded my arms.

Truth be told, the only reason I was feeling a little better was because he was right there. I was sure if I was out of his presence, I would go back to those feelings I had earlier, but he didn't need to know all that.

"Good, because I was wondering if I could take you out tomorrow," he said.

"I don't know. Tomorrow is Monday, and I have to be at my shop early. Mondays are my busiest days," I said.

Once a week, I'd stop by all my businesses to make sure that they were straight, not to mention that I also did hair at both of my salons. A heffa be beat on a Monday.

"Shit, what's the name of your shop?"

"Mimi's, why?" I asked.

"You talking about the shop next to Brother's barbershop?" he asked.

"Yeah, that's one of them," I proudly answered.

I was always proud of my shops. After all, I've come a long way to get where I am.

"Mad people be talking about your shop. I might have to come through and let you do what it do," he replied, laughing.

"I might be able to do that," I stated.

"What else will you be able to do?" he asked, obviously flirting.

"Hmm, what would you like for me to do?" I asked in a sexy tone.

"Well, there's a lot I would like for you to do, but first—" he became silent and pulled me into his arms.

He then kissed me. At first, I didn't return the kiss because I was caught off guard. But after a few seconds, I returned the favor. We kissed for what seemed like hours but was actually only minutes. I'm sure we wouldn't have stopped if it wasn't for my phone ringing. I pulled back and looked at my phone to see that it was Kay calling me.

"This nigga got a lot of nerves." I stood there, shaking my head.

I sent that shit to voice mail. I was about to say something when my phone started ringing again. I looked at it and noticed it was Kaylin calling again. I did the same thing I did before. I sent his ass straight to the voice mail.

"I'm sorry, handsome. Now, where were we?" I asked, pulling Jay close to me, but before my lips could touch his, my phone started ringing again. I swear this nigga was starting to piss me off all over again.

"You might want to get that," he said.

I shot him a dirty look and rolled my eyes at him.

"I wish the hell I would. You do remember what just happened, not even an hour ago, right?" I asked, with anger in my voice. I was getting mad with him for telling me to answer that shit.

"Hey, don't get angry with me. I'm just saying, maybe it's important," he replied, throwing his hand up as if he surrendered.

I had to check myself. I mean, why was I getting mad with him? He has been nothing but a complete gentleman, and here I was trying to fuck shit up before it happened.

"Look, Jay, my bad for screaming at you and shit. I didn't really mean to. You just caught me off guard with that shit, but I'm 'bout to bounce on outta here," I said.

I sent Troy a text, letting her know that I was ready to go. As I turned to leave, Jay stopped me.

"It's cool, ma. I know you mad and all, but don't let that nigga get to you like that. From what I've seen so far, you're a real cool and down-to-earth chick, and I like that about you. I wanna get to know you a whole lot better," he said, letting go of my arms.

"I'd like nothing more than getting to know you also, but things are really complicated right now. There are a lot of things that I have to take care of," I said, backing away.

"While you're taking care of everything, tell me, who's going to be taking care of you?" he asked, stopping me in my tracks.

Shit, how could I respond to his question when I didn't even have an answer? I came up with the only thing I was able to say.

"I can take care of myself. I've basically been doing it my whole life."

"Let me take care of you, Mimi," he said.

The way he said it made me swallow real hard. Beside Troy and my kids, I think this was the first time someone actually showed concern for me.

"I don't know, Jay, I just met you. I'm already going through some shit right now. I don't have time to be adding another nigga into the equation."

"We don't have to start off like that, Mimi. Let's be friends, take things slow. I'm not like your man. I wouldn't do you like that, ma. Let me be here for you," he said.

I really had to think about this. I mean, I didn't even know dude like that. For all I know, he could be a serial killer or something. He was cute and all, but I've learned from Kay that everything that glitters ain't gold. I was already in a fucked-up situation. I was not trying to go down that road again.

"Let me think about it. Give me some time," I said. I wasn't too sure of what I was about to do.

"Okay, that's fine," he replied.

I wanted to say something, but then I noticed Mark walking up. I said good night to him, then headed to Troy's car. I couldn't even get in the car good enough before she started talking shit.

"It's about fucking time. Bitch, what took you so damn long? Kay's been blowing my phone up. I had to power the shit off before Mark went to thinking that I had a man and shit," she laughed as we left the park, headed in the direction of my house.

"Shit, he was blowing mine up too, but I don't have time for Kay's ass. I'm about to do me," I replied, serious as a heart attack.

"Now, *that's* what the fuck I'm talking about," she said, pulling up in front of my house.

I reached for the blunt that we'd rolled, and then lit it. I let the smoke fill my lungs and then lay back. I didn't know my plans as of yet, but I did know I wasn't about to be anyone's fool anymore. If Jayden knew like I knew, he'd better come correct.

Troy

Now, normally, I didn't say shit, but things between Mimi and Kay have been real crazy lately. Mimi is my girl, and I would go with her to the end, which is why when she left Louisiana, I left with her. We were supposed to be coming down here to start over fresh, but Kaylin's ass was always in some shit. To be honest, I don't know how they lasted this long. If you asked me, she should've been left his ass a long time ago. I was ready for my girl to finally open her eyes and see that he really ain't shit, because if they kept this up, somebody was going to get hurt. It would really hurt me if something was to happen to her.

You see, Mimi and I grew up pretty much alike. Went through the same old bullshit, did almost the same shit. Only thing is, Mimi was an only child. She never knew her father because he left before she was born, which was why her mother had put her through hell. I, on the other hand, have two brothers and a sister I've never known. My mother was all fucked up and shit, so I never really fucked with her like that. I knew my father, but not in the way I should have. My father was a heartless man. He had to be for the shit he did to me. One night while I was asleep, my father came into my room and started touching me. I didn't think much of it because I was so young. Well, one day turned into weeks, weeks into months, and months into years until I got out. I graduated and left with Mimi, which was the best thing that ever happened to me. That's why I'd do anything for her . . . not because I feel obligated, but because I love her, and she's family.

When we first came out here, everything was great. Mimi went back to school and got another degree. I, on the other hand, held down a job. Then, Mimi came up with this brilliant plan to invest her money in some real estate. That's how she ended up with the club, followed by the salon. Her salon was doing so good that she had to open up a second one, with me being the manager and all. And to top it off, she did it all with Kaylin's money. I ain't saying that my girl was a gold digger, but she most definitely wasn't fucking with no broke nigga.

Like most men, though, Kay had always been a player. He played Mimi when she was in Louisiana, but what he didn't expect or even know was that Mimi played his ass back. This was why she ended up leaving Louisiana, with hopes of starting off fresh. He ended up coming with her. Kay really thought that he was the only one cheating, but he got another think coming. Once Mimi found out about all the chicks he was messing with, she sought revenge. The straw that broke the camel's back was when Mimi found out that Kay had slept with our childhood friend, Stacy. Now that wasn't right at all, because he knew what the girl had been through. Hell, he was the one who ended that situation for her. So I don't see how he could've done some shit like that, but to each his own, I guess.

Mimi just brushed it off as if it was nothing. Well, that's what I thought until—well, until she did what she did. I couldn't be mad either. An eye for an eye summed it all up. What neither I nor Mimi expected was for her blast from the past, or her secrets, to resurface. She'd been paying him to keep their secret hidden. Like people say, though, what's done in the dark comes to the light. I hoped my girl came out on top, but either way, I was going to be right there with her.

Kaylin

I'd been calling Mimi's phone ever since I left Star's apartment, but she didn't answer me once. I knew she could be a li'l stubborn and shit, so I decided to call Troy's phone instead, but she wasn't answering either. I hated when that shit happened, and that's why I been trying my hardest to keep that shit separate from my life, but I guess I wasn't trying hard enough. Shit had really been crazy out here, so crazy that I was starting to wonder if it was all worth it. I mean, I already had my money stacked, a good business, and my family. It had me wondering why I was still doing all this in the first place. Between working, my side pieces, and my woman, shit, I'd be beat. I barely had enough time to spend with my family. It had been a minute since Mimi had caught me slipping. The last time I got caught messing around was when I was messing with Stacy, and that was a very long-ass time ago. Speaking of Stacy, I swear she'd been getting on my last fucking nerves. Matter of fact, if it wasn't for my son, her ass would've been cut the fuck off. She was starting to get too needy and demanding. I had no idea why I moved her ass up there in the first place, because if Mimi found that shit out, it wouldn't be anything nice.

You see, Stacy and Mimi were close friends back then, but it was cut short because of Stacy and me having a relationship. It was kind of fucked up too, because they were supposed to be good friends, but you know everyone has a "supposed-to-be" friend, who secretly be hating. For Mimi, Stacy was the one. To be honest, she was the one who pursued me. Yeah, I knew it wasn't right, but I couldn't resist pussy—ever.

Thinking about Stacy reminded me that I needed to check on my son. I haven't seen him in a couple of days. I really needed to tell Mimi about him, but I didn't know how. Shit, if my cheating didn't make her leave, I knew this would. I should've told her about him, but I couldn't. I was too scared of losing her.

I slowly came out of my thoughts as I pulled into the driveway of my home. I looked up at the house and saw it was in total darkness, which could only mean that Mimi wasn't home. I wondered where the hell she could be at. Shit, the sun's about to come up. Shaking my head, I turned off my car and then got out. I walked to the trunk and grabbed my bag and walked toward the house. Before I could get to the door, I noticed my house keys were missing off of my key ring. The only person who could've taken them was Mimi. This was that bullshit that I didn't have time for. I pulled my phone out and tried to call her, but only got her voice mail.

I checked to see if the spare was there, but it wasn't. Now I knew for damn sure that her ass was tripping.

I decided to wait to see if she was going to show her ass. Hopefully, it would be sooner rather than later. I called Stacy to see what's been up with my li'l man.

"Hello," she answered like she was wide awake.

"Girl, you sound wide awake. What the hell you doing up this time of the morning anyway?" I asked.

"First of all, the last time I checked, I was grown, and you were Kaylin's daddy, not mine," she responded with an attitude. That's why I could've never fucked with her ass like that. She's too damn flip for me, and I hated a chick with a stank attitude. That's why I never respected her ass. She'll always be a bitch to me.

"Look, bitch, check that attitude and tone it before you make me fuck you up. Now, I'm going to ask you one more fucking time, why does it sound like your ass is wide awake and shit?"

Sucking her teeth, she screamed, "Because I just came from Club K3, Kay! Damn!"

"What the fuck were you doing at my woman's club, and where the fuck my son at?"

"Nigga, what the fuck you mean? I went to a fucking party. I was tired of sitting 'round the house all day, and your son is at one of my friend's house," she replied.

I grabbed a cigarette to calm my nerves. I was pacing back and forth, because right now, all I wanted to do was fuck this bitch up. Shit, my nerves was that damn bad. There were three things in this world that I didn't play about: my kids, my woman, and my money, all in that order.

"Bitch, I'll be over there later on, and when I get there, my son better be there, or we're going to have a lot of fucking problems. Ya dig?"

I didn't give her bitch ass time to answer before I hung up the phone. She thought I was fucking with her, but I was not. If my son wasn't there when I got there, I was gonna show her who was the fucking boss. Fuck, I paid all her bills and shit. The only thing I asked her stupid, stank ass to do was to take care of my son and to stay away from Mimi and my family. Sometimes, I regret sleeping with that ho. She's never done shit the right way. The bitch liked testing me, but I was gonna put her in her place . . . very soon. Sometimes, I thought she be doing that shit just to cause problems. Sooner or later, I was going to have to put my foot up her no-good, trifling ass.

Looking up, I didn't even notice Mimi and Troy standing there. I knew we were about to have more problems, because I'm pretty damn sure that they overheard my conversation with Stacy just now.

"Where were you, and why wasn't you answering the phone?" I asked. She didn't even answer me. She brushed right by me and walked to the front door like I wasn't talking to her. Shit, I wasn't having all that.

"Mimi, I know you hear me talking to yo' ass," I said, but she kept on ignoring me. I looked back at Troy, but she rolled her eyes and shook her head. These bitches tripping. They don't want to fuck with me right now. I turned to see that Mimi had done made it into the house.

"Mimi," I called out once I had gotten inside, but she said nothing. I walked over to see if she was in the kitchen, but she wasn't there. I then walked into the living room, only to see that she wasn't in there either. I know where she was, though. As I walked up the stairs, I made a mental note to check all of my bitches. They asses were trying to cut up, but I wasn't going to let them.

I made it to our room, where I found Mimi putting clothes in her suitcases. Now I know like hell she wasn't trying to leave me. She must really be out of her mind if she thought that I was going to let that shit happen.

"Mimi, what's up? I know you ain't trying to leave me," I said, looking at her from the doorway.

"Shit, nigga, if you think that me or my kids are staying here, then you must be out yo' rabbit-ass mind, Kay," she replied.

At the mention of my kids, I moved over to the bed where she was packing. She must be tripping, because she ain't taking my fucking kids nowhere without me. I ain't having that. We're a family, which means we're supposed to be together and get through shit like this together.

"Look, ma, I know I messed up and shit, but you ain't taking my kids nowhere," I said.

She laughed, shook her head, and went back to packing. I looked on. Honestly, that was all I could do. I knew if I did anything else, it wouldn't be talking. She walked out of the room, and I followed behind her into the kids' room.

"Mimi, I said you wasn't taking my kids anywhere." I pulled her arm, trying to stop her before she could make it out of the room.

"Nigga, you better get ya fucking hands off of me," she replied.

I swear if she wasn't my woman, I would've beaten the fuck out of her. I hated when a bitch got flip out the mouth.

"Mimi, you gon' have to chill with yo' smart-ass mouth. I ain't got time to play with yo' ass," I said, then released her arm.

"Like you have time for me any other time, huh? Look, just move out of my way so I can get out of here, Kay," she said, trying to move, but I blocked her.

"Mimi, I'm sorry. I really am."

I really was. This was the woman that I wanted to spend the rest of my life with, and I wasn't about to let her go.

"Yeah, I know—you're sorry. A *sorry* excuse for a man, now move out of my way."

She moved past me. Words couldn't explain how I was feeling right now. I fucked up royally, and I knew that I would have to pay for it.

"What can I do to make this right?" I walked up behind her, asking softly.

"There's nothing you can do right now, Kay. Just let me be, give me my space. Shit, I might as well find me a nigga who's going to appreciate me, because, obviously, you don't," she replied while walking down the stairs with her bags.

"Don't get fucked up. If I find out that you got another man, I'ma dead you and him, and that's on everything that I love," I snarled, mad as fuck.

She must be out of her mind if she thought that I was going to let her mess around on me. Yeah, I know I sounded selfish, but fuck all that—she belonged to me.

"Yeah, well, watch me, nigga," she said, walking out the door to leave.

I followed her outside where I grabbed her and looked dead in her eyes and said, "Please believe that what I said ain't a threat. It's a promise."

"Fuck you, nigga! Go back to that bitch you was just with. Or better yet, go back over to Jade's house. I mean, you was over there earlier, huh?" she said, getting into her car.

I stood there like a dummy, wondering how the fuck she knew I was over there.

"What? Cat got your tongue? Now you can't speak?" she asked.

She backed her car out of the garage. "Stupid ass, standing there looking like a fucking fool. Bitch, yeah, I know, which is why you should keep ya pieces in line and stop them bitches from calling my phone," she said.

"How you know where I was?" I asked.

"Fuck you, nigga! Never dish out shit that you can't take. Watch me work," she said before she pulled off.

I can see now that this shit wasn't going to be easy to overcome. But one thing I knew for sure was that I wasn't losing my family for no one or nothing.

Mimi

Kaylin could save all that "I'd kill you before I let you leave me" bullshit. He wasn't thinking about all that when he repeatedly cheated on me. I don't understand how a nigga could dish out this and that, but couldn't take it in return. I mean, if you didn't want ya girl cheating on you, then why you cheating on her? Shit just didn't make no damn sense. Kay needed his ass whooped, for real. I had been putting up with his cheating ways for too damn long.

Here I was, twenty-six years old, a mother of three, and I had to put up with his shit. He's too damn grown for all that. I don't have time to be trying to raise a grown-ass man. If his mama ain't did it, then I wasn't gon' do it either. I don't have time for all this. I have my club, salons, and rental properties to see about. Most of all, I have Kailay, Kayson, and Kaylon. I have zero time for bullshit. Not to mention, I've been confronted by my past.

Tyreek had been trying to get me to leave Kaylin for him, but I wasn't trying to go there. He was good people and all, but what we did was on some revenge-type shit. I only fucked him because Kay was fucking my friend Stacy. I fucked his friend to get even. There was no love between Tyreek and me. I didn't have any type of feeling for him in that way. He wasn't trying to hear all that, though. He has been threatening to tell Kay all about us and our secret. I tried paying his ass, but that only lasted for so long, and now I just didn't know what to do anymore.

I rode through the city with no destination in mind until I finally decided to get a room. Pulling up into the Ritz Carlton, I handed the valet my keys and proceeded inside to book me a room. After I booked my room, I called to check on my children, and then I headed upstairs. I was barely in the door before my phone started to ring. I glanced at it and noticed it was Kaylin, so I sent him to the voice mail and added him to my block list. I wasn't in the mood for his bullshit.

After the day I had, I needed a drink, so I went over to the minibar and fixed one. I called Troy up. I knew she had to be mad, because I hadn't called her back as yet. Shit, my mind was so far away from here.

"It's about damn time. I was just about to call ya ass," she replied with an attitude.

"Girl, I forgot to call you. My mind is all over the place right now, boo," I replied while fixing me another drink.

"Don't know why. You could have come here anyways. You know that you're always welcome here. What, my place isn't good enough for you?" she asked, pissing me off. She was becoming a little too clingy for me.

"Troy, chill with all that. I told you that I needed to be alone right now," I replied, throwing back a shot of Patrón, and it didn't even burn my chest. Shit, I need this type of therapy right now.

"Well, I understand all that, but I still wanted you here with me or me there with you," she responded.

I rolled my eyes as if she could see me, because she was starting to work on my last damn nerves.

"Girl, I'm going to be all right. Besides, if Kaylin chooses to look for me, your place would've been the first place he'd look," I slurred.

Those shots really had me feeling it. That's why I didn't like to drink, because I'd get drunk much too quickly.

"Bitch, you sound like you've been drinking. You know you can't drink," she said, laughing.

"Shit, I have. I need a whole damn bar to myself after the night I had," I said, laughing at myself. I looked over to see that I drank almost a whole bottle within twenty minutes.

"All right, girl, I'ma let you go get your drunk ass some rest. It sounds like you might not make it to work later on," she said.

"Girl, honestly, right now, work is the last thing on my mind. I'm thinking about taking the next couple of days off," I said, then made my way to the bathroom.

"That's cool. You know I'm going to hold the salon down. I'm going to send Candy to the other one. Just take all the time that you need," she responded.

"All right, girl, I'm about to take me a shower and get me some rest. I'll call you tomorrow. Thanks for having my back. Love you, Troy."

"Always and forever, love you too," she replied before hanging up the phone.

I sat there thinking about my life and how it got this far. In a way, I was no better than my mother. In fact, I was just like her. Let a nigga use the fuck out of me. Only difference is that I never allowed a nigga to beat on me. I remember when I was younger, my mother used to treat me all kinds of fucked-up ways. I had to steal to get whatever I wanted. I barely had clothes on my back or food to eat. Life in Louisiana was hard for me. That was until I met Kaylin.

Life before Becoming a Kept Bitch

You'd have thought that people would be happy that they were having a baby. Shit, some people go all out, having parties and shit. Some even start planning shit ahead of time. Not my parents, though. My parents were among those who didn't give two fucks about having a child. In fact, they'd probably wished that I was never born.

My mother, Marie Washington, and my father, Julius Baker, had been together for five years, on and off. They were natives of New Orleans, Louisiana. They lived in the Lower Ninth Ward. If you let them tell it, they didn't have a problem, but if I can recall correctly, we were living in an area where there were crackheads, prostitutes, pimps, drug dealers, and mass murderers. It was a *big fucking problem!* Not to mention that they were living off of the government. Please—that shit has "problem" written all over it. As if all of that wasn't bad enough, she had a "sometime man." What is a "sometime man" you ask? It's a man that you'd only see about four–five times a week and mainly at night. If having a man like that wasn't a problem, then she was too hard the fuck up. The man barely took her out, and if he did take her anywhere, it would be to a function that took place at night. He'd always claim that he was too busy or at work, but I didn't know of a job in New Orleans that would keep you away all the fucking time and only paid minimum wage.

I don't know how she put up with that shit. Me, personally, I wouldn't have been able to deal. Any woman in her right mind would know that her man was cheating on her with another woman. Not my mother, though. She was naive and fucking country as hell. She was a simple-minded bitch who blamed me for making that nigga leave, but I ain't did shit.

If they didn't want to have a baby, then they should've been using condoms, she should've been on birth control, or she shouldn't have been fucking him at all.

My father wasn't shit either. That nigga left when he knew he had a child on the way. He didn't even have the decency to wait until I was born. Once my mother told him that she was pregnant, he told her to get an abortion. Once she stated that she wasn't killing her child, he packed the little shit that he had at her house and bounced, leaving me to feel the wrath of a scorned hood bitch. If I ever find out where he is, I'd probably fuck him up. That nigga was the reason why I'd never got to experience real love. He's the reason why I wasn't too sure about myself, and why I allowed people to walk all over me. Since the day that the nigga walked out of our lives, it's been a living hell for me.

My mother treated me like shit on the bottom of your shoes. I was forced to get everything that I needed on my own: clothes, shoes, bras, and pads. I had to make my own way, and I was only sixteen years old. Who in their right mind would hire me when I was sixteen and still in high school? On the mornings that I'd have to go to school, she'd wake me up extra early so that I could clean up whatever mess that her drunken ass would put down. Sometimes, I think her ass did that shit on purpose, so by the time that it would be time to go to school, I'd be dog tired. The only thing that I'd have time to do is wash my ass, brush my teeth, and comb my hair. I didn't even have enough time to eat, and if I did, I'd have to walk them thirty minutes to get to school. Shit, half of the time, there wasn't shit in the refrigerator to eat or drink, and I'd have to go to school hungry. That bitch was evil as fuck, and I was the only person who'd get to see it. She was nice to everybody else—except me. At times, I'd lock myself in my room, because she always called me out my name if I'd pass by her. Sometimes she'd be mean just because she could. I got used to that. At times, the shit didn't even hurt me anymore. Whatever she said, I accepted and ran with it, because I knew she'd fuck me up for real if I didn't obey her.

The bitch often went off for no fucking reason at all. That ho really needed to get her a life and stop fucking with mine.

She needed to stop drinking, because that's when she was at her worst. All she did was fuck with me, and I was just about tired of her shit.

"Amina, do you hear me?" my mother asked, loud as hell.

"Yes, I hear you," I replied, still in a groggy state.

Truth be told, I didn't hear a fucking word that she said. I was already tired, plus, I had school in the morning, and she had me up cleaning after her drunken ass once again.

"Well, what the hell are you standing there for? Get to cleaning up this fucking mess. It looks like a pigpen up in here," she said, clutching a bottle of vodka in her hand.

"Yeah, because you're the pig that did this," I mumbled under my breath.

"What did you say?" she asked, walking close to me.

"Nothing, I asked for the broom," I lied.

"It's wherever you left the bitch yesterday," she replied as she took a sip from her bottle of vodka.

After giving me my instructions, she went to her room, where she'd finish her bottle and fell asleep. I'd feel much better if she stayed in there and never came out. I had a drunk for a mother. What type of woman do you know would drink her life away, and all because some nigga ain't gave a fuck about her?

I looked around and shook my head. There were beer cans and empty bottles all over the living room. I just cleaned that shit up yesterday and here she went, making a mess all over again. I proceeded to the kitchen where I almost lost it. The kitchen sink was filled with dirty dishes. Shit, we didn't have no fucking food in the refrigerator, so I wondered where the fuck all these dirty dishes came from. I couldn't keep doing this, I thought to myself. I went into the cabinet to get a garbage bag, and when I opened it, I saw two huge fucking rats in there. They didn't even look like rats. They looked like fucking armadillos. The shit wasn't surprising, though, because with a house as filthy as this, you're liable to see all kinds of insects and rodents in the bitch.

After getting the garbage bag from out of the cabinet, I proceeded to the living room. I walked around, picking up trash and dumping it into the bag. I even ran across a needle.

Now, only the Lord knows that I wasn't ready, but if my mother was doing anything besides drinking, then I was most definitely about to bounce. It was bad enough that I had to put up with a drunken bitch, but to put up with a bitch on drugs was a different story. I shook my head in disgust, placed it in the bag, and continued picking up the rest of the trash. When I was done picking up trash, I grabbed the broom and swept the floor. I took a bucket, filled it up with dishwashing liquid and hot water, and mopped the living-room floor. Even though the couch was torn up, I went into the hall closet and removed an all-white blanket. When I was done spraying air freshener, I placed the blanket on the sofa and fixed that shit up the best way that I knew how.

After I finished cleaning the living room, I moved to the kitchen. I knew that this shit wasn't going to be a major task. I started with the trash, emptied soda cans, pizza boxes, takeout plates, and again, liquor bottles. I never saw a woman who drank as much as my mother did. My father really did a number on her sad ass. After I picked up all the trash, I tied the bag and removed all the dishes from out of the sink. I rinsed out the sink and proceeded to let some fresh hot water run. I then added some dishwashing liquid, bleach, and baking soda to the water. Don't ask me why. I had seen my auntie do that shit one day while I was at her house. Ever since then, I'd wash dishes like that. It actually cleaned the dishes a whole lot better too. It took me forever to wash all them dishes. Shit, I had to throw away some because they were just too damn dirty. When I was finished with the dishes, I swept and mopped the floor.

That wasn't all, though. After cleaning up all that, I also cleaned up the bathroom. When I was done, it was fifteen minutes to seven. I knew that I was going to miss the bus, so I wasn't rushing. I'd just have to walk to school.

Leaving my room, I ran into this botched-looking nigga. I mean the nigga was ugly as fuck, plus, he was fat. This bitch really done lost her fucking mind and shit. She got this ratchet-ass nigga sleeping here. He must be some nigga she met at a bar, or the nigga she was with when doing her new hobby. I was about to walk off, but he got in my way.

"Umm, excuse you," I said, as I tried to move past him, but he wouldn't move.

"Hey, pretty lady, what's your name?" he asked.

"None of ya business. Now move."

"I know you have a name, and I ain't moving until you tell me," he said, walking closer to me.

"I told you my name already. It's none of ya business," I replied as I tried to push past him. He grabbed me and pinned my body against the wall.

"I see you like to be smart, but let me see how smart you are after this," he said, as he started kissing my neck. I tried to wiggle my way from his grasp, but I couldn't.

I started to scream so that I could get my mother's attention. Knowing her, her drunken ass was probably knocked out and couldn't hear shit.

"Please stop," I begged.

"Nah. Fuck all that." He took his hand and stuck it in my shorts. He was about to get a rude awakening because my pussy was sweaty as fuck. Taking his finger, he stuck one inside of me. To say I was disgusted would be an understatement. I wanted to fuck this nigga up.

Taking my right leg, I kicked him as hard as I could. He ended up letting me go, so I ran to the bathroom and yelled.

"You ugly, fat fucker. I hope ya perverted ass enjoyed that, because the next time you pull some shit like that, I will fuck you up. Oh, and by the way, smell ya hand with ya ugly ass."

I hurriedly closed the door and leaned against it. I didn't move until I heard the front door open and shut, and I peeked out the window to make sure that his chubby ass was gone. After making sure that "Gorilla Zoe" was gone, I turned the water on to take a quick bath. It was already 7:20 a.m. and school started at 8:00 a.m. If I didn't get it pushing, I was going to be late.

After taking a bath, I quickly threw on my clothes, brushed my teeth, and threw my hair into a ponytail. When I was done with all that, I headed to my room where I threw on my slippers; then I grabbed my book bag, and I was headed out. Before I had a chance to make it all the way outside, this bitch called me.

"Amina," she said, sounding drunk as hell.

"What?" I yelled. I did that shit because I knew that bitch had to be hungover.

"Shhh. Bitch, what the fuck is you hollering for?" she replied, covering her ears.

"You called me, I was just trying to see what you wanted," I responded.

"I wanted to make sure that everything is all cleaned up. I also wanted to remind you to have your fast ass in the house before seven, or else you're going to sleep outside with the people who are on the fucking streets. Oh, and make sure you get something to eat, because we don't have a damn thing in here to eat," she responded, as she reached her hand in her pants to scratch her ass.

I swear the woman was beyond trifling. All she wanted to do was drink, be filthy, and put shit all over the place. She barely took a bath, so that explained why she was itchy all the fucking time. She was just nasty as fuck. She fucked herself up when she gave a fuck about a nigga leaving her. Before she could say anything else, I left. I ain't have time for her bullshit. It was bad enough that I had to walk to school, thanks to her drunken trifling ass.

Outside was already hot as hell. One thing about Louisiana's weather was that when it was hot, it was hot as fuck. By the time that I got to school, I would probably be all stinky and sweaty. Lord knows I ain't got time for that. I had enough of these bitches fucking with me already. I secured my backpack on my back and began my journey.

Halfway there, a pimped out Caprice pulled up beside me. I didn't know who the car belonged to, so I kept on walking. Seeing that I wasn't stopping, the driver decided to roll the window down.

"Say, shorty," he said, but I ignored his ass and kept on walking.

I didn't have time for these busted-ass niggas. I was trying to get to school where I knew I could better myself and get the fuck out of Louisiana. Period.

"Ma, I know you hear me talking to you," he said, as he rode beside me.

I stopped and turned toward his car. I couldn't front. Dude was cute as fuck, but he was light-skinned. I was always into dark-skinned dudes, but I guess he'd do.

"Who you talking to—me?" I asked, looking around. I walked over to the car and peeked my head through the window. He ain't know it, but I was trying to see what he was about.

"You the only one out there, huh?" he shot back at me.

"Well, I have a name, and I know damn well that it ain't shorty," I said, as I got closer to his car.

He had a baby face, a light complexion, braids, and some cute little dimples. His whole image screamed, "He's a drug dealer."

"Well, if I knew ya name, then I'd be able to call you by it," he said.

"Well, my name is Amina Washington," I replied, with my hands on my hips.

"Amina, I like that. But I think I'm going to call you Mimi," he said.

"And what's your game? I meant name?" I asked him.

"My name is Kaylin Williams," he said, licking his lips.

"Kaylin, hmm. I guess I'm going to call you Kay," I replied.

"Well, Ms. Mimi, where are you headed?"

"Well, Kay, I was on my way to school."

"School—you still in school?"

"Yes, I'm a junior in school."

"Well, you sure don't long look like you're in high school. How old are you?"

"I'm sixteen, but I'll be seventeen in April," I said, smiling. "Look, I'd love to chat with you and all, but I have to get to school. I only have minutes until the bell rings."

"Let me give you a ride then," he said, as he reached over to open the door from the inside.

"Okay, thanks," I replied as I got into his car. He waited until I was in the car completely with the door closed, and then he pulled off.

"So, Mimi, what school do you go to?"

"I go to G. W. Carver High. Why?"

"Humph, I just asked, li'l mama. Besides, I'm giving you a ride, ya know," he said, smiling. I couldn't help but laugh also.

"Oh, yeah, well, what's up with you? What do you do? How old are you?" I asked.

"Well, I'm twenty-one. I'll be twenty-two in May, and I'm in college. I'm trying to get a degree in business," he replied as he pulled into the school's parking lot. Once we made it to the front entrance, I saw my girls Troy and Stacy waiting on me.

"Well, that's good. I wish you luck with all of that," I responded, as I opened the door to get out.

"Hold up, shorty. I don't get no good-bye, hug, or nothing?" he asked, sounding corny as hell.

I reached over to give him a hug, and he kissed me on my cheek. If I wasn't so black, you'd probably seen me blushing down.

"Say, here, take my number and call me when you get out of school later," he said, handing me a piece of paper with his number on it.

"All right," I said, taking the paper out of his hand.

I grabbed my backpack and got out. I waved good-bye and went to meet my friends. I knew when I got over there, they'd have a million and one questions to ask me, but right now, I was trying to head to a late breakfast, because I was starving.

Mimi

My friends had been getting on my nerves since the morning, and it was only fourth period. I hadn't told them a damn thing about Kaylin, and I didn't plan on it. You see, while they might be my friends, I never told them all my business. I'd always seen shit where a girl would tell her friend about her man, then the next thing you know, the friend was fucking him. No, no, no, I couldn't deal with no shit like that. The only one I'd really tell my business to was Troy. Troy was not like everybody else. She wasn't mean, and she didn't have to fake it to make it. I could tell Troy anything and not one time did she judge me. She was my true friend. Whenever I didn't have anything to eat or clean clothes to go on my back, I could always go to her. That was my bitch there.

I sat in Mr. Walker's math class bugging. I wasn't paying attention to what he was teaching or to my friends, for that matter. The only thing on my mind right now was Kaylin. Dude was so fucking cute and fine, that the shit should've been a crime. Every time I thought about him, I got this weird feeling in my stomach. I held on closely to his number. I was hoping that I'd get a chance to see him again. But a person like that would never want a chick like me, I thought.

I made up my mind right then and there that I was going to throw his number away. I'd be out of my mind to think that he actually wanted me, I thought to myself. I put all thoughts and hopes of possibly being with Kay out of my mind. I then grabbed my backpack and took down notes for the remainder of the class.

At 2:30, the bell rang, indicating that class was over. I grabbed my book bag and went to my locker. Since it was Friday and we didn't have any homework, I'd be leaving all my things in my locker for the weekend. Before I had time to even open my locker, here came my friends with they nosy asses.

"So, Amina, are you going to tell us or not?" I heard Stacy ask, but like before, I ignored her ass, and I continued to do what I was doing. I looked at my friends and rolled my eyes. They were so fucking nosy, but if the shoe was on the other foot, they'd do me the same damn way.

"Well, excuse me. You don't have to act all stuck up," Troy said, once she noticed that I wasn't playing.

"I'm not acting stuck up. I just don't have nothing to tell," I said, closing my locker. I turned around and leaned against it. Folding my arms across my chest, I stared at them.

"Well, okay," Troy replied.

"Come on, let's go," I said to them.

"What are we getting into tonight?" Troy asked as we walked down the hallway.

"Girl, y'all know I can't go nowhere or else I'll be outside, sleeping with them crackheads," I answered.

"You could always sleep at my house," she said, getting a li'l too excited.

I looked at her like she was crazy. She and I both knew that she didn't like staying at her own house. So why in the hell she thought I would want to be there?

"Nah, I'll pass," I responded, as we exited the school building.

"I'm going by Mimi's. Stacy, are you coming?"

"Nah, I'll pass," she replied, and walked off to catch her bus.

I looked at Troy, then Troy looked at me for an answer, and I hunched my shoulders indicating that I didn't have one. I had no idea what was going on, but Stacy's been acting funny lately. I couldn't put my finger on it, but homegirl had been throwing major shade. I didn't have time for Stacy. Truth be told, I didn't know how we became friends in the first place. She was always one to think that she was better than everybody else. Even though we all came from the projects, she always felt like she was more than what she really was. I hated to be around a person like that, because if you were any better than us, you wouldn't be living in the PJs and going to public school. I left that for her to deal with, but the minute she got out of pocket with it, I was going to put her in her place.

"Girl, why the hell is your friend bugging, though?" I asked once we were seated on the bus.

"Who knows? I don't have the slightest clue. Are you going to tell me about ole boy, or do I have to find out on my own?"

"I was going to tell you, girl, you know how I do it. I don't tell my business to anybody but you," I said, as I looked out the window.

"So, are you?" she asked, squirming in her seat. Shit, she was happy, like she was the one who met him and not me.

"Well, his name is Kaylin. He's twenty-one, and he's in college. He says he going to get his degree in business, but he never told me how he got them fresh clothes and shoes that he had on. Nor did he tell me how he's twenty-one with his own whip. He never mentioned anything about a job, so I could only think of one thing," I said, looking at her and smiling.

"D-boy," we both screamed at the same time.

We've always talked about wanting a D-boy, who could supply our every need, but we've never actually started the task of getting him.

"Girl, we don't know that for sure, and besides, I threw his number away in the garbage can at school," I said to her.

"Bitch, is you crazy? Why the hell would you do that?" she asked me.

"Because, what would a nigga like him want with a chick like me? I'm from the projects. I don't have a pot to piss in or a window to throw that bitch out of. My mother treats me like shit, and my father left me. Shit, I got to steal just so that I could have something to eat and clothes on my back. I don't have a damn thing to offer him," I replied, as I looked straight-ahead.

Truth is, I wasn't too sure about myself. I was never close with a man; I never knew what it felt like to be wanted or loved. I lived in the fucking projects with rats and roaches. I sometimes have to wear my clothes two or three times a week. I have absolutely nothing, and my mother made sure of it.

"But it's not like that. He doesn't know you or where you come from. He doesn't know that you barely have food to eat or clothes on your back. He doesn't know that your mother treats you like shit, or that you stay in the projects. Maybe he just likes you. To be honest, Mimi, you are a beautiful girl. Any man or boy in his right mind would want you. Stop selling yourself short just because of the things that your mother does to you. You don't know what he wants. He gave you his number, so I think that you should call him," Troy replied, sounding like an old lady.

You see, that's why I loved that girl. She always knew what to say, when to say it, and how to say it.

"I know, right? But I just don't want anyone looking down on me for something that I don't have or the way that I live," I said to her.

"Like I said before, you don't know what he wants or don't want. You can't knock it until you try it. Take it slow, get to know him," she replied.

"Too late, I already threw his number away in the trash," I responded to her.

"Well, if it was meant to be, then y'all find each other again," she said as the bus stopped at our spot.

We got off the bus and started walking. The street was kind of busy since it was a Friday, so it took us a little longer than it normally took.

As we walked down the street, we witnessed shit that we shouldn't have. On one corner, there were crackheads and D-boys, and on another corner, there were hoes and pimps. Say what you want to, but I'd hate to see the streets in the next two weeks for Mardi Gras. They probably have all kind of shit happening on the blocks, including murder. That's why I'd be happy when I graduate high school and left this piece of dump.

Walking to the building where I lived, I spotted Gorilla Zoe from earlier. I said absolutely nothing as I put my head down and picked up the pace.

"Bitch, why the hell is you walking fast like that?" Troy asked as she sped up, trying to stay close by me.

"Girl, I have to use the restroom bad," I lied.

When I made it to the front door, I prayed that my mother wasn't there and that the house was cleaned. Opening the door, I was beyond surprised to see that the house was indeed clean.

"Wow! I can't believe this shit," I mumbled to myself.

"What did you say?" Troy asked.

"Nothing, come on. Let's go to my room," I said to her.

I raised my index finger to my lips, letting her know to be quiet, as we quickly walked to my room. We sat down on the bed talking, but I couldn't get Kaylin out of my mind. I wondered what it'd be like to be loved and wanted . . . to have someone who won't treat me bad or bring me down. I fantasized about leaving this bitch and telling my bitch of a mother to go fuck herself. *Only, if only that shit could be true,* I thought to myself.

"What you over there daydreaming about?" she asked me.

"Life," I simply replied.

"Believe it or not, things are going to be all right, Mimi. Just wait and see," she responded.

All I did was shake my head. I really hoped so, because I didn't know if I could continue living like that.

"Yo, let's go to the corner store right quick," I said to her.

"A'ight," she said.

I could've sworn that I heard noise coming out of my mother's room, but I ain't pay no mind to it. I wasn't trying to be bothered with her right now.

We quietly walked past her room and left. We met up with this dude name Lucky. Lucky was a cool dude. He just was on that shit bad. He'd wash the fuck out of your car, and he'd only charge you ten dollars to do it.

"Say, li'l Mimi, do you have a dollar?" he asked me.

"Nah, Lucky, I don't have a dollar."

"Here," Troy said, handing him a dollar bill.

After dealing with Lucky's old begging ass, we headed to the store. As we walked down the street, a black Escalade pulled up. I had no clue who the driver was, so I kept on walking. Seeing that we weren't stopping, the truck followed us. I was kind of nervous, so I started picking up speed. I was about to take off running when the driver rolled down his window.

"Say, li'l mama, where you going at like that?" I heard a man say from the driver's side.

When I looked back, I saw a dark-skinned dude with dreads in his head. Homeboy was a cutie too. I walked closer to the truck, and that's when I noticed Kaylin sitting on the passenger's side.

"'Sup, Mimi?"

"Hey, Kay," I replied, nodding my head.

He jumped out of the truck and walked toward me. "Where you going?" he asked, once he was close to me.

"I'm about to run to the store real quick," I said to him.

"Word? I thought I told you to call me once you got off from school," he said, getting all in my face.

"I forgot," I said blushing.

"I bet you did, huh? Come on, let's go in the store."

"Come on, Troy," I called out to my best friend.

I followed behind him like a lost puppy. I couldn't believe that dude wanted me. Walking into the store, I grabbed two bags of chips, a sandwich, some candies, and two cold drinks, all of which I was going to need to get me through this weekend, because I knew for a fact that my mother wasn't worrying about if I ate or not.

After I got everything that I needed, I went to look for Troy. When I found her, she was talking to some dude, so I waved to let her know that I was ready to check out. I looked around for Kaylin, and I saw him talking to some chick at the counter. I walked past him to the register. He wasn't my man, and I most definitely wasn't looking for trouble.

I waited for Troy to come so that we could pay for our things. When we were finished, I grabbed my bag, politely passed right by Kaylin, and left the store. I wasn't about to let no nigga play me. Ain't no way I was going through that shit there.

We left the store and made our way back to my house.

"So what, bitch? You just going to leave him like that?" Troy asked.

"Girl, yes. You seen that shit. I'm not a fucking groupie. I don't have time to be beefing over a nigga who ain't for me," I replied to her.

I gave her the side eye, because she was starting to sound very thirsty to me.

"Well, I told you to give him some time. Shit, let him warm up to you," she replied.

I stopped in my tracks and looked her in the eyes so that she could hear me. "Troy, do you hear me, because apparently you didn't? Didn't you see him in the store talking to some other bitch while I was in there? You want me to play myself behind a nigga like that—baby, please, it's not that damn serious."

"Well, okay, damn, Mimi! Don't chew my head off," she said.

I said nothing as I started walking. Shit, I really wanted him, but I wasn't trying to be let down by anyone again.

"Just come on, girl," I said, grabbing her arm.

We were about to enter my building until someone called out to us.

"Say, Mimi," I heard a voice say behind me. I started not to turn around, because I knew exactly who that voice belonged to. I turned around to find Kaylin trailing behind me.

"Where you going at, ma?" he asked, once he reached me.

"I'm going inside to my house. Why?" I replied, looking at him from head to toe.

"Why you left the store without saying good-bye?" he asked.

"The same reason why you were talking to some chick, and I didn't interrupt you. It was none of your business," I shot back at him.

He looked at me and started smiling, showing off his dimples.

"Aww, are you jealous?" he asked.

"Jealous? Why would I be jealous? You ain't my man," I responded.

"No, but I want to be." Damn, he just threw it out there.

Hmm. "Is that so?" I asked.

"Yes, why else would I chase you down after you left me in a corner store?" he replied.

"I don't know."

"Well, can I?" he asked, staring at me.

He had me feeling all nervous and shit. I wanted to back into a corner somewhere.

"Can you wh—wh—what?" I replied, stuttering.

"Can I be your man?" he asked.

Oh, shit, this dude is for real, I thought to myself. Never in a million years did I think something like this would happen to me. I was always the one to think that the world would pass me by, and I'd never be able to experience love. I barely could get it from my mother, so why would someone else waste their time loving me?

"Can we take it one step at a time? I'm kind of new to this," I said to him. I really did like him and all, but I wasn't in no rush.

"Cool, that's fine," he replied. "How about I take you to the movies then? We could make this a double date, I'll bring my boy, and you bring your girl right there."

I stood there thinking about it, wondering if it would be a good idea to even put up with him. I didn't know this dude from a can of paint. I never even asked him if he had a girlfriend. For all I knew, he could be a serial killer and whatnot. Who was I kidding? I was only making up excuses so I wouldn't go. Maybe this was what I needed. Maybe it was time for me to really start living my life, instead of being my mother's maid and stress reliever. Maybe this was a good idea after all. I guess I was taking too long, because Troy ended up nudging me in the back.

"Remember what I told you earlier, Mimi." She slowly walked over to me and whispered in my ear.

I looked at Kaylin and tried to speak, but no words came out of my mouth. Damn, this nigga already had me speechless.

"Sure, I'd love to go to the movies," I finally managed to get out.

"Cool, I'll be back to pick you up at eight," he replied.

He then walked up to me and hugged me, followed by a kiss on the cheek.

"What apartment do you live in?" he asked.

I quickly pointed to the apartment on the right.

"A'ight, see you at eight, pretty lady."

I waited until he was gone to show my excitement. Both Troy and I were jumping and screaming. We had to go inside because we were drawing so much attention to ourselves. Once we made it inside, we ran to my room, not caring if my mother was home or not.

"Bitch, I can't believe you're going on a date," Troy said, once we were seated on the bed.

"Girl, me either. I never been on a date before. Shit, I never been close to a boy before," I replied, suddenly becoming nervous.

"Oh, Troy, I can't go. I don't have anything to put on. What if he doesn't like my hair?"

"Girl, stop all that mess. I have a couple of outfits in my bag. And you know if I don't do your hair, then you're more than capable of doing it," she said, sounding like she was the oldest of us.

I watched as Troy pulled out a bunch of clothes. I mean, I didn't know if she thought we had more than the weekend off from school, because she brought clothes like she was spending one or two weeks here. We found the perfect outfits, and we decided to do each other's hair. Once we were finished with all of that, we headed to the bathroom, where we both took turns taking a bath, while the other one waited.

We were putting the finishing touches on our outfits when someone started knocking on the door. I thought that it was Kaylin, so I went to answer it. I opened the door . . . and tried to lock it quickly. Standing there looking like King Kong himself was Gorilla Zoe's ugly ass, and then he had the nerve to have a smile on his face.

"Well, hey, there, pretty lady. You miss me?" he said walking through the door.

"Look, black and ugly, I don't know you nor will I ever miss you," I said, turning around. I started walking away, but he stopped me.

"Look, bitch, we could do this the easy way or the hard way. Either way, I'm going to get me some of this," he replied as he tried to put his hand under my dress.

"Mimi, who's at the do—" she started to say but stopped at the sight of this nigga's hand traveling up my dress.

"What the fuck is going on here?" she asked, walking toward us.

"Nothing! Mind your business, little girl," I heard the Gorilla say.

I didn't say anything as I hung my head low, so she wouldn't be able to see the tears that were falling down my cheek.

"That *is* my business, and I tell you what, if I catch you putting your hands on her one more fucking time, I'll kill ya," she spoke through gritted teeth.

"Come on, Mimi, let's go."

She took my hand as we walked back to my room. I wanted so badly to call the date off with Kaylin because I was no longer in the mood, but I didn't. I wasn't about to let no one spoil my night.

"Are you okay, Mimi? Do you want to call this date off?" she asked.

I picked my head up and wiped the tears from my face. I was tired of people thinking that they could get over on me, and I was tired of me letting them.

"No, I'm okay," I replied, as I cleaned up my face.

"Are you sure? Because we don't have to go. We could just stay home and chill for the rest of the night," she responded.

"I'm all right, Troy, come on, they'll be here any minute now."

I quickly refreshed my face and fixed my hair. Right when I was about to look out of the window, someone started knocking on the door. Since we were sure that it was Kaylin this time, we grabbed our purses, took one last look in the mirror, and headed out.

As I opened the door, my heart literally skipped a beat. Standing there looking good as ever . . . was Kaylin and the dude that I saw earlier. I wasn't one to believe in love at first sight, but after tonight . . . that quickly changed.

"Dang, ma, you look better than you did before," Kaylin said, as he pulled me in for a hug.

"You don't look so bad yourself," I replied, smiling.

"Y'all ready?" he asked.

"Yes."

I turned to shut the door, and I locked eyes with Gorilla Zoe's ass. The way he looked at me sent chills up my spine. I hurried and closed the door. This creepy-ass nigga better stay away from me. If he laid one more finger on me, I'd kill him, I thought to myself.

***

Kay and his friend Chris took us out to eat after we left the movies. I was happy because he was the perfect gentleman. He opened the door when it needed to be. He paid for everything that I wanted. He took his time. He never tried to take advantage of me. That was cool in my book, because Troy was the only other person who actually treated me right.

Needless to say, after that night, I ended up making Kaylin my boyfriend. Whatever I needed, he made sure that I had it. I didn't go a day without something, nor did I have to steal or con people out of it anymore. I finally found someone who was all for me, someone who wanted nothing from me but gave me everything that I needed and more. Shit, I wasn't trying to complain. I've been through so much, that a little sunshine after the rain wouldn't hurt a bit.

The weekend passed by superfast, and here it was, Monday again. I spent the whole weekend with Kaylin, and I had to say that I was catching strong feelings for him. I mean, who wouldn't catch feelings after a man who gave them damn near everything that their heart desired? But it was not just the material things. He spent time with me, he was always there when I needed him, and he cared about me too. I had it so bad that I found myself constantly thinking about him, wanting to be near him. Shit, I was acting all sprung, and I haven't had sex with him as yet.

My mother's been giving me a pass lately also. She wasn't waking me up like she would normally do, nor was she fucking with me. I'd say that this was the first time in a while that I didn't go to school hungry or tired. I guess it was because I was still her damn slave and I kept the house cleaned. I also stocked the refrigerator up sometimes, but that was only when I knew that Kaylin and my friends were coming over. Other than that, I'd let her ass starve like she did me. She was lucky that I was a firm believer of "Never Throw Stone for Stone."

I was lying in bed because I was completely tired. It was crunch time. I had a ton of homework, not to mention that I had math, English, and science exams to study for. Man, I was beat. I also have to braid Kaylin's and Troy's hair tomorrow, and roller set mine. I wanted so bad to reschedule, but they were my babies. I couldn't tell them no. Instead, I decided to take a bath, hoping that it would wake me up. Dragging my body out of the bed, I grabbed my nightclothes and headed to the bathroom.

On my way there, I heard my mother and some man fussing. I did like I'd normally do, and went about my business. That was her problem, because if she liked it, then I loved it. I wasn't trying to get in her business, knowing that whoever she was fussing with would be right back the next day. I didn't understand how she could let men continue to treat her that way. *Couldn't be me,* I thought to myself.

I proceeded to the bathroom where I was immediately disgusted. I knew when I left this morning that the bathroom was clean, but it looked like a fucking tornado ran through this mutherfucka. There were clothes, liquor bottles, and trash all over the fucking place. To make matters worse, when I pulled the shower curtain back, the tub was filthy, like someone threw a bucket full of mud and left it there. I don't know how someone could live like this. I knew for a fact that the first chance I got, I was leaving this hellhole. She'd have to put up with this shit her damn self. She's lucky that I really wanted to take a bath, or else I would've left that bitch just like that.

Putting my feelings to the side, I went to the hall closet and grabbed some bleach, Comet, a garbage bag, and the broom and mop. I started picking up the trash first, and then I swept and mopped the floor. The floor had all kinds of shit on it. I even found another needle. It took me about half an hour, but I was finally about to get it done. I was even more tired than before when I finished. Finally, I ran me a nice hot bath, added bubble bath to it, and got in. I placed my *Xscape* CD in the radio, and then I got in.

Not even a good twenty minutes into my bath, someone came knocking at the door. If they had common sense, then they would've known that someone was in there. Better yet, the radio playing should've given they asses a huge hint. I ignored whoever it was and continued my bath. You'd think that they would leave, but they kept on knocking. I lowered the music down a little bit.

"Man, what?" I screamed, but no one said anything. I was about to turn the radio back up when they started knocking again. I'd be damned if they didn't fucking know that I was in there.

"Who the hell is it?" I asked, in a pissed off tone, but like before, no one answered.

I got out, wrapped a towel around my wet body, and went to answer the door. When I opened the door, no one was there. I was about to peek my head out of the door when someone came rushing in. Whoever it was pushed the door so hard, that they made me hurt my back.

"What the fuck!" I said.

I looked up to see that it was the gorilla standing there.

"What the fuck do you want?"

"You know what I want. I told you that I was going to get me some one way or the other," he replied, as he ripped the towel off of my body. I tried to crawl away, but he grabbed my ankle and pulled me back.

"Where you going, li'l bitch? I don't hear you talking all that shit now," he said, as he got down on his knees.

I used my other foot and kicked him in his face. He ended up letting me go. That's when I got up and ran to my room. I was about to close the door, but like before, his big ass ran in behind me.

"Oh, you're going to pay for what you just did, bitch," he said, as he started walking toward me. I backed up and tried to put as much distance between us as I could. Soon, there was no more room for me to back up as he came toward me. I quickly tried to run past him, but he caught me before I could go anywhere.

"Yeah, bitch, I got you now," he said, as he started slapping me. "That's for kicking me in my face."

"No, please, stop," I said, trying my best to fight him off, but the more I fought him, the weaker I got.

"You tried to play me the other day, huh? I waited for this moment. I even waited until you took a bath this time," he said, as his hand traveled in between my legs. I crossed my legs at my ankles and squeezed them closed, with hopes that he would just let me go.

"Please, just let me go," I begged, but my pleas fell on deaf ears.

"Nah, ma, I've been waiting for this. I'm getting me some pussy tonight. Now, shut the fuck up," he said, as he tried to pry my legs open, but they weren't budging.

"Bitch, you can try all you want, but you going to open your legs whether you like it or not."

He threw me on top of the bed. He then punched me in my stomach, making me open my legs. He then took one of his fingers and inserted it into my vagina.

"That's what I'm talking about. You must be still a virgin," he replied. He then took a glob of spit and rubbed it over my vagina.

Watching him do that shit made me sick to my stomach.

"Please, stop. If you stop, I promise that I won't tell anyone. This will be our little secret," I said, trying to reason with him.

"Bitch, didn't I just say for you to shut the fuck up?" He kept slapping me in the face.

He must've slapped me about six times. By the time that the last lick went across my face, I was ready to give up.

"Yeah, that's right. Stop fighting me. You already know you want," he said, as he took his shriveled-up dick out.

Positioning his head at the entrance of my vagina, he tried to enter me. As he was pumping, tears were rolling down my face. Not only because it hurt me physically, but mentally and emotionally also.

His big ass started grunting, moaning, and I swear his breath smelled like dry shit. I started gagging and shaking as he was humping and pumping. I closed my eyes and started counting down from one hundred, imagining that I was somewhere else. By the time I made it to seventy-five, he was finishing up and it wasn't long before I felt his seeds flowing through me.

"If you tell anyone what happened here, I'll kill you," he said, as he put his dick inside his pants. Out of the corner of my eye, I saw something move. When I looked toward the door, I saw my mother standing there. I started crying again as I thought about her watching him raping me and not doing anything. I turned to see if she was still there, but she wasn't. I never knew someone could hate their own child like my mother hated me. No man could be the cause of all that hatred, and if it was then, that was a damn shame.

"You heard what I said, huh? If you tell anyone about what happened tonight, I will kill you and your mother," he said, as he headed for the door.

I sat there wishing that he would've killed me, because nothing was worse than what he did to me. He took my most prized possession without my permission, and there was no way for me to get that back.

I lay there waiting as he left. Soon as he was gone, I grabbed my nightgown and ran to the bathroom. Once I was in the bathroom, I ran mostly hot water in the tub. When I was satisfied with the temperature, I got in, balling up into a fetal position. I sat there wondering what my life would've been like if I had a parent that actually cared about me. The kind of parent who'd let me make my own mistakes, but will be there along the way, whenever I needed them, night or day. Parents who'd look at you for no specific reason, and say I love you. Instead, I got stuck with a set of fucked-up parents.

I wanted to be able to feel something, anything—but there wasn't nothing left to feel. They've taken away all that I had already. I didn't have an ounce of fight left in me.

After sitting in all that hot-ass water, I got out and dried off. Placing my nightgown over my head, I headed to my room. When I got in my room, I became nauseated. There were clothes all over the place. It smelled like pussy in this bitch, and the sheets had blood on them. *Jesus, if you're really up there, then take the wheel*, I said to myself.

I went ahead and started picking everything up. When I got to the sheets, I rolled them up and threw them in the trash. I didn't need a reminder of that. After picking up everything in my room, I went into the hall closet and grabbed a fresh sheet. When I was done placing the sheet on the bed, I grabbed my phone and told both Troy and Kaylin that I was sick, and I wasn't able to do their hair. They tried to put up a fuss and come to check on me, but I insisted that I was fine and said that I'd call them later. I powered my phone off, took two Tylenols, balled up into a fetal position, and cried myself to sleep.

Troy

I didn't know what was going on, but Mimi had been block-ing me. I tried to see her when she first said that she wasn't feeling good, but she told me that she was okay and that she'll call me tomorrow. Well, tomorrow done turned into two whole damn weeks, and I hadn't heard or seen my best friend. She wasn't even coming to school, which threw me for a loop. Mimi never missed school. Even when she was tired from one of her mother's spats, she still came to school. I know that shit had to be serious.

I was tired of Stacy's salt-throwing ass. I never seen some-one who was such a fucking hater. Whenever I said something about Mimi and Kaylin or mentioned the date that we had, she would roll her eyes or suck her teeth. I paid her ass no mind at all. She's mad because Mimi found herself a man and she didn't. Oh, well, she better get used to the shit, because Mimi really liked Kay. Besides, I missed my friend, and I wanted to see her, which was why I'd caught the school bus to her house. Since we had exams this week, I thought I'd share my notes with her and we could study together.

I was almost to Mimi's apartment building when someone called out to me.

"Yo, Troy, come here right quick, ma."

I turned around and saw Kaylin jogging toward me. That's why Mimi's ass was probably ducking me, because she was spending time with Kaylin. *Shit, I wish she would've told me that though,* I thought to myself.

"So you're the reason that Mimi's been dodging me, nigga?" I said, rolling my eyes at him.

"Nah, ma, I thought that was all you. I ain't talked to shorty in a week or so. She told me that she was sick and shit. I came here today to check on her," he replied, looking at me.

"For real, Kay, you haven't been here with Mimi? Because I haven't talked to or seen her in two weeks either," I said, getting worried.

"Like I said, ma, I haven't talked to Mimi in a week. I was getting worried, and I thought that she found her someone new, so I came to check on her today and shit," he replied, moving his arms.

That was all I needed to hear. I strolled across the playground at full speed, trying to get to the apartment where Mimi and her mother stayed. As I was walking, I said a silent prayer, hoping that my friend was all right. For someone's sake, they better hope she was.

Once I made it to the door, I started knocking like I was the police. I was knocking so loud that I made the neighbors open their doors. Shit, I didn't give a fuck, nor was I going to stop. Something was wrong with my best friend, and I wasn't leaving until I found out. I stood there banging for about five whole minutes until this big, black, ugly-ass, gorilla-looking nigga came to open the door with no shirt on. If he knew better, he'd do better and put his titties up somewhere.

"Little bitch, what is your fucking problem, and why the fuck you knocking like the police and shit?" he said, angrily.

"Look, I don't know who the fuck you is, but I didn't come here to see you. I came here to see Mimi, and I ain't leaving until I see her," I replied, matching his tone.

I don't know who this gorilla-looking nigga thought he was, but clearly, his ugly ass had the wrong one today.

"Look, bitch, Mimi ain't here, now, I suggest you take your little friend right here and get the fuck out," he said, pointing to Kaylin. By that time, I guess Kaylin was tired of his shit too, because the next thing I knew, he had his gun pointed in that nigga's face.

"Look, man, we didn't come here for any trouble. All we came over here for was to see Mimi, but you over here trying to make shit hard. Now, this gon' be our last time asking you, where the fuck Amina's at?" he said, getting all in that nigga's face.

It was like that nigga blacked out and went into another world. Shit, he had me scared for a minute.

"She's in her room," his big ass replied as if he was all out of breath.

Pushing past him, I hurriedly ran into the house. When I got in Mimi's room, I almost lost it. She was lying there with no clothes on. I quickly ran over to check on her.

"Mimi," I yelled, shaking her, but she wasn't responding to me.

"Mimi, please get up, baby."

I guess Kaylin heard me hollering and decided to come see what was going on. Just like before, when he first entered the room, he lost it.

"What the fuck happened?" he asked me.

"I don't know. She was like this when I got in here," I replied to him.

"I swear if he put his hands on my girl, I'm going to kill him," he said, removing his gun from his waist.

He then started kicking shit and screaming all kinds of threats. Right now really wasn't the time, so I had to stop him.

"Kay, come on. We have to get her to the hospital," I said to him.

Wherever he was, he wasn't too far gone, because once I said that, he was back to himself. Running to my aid, he helped me throw some clothes on her and carried her out. When we got outside, there were people all over, but we didn't pay them any mind. I rushed to Kaylin's car and got in the backseat with Mimi, while he jumped in the front. When we were secured safely in the car, he sped off. We decided to take her to Tulane Medical Center since it was closer.

Pulling up to the hospital, we almost ran over a couple that was standing by the emergency entrance. Kaylin got out and ran to get a doctor, while I stayed with Mimi.

"Mimi, if you can hear me, hold on. I promise that it will be all right. All you have to do is hold on," I said, stroking her hair. Just as I looked up, someone was opening the door.

"Thank you, ma'am, we have it from here," a doctor said to me.

Moving to the side, I watched as they placed her on a gurney, and then ran through the door, down a hallway, and into a room. I watched, knowing that I wasn't able to go in the room with her. I went to go sit in the waiting room. When I got to the waiting room, I looked around for Kaylin, but he wasn't anywhere in sight.

I took a seat in the corner and watched as people came in and out of the waiting room. I sat there hoping that Kaylin would show up, but he didn't. Two hours went by, and there was still no word on Mimi or Kaylin. I was totally exhausted, so I ended up falling asleep.

Mimi

When I came to, I was in the hospital. I thought for sure that I'd be in a much better place, but I wasn't. I was somehow still on this fucked-up earth. Looking around, I didn't see anyone in the room with me, so I pushed the button to call the nurse. While I was waiting for the nurse, I thought about the events that had happened.

After I was raped and beaten, I decided to take a couple of days off from school, since I wasn't feeling too good. It had been three days since I first was raped, and I thought the nigga was going to leave me alone, boy, was I wrong. On the fourth day of my "vacation from school," he came in my room while I was asleep. I tried to pretend like I was asleep, but it didn't matter if I was asleep or not—he still ended up raping me, all while my dumb-ass mother would be in the other room letting it go down. I was tired of being mentally and physically abused, so I tried ending it all, and that's how I ended up being in here today. I was about to hit the button to call the nurse again, but she ended up coming.

"Well, hello, there, Ms. Washington. It's nice to have you back," she said, smiling.

"How did I get here?" I asked her.

"I'll get the doctor, and he'll be able to tell you all that," she replied.

"Is there anyone here waiting to see me?" I asked, wondering if Troy or Kaylin were here.

"I don't know, but I'll check for you. Just let me get your vitals," she replied. After she did what she had to do, she left. A couple of minutes later, Troy came walking through the door. We both broke down crying instantly.

"Mimi, tell me what's going on, please," she said.

"I promise that I'll tell you, but not right now," I replied sadly.

I wanted to tell her so bad, but I didn't know how to tell her. I couldn't find the right words to tell my best friend that I was being raped repeatedly by some nigga and my mother just sat there and let it happen.

"Mimi, don't you ever scare me like that again," she said, hugging me.

"I'm sorry, I couldn't take it anymore," I replied, wiping my face.

"Whatever it is, it's going to be all right. I promise," she said, hugging me tightly. We stayed like that for about twenty minutes until the doctor interrupted us.

"Hello, Ms. Washington. I'm Doctor Davis. I'm the doctor who's been working on you since you came in here."

"Okay."

"I have a couple of questions that I would like to ask you," he said. He then looked from me to Troy.

"Privately."

I knew what he wanted to ask me and truth be told, I didn't want Troy to be there either. But she was my best friend. She was going to find out one way or another. So I decided to let her stay and hear it from both of us.

"It's okay, Doctor Davis. You can say whatever you have to say or ask whatever questions that you have to ask in front of her. She's my family," I replied, squeezing Troy's hand.

"Well, ma'am, were you aware that you are pregnant?" he asked, looking at me. I went to answer him, but my voice got stuck in my throat. I wasn't even having sex voluntarily, and yet, I was pregnant.

"No, sir," I finally managed to say, as tears rolled down my face.

"Well, it seemed that you were, but you had a miscarriage a few days ago. Now we're going to have to run some more tests, just to be sure that everything is fine," he said, looking over the rim of his glasses.

"Now, another thing, while I was doing a physical exam on you, I noticed that there were severe injuries, cuts, and bruises across your body as a result of violent restraint, together with injuries to the genital region. I know these types of symptoms, so I have to ask . . . Were you raped?"

At the mention of the word *rape,* I cried harder. I knew for a fact that I was raped—hell, even the doctor knew, but I still didn't want to tell anyone. So I told him a lie.

"No, I wasn't raped," I replied.

"Are you sure?" he asked, looking from me to Troy.

"I'm positive," I responded.

I didn't know why I was protecting someone who raped me, but I was. I guess it was because he'd threatened to kill me, and I was scared.

"Well, okay. I'm going to send the nurse in so that she can draw some more blood, and then I can get these tests done. Hopefully, you'll be out of here day after tomorrow," he replied.

"If you need anything, hit that call button, and the nurse will come. Take care of yourself and have a good day."

Like he said, the nurse came in and drew blood from my arm. She then checked my vital signs again and asked if I needed anything. Once I told her that I didn't, she left.

"Mimi, can you please tell me what the fuck is going on? That man said that you were raped," Troy said, as she took a seat on the bed next to me.

I looked at her, then at the door. I was trying to make sure that no one was there.

"Remember the day that I was supposed to do you and Kaylin's hair?" I asked her.

She nodded her head.

"Well, I was feeling tired, and I decided to take me a bath, so I wouldn't fall asleep. When I got in the bathroom, it was dirty, so I cleaned it up. When I was done cleaning, I ran my bathwater, threw on my favorite CD, and got in. While I was in the tub, someone came knocking on the door. I ignored them the first time, but they kept on knocking. So I got up to see who it was. When I opened the door, no one was there, but when I went to close the door, someone came crashing into the bathroom, making me hurt my back. When I looked to see who it was, I got the shock of my life. It was the same black, ugly, gorilla-looking dude who was there with my mother."

"You mean the man who was there earlier?" Troy asked me.

"Yeah." That's when I broke down crying.

"I tried to get away from him, I really did. He raped and beat me. I ended up taking a couple of days off from school, I was hurting both mentally and physically, and I didn't want anyone to see me. I thought that he would've left me alone, but he didn't. He ended up raping me on Wednesday and every day after that. You know what was so fucked up about the whole situation? My mother would watch him from the door as he was raping me. She didn't even try stopping him. I can't imagine having kids and let some nigga violate them like that, without me doing anything. I lay in the bed for hours, just crying myself to sleep, but today was different. Today, I wanted it all to end, so I took some pills and tried to kill myself, but I didn't die. I ended up in here."

It was hard to do, but I finally told her. I didn't want to, but I had to. She was always there when I needed her. Hell, she was going through something similar. That's why I didn't want to tell her, because she already had her own burden to bear, but I knew that she would understand. I couldn't keep something like that from her, and I didn't want to hold all that in.

"Troy, you have to promise that you won't tell Kaylin. I don't want him to do anything stupid."

"I promise I won't tell him anything, but that don't mean that I won't handle that fat fucker on my own," she replied, rocking back and forth.

I was about to say something, but something caught my eyes. Looking to see what or who it was, I spotted Kaylin in the corner by the door. Before I could say anything to him, he left. I had an idea of where he was going, which was why I said a silent prayer asking the Lord to protect him and to keep him out of harm's way.

Back to the Moment

After the trip down memory lane, I finished the bottle that I was drinking. Lord knows that I wouldn't wish that life there on my worst enemy. A life like that was not one that someone needed to live. After getting myself drunk, I hopped in the shower. When I was done, I lay across the bed and fell asleep.

Kaylin

If Mimi thought that I was playing with her, all she had to do is test me and find out. I've been calling her ass for a minute nonstop, but her phone is going straight to voice mail. She must have put me on the block list or something. I couldn't even get through calling her privately. Fuck it, I thought. I'ma let her ass cool off for a minute. Then we're going to have to sit down and work this out. I might even tell her about Stacy and Kaylin Jr. Nah, I won't do no dumb shit like that. I'ma try my best to keep them away from Mimi. I might even move them to another state. Shit, I think that's what I'm going to do. I'ma have to do something if I planned on keeping my lady.

After the fight we had last night, I went back inside. I swear I was missing my lady so much. I wish my kids were at least home so we could spend the day together. I haven't been myself lately. I used to take my kids out for fun every week-end, but I been slacking. It's a good thing I hired a couple of people to manage my strip clubs, or I would've been assed out. That's why I've really considered quitting that nightlife to walk on a straight and narrow path. I couldn't keep neglecting my responsibilities like this. Something had to give, and soon.

After I made sure that everything was locked and secured, I went upstairs to take a shower. Getting out of the shower, I tried to call Mimi's phone again. I got the voice mail yet again, so I lay down and went to sleep.

I was awakened out of my sleep by the doorbell ringing. Looking over, I realized that it was a little after 10:00 a.m. I looked over for Mimi, but her spot was empty. Hearing the doorbell again, I got up to answer the door. When I got to the door, my kids and their babysitter, Ms. Emma, were standing there.

"Daddy!" my kids yelled, running to me once I opened the door.

"Morning, Mr. Williams," Ms. Emma said.

"Good morning, Ms. Emma," I replied back.

"Ms. Mimi was supposed to come get them at eight, but she never came. That's not like her. Is something wrong?" she asked, walking into the den.

"There's nothing wrong, Ms. Emma. Mimi's just busy. It must have slipped her mind," I said, pulling out some money and handing it to her.

"Okay, I have to go. I'm running late for my appointment. Have a good day," she said to me.

She walked over to the kids, kissed each of them on their forehead, and said good-bye.

After seeing her out, I followed the sound of cartoons and laughter to the living room, then I sat on the couch with my sons, K2 and K3.

"Daddy, where's Mommy?" Kayson asked, looking at me.

"Yeah, where's Mommy?" Kaylon chimed in, repeating the question before I could answer. Like I said before, my little men were Mama's boys.

"Mommy's not here right now. What, y'all don't want to spend any time with ya old man?" I asked.

"Daddy, can we go to IHOP for breakfast? Because I'm hungry," Kailay asked.

"Yes, baby, Daddy will take you to IHOP. How about you guys? Do y'all want to come too?" I asked Two and Three, as my sons were affectionately known.

"Yesssssss," they both screamed together.

"After that, can we go see Mommy?" Three asked.

"Sure, li'l man. We can go see Mommy," I replied.

"Kailay, why don't you go ahead and get dressed, while I dress me and these two," I said, pointing between my two boys.

"Okay, Daddy," she replied, heading for the stairs.

"How about us three guys dress alike today?" I said.

"Nah, Daddy, I love you and all, but we gotta have our own swag. We don't want to dress like you," Kayson said, heading to his room with his brother following behind him. I swear at only four years old, them little niggas thought they were fourteen.

I shook my head, and then I headed for my room. I looked around and sighed. *Mimi needs to bring her ass home,* I thought. I walked into the bathroom and quickly took a shower. After showering, I then proceeded to get dressed. Wanting to be simple, yet fresh, I threw on a fresh white V-neck, some blue True Religion jeans, and some fresh white Js. I then threw on my jewelry and headed to check on my kids. I made my way to Kailay's, where I looked on as she strapped on her sandals.

"Has anyone ever told you how beautiful you are?" I walked up to her and asked.

"Yes, Daddy. I get it from my momma," she responded.

"You surely do. Come on, beautiful, let's go check on ya brothers," I said, as we headed toward the boys' rooms.

"Two, you all right in here?" I asked, looking at my son.

"Aww, Daddy, I told you that I wanted my own swag," he said, looking me up and down. Just like me, he was dressed simple in a fresh all-white tee, his True Religions, and white Jordans. I have to admit, he looks like my mini-me, hair, clothes, and all.

"I betcha y'all ain't as fresh as me," Three said, walking into the room wearing the exact same thing as his brother and me. I had to laugh, because they wanted their own swag, but still ended up dressed like me. Like father, like sons, I said to myself.

"I thought y'all wanted y'all own swag. Looks like y'all wanna be like Daddy to me," I said, looking at them. "Come on, y'all, let's go."

Once we were all downstairs, I locked up and headed to the garage. Since I had my kids, I pulled out my red Yukon Denali. After strapping my kids in, I began pulling out of the garage. Before I could get to the end of the driveway, I noticed a yellow envelope taped to my front door. I got out and went to retrieve it. Making my way back to the truck, I stuck the envelope inside of the glove compartment.

On my way to IHOP, I tried calling Mimi—still no answer. I was becoming angrier by the second. I mean, the least she could've done is call to check up on the kids, but instead, she wanted to act like a bitch. I was gonna put my foot up her ass when I saw her.

I pulled into IHOP's parking lot and found a place to park. Finding a table was quick, because it wasn't packed in here like it would normally be. Once seated, we ordered, then waited. As we were waiting, I could've sworn that I saw Stacy and Kaylin headed to the bathroom. I hope I was wrong, because Lord knows that I didn't need this right now. If my kids saw him, they're gonna know what's up. Shit, he looked exactly like me, Two, and Three.

I turned around once the waiter set our food down. I thanked her, and we all proceeded to eat. We talked in between bites, but for the most part, there was more eating and less talking. Halfway through the meal, Kayson and Kaylon started asking about Mimi. I was about to answer them when I heard someone scream.

"Daddy!" Kaylin Jr. screamed, running toward our table. I didn't know what to say. All of my kids were looking at me and my oldest son, who they knew nothing about. Turning around, I noticed Stacy walking up. I grabbed Junior and met her before she could even make it to the table.

"What the fuck! I told you about staying in your lane," I said, heated. This bitch was really trying to test me.

"What the fuck you mean staying in my lane, nigga? We came to get some fucking breakfast," she said, in a loud tone.

"Lower your fucking voice, and why outta all the places did y'all come here?" I asked.

"How the fuck you expect us to know that you and them damn kids was going to be here? I went to get your son like you said. On my way home, he said he was hungry, so we came here," she responded, waving her hand all over the place.

I really didn't want to make a scene, especially not while my kids were with me.

"Look, man, I'ma need for y'all to bounce," I said, referring to her and Kaylin.

"What? You expect *us* to leave, because you and *your* precious kids are here? My child belongs to you too, Kaylin, or have you forgotten that?" she replied with venom.

"Daddy, can I meet my sister and brothers?" my li'l man asked. Stooping down to his level, I looked into his eyes and kissed him on his forehead.

"Not now, Kay, but you'll get to meet them real soon, okay? Daddy just has to get something straight first," I replied back to him.

"Okay," he responded sadly.

"Hey, li'l man, don't be sad. Daddy will come check on you later on, okay?" I said.

"You promise?" he asked.

"Yes, I promise," I replied, standing up. I then looked back at my kids who were watching my every move. I turned around and gave Stacy a stern look.

"Take him home. I'll be there later," I told her and walked off.

"Yeah, whatever, nigga. Come on, Kaylin," she replied, grabbing him by the hand and storming off.

I watched as they both hopped in the car and left. I then turned and went back to the table with my kids.

"Daddy, who's that boy and why does he look like you?" Kailay asked.

"Yeah, why he look like us?" Kayson asked.

"And why did he just call you Daddy?" Kaylon asked.

"Not right now, y'all. We'll talk about it later. How about we go to the park?" I said to them.

My kids were never ones to beat around the bush. I knew this was going to happen, but what was I supposed to tell them? I couldn't tell them that they had a brother, because then, they'd tell Mimi, and I'm sure that I'd lose them all forever. I have to tell them, but not now. I'd wait for the right time . . . if that time ever comes.

Mimi

I got woken up by the sun beaming into my room. I tried sitting up, but I was stopped instantly by my throbbing head. I located my purse to see if I had anything that I could take for my head, but I found nothing. *Just my fucking luck,* I thought to myself. When I couldn't find anything to take, I lay back down and somehow ended up falling asleep again.

An hour later, my phone woke me up. Thinking that it was Kaylin calling, I answered with an attitude.

"What do you want?" I asked.

"Ummm, hey, good morning. I was calling to check on you, but if it's a bad time, then I can call you back," I heard a voice say.

"I'm so sorry, Jayden, I had no idea that this was you calling me," I said, feeling bad for going off on him.

"It's cool, ma. I was just calling to check on you," he responded.

"Other than sleeping in a hotel and having a hangover with nothing to take for it, I guess I'm fine," I said, getting up from the bed.

"What hotel you at, ma?" he asked me.

"I'm at the Ritz Carlton, room 1302. Why?" I asked.

"Oh, really? That's the same hotel I'm at. In room 1305," he said, getting excited.

"Well, well, well," was all I said.

"Check it, ma, have you eaten breakfast yet?"

"No, I haven't. Why? You want to feed me?"

If I kept this up, no telling how much trouble I'd get myself in.

"Why don't I order us some room service and bring you something for your headache?"

"Sure, that's cool."

"Your room or mines?" he asked,

"My room would be fine."

"All right, give me about half an hour to get everything ready and I'll be there."

"Okay, I'll be waiting."

After I hung up with him, I went to take a shower. When I was finished, I combed my hair and threw on some sweats and a tee shirt with my house slippers. I didn't know what to call this thing that Jayden and I had going on, and I really didn't care. I meant it when I said I was tired of trying to please everybody but myself. Today was the day that I started living my life for me.

Jayden

Things couldn't have been better for me right now. Originally, my plans were to make the drop, then head out, but those plans changed when I ran into Mimi at the gas station. I wasn't supposed to be making the drop in the first place. That was one of my homeboy's jobs, but he couldn't make it, so I had to do it. I was actually pissed about it, but now, I was glad that I came after all.

When I first laid eyes on Mimi, I knew from that moment that I had to have her. Shorty was fine as all outdoors, and she had class. Not to mention that her beautiful chocolate skin was flawless, and it had a glow to it. So when I saw her coming inside of the store, I bumped her, making her drop her phone. It was the only way that I thought I could get her to notice me. I was even happy to buy her another phone, because it meant that I would get to see her again.

What I wasn't expecting was for her to have a boyfriend. That shit there pissed me off. I was glad when I heard that they were having problems. Baby girl got hands on her. The way she whooped ole girl's ass was crazy. She even went after her old man. I kind of got mad when that nigga pushed her. That shit really pisses me off, ya dig? Where I came from, men didn't put their hands on a woman. That's why I stopped her from going after him again. If it wasn't for the fact that I had a shitload of drugs in the car, then I would've done him something dirty. Instead, I got Mimi out of there and headed to my hotel room.

I sat in my hotel room, staring at my phone all night hoping that Mimi would call. When I got tired of waiting for her to call, I took a shower and went to sleep. The next morning when I woke up, the sun was shining. I checked my phone to see if I had any missed calls from Mimi, but I didn't have any. Tired of waiting, I decided to call her. I was happy as hell when she said she was in the same hotel as me. Just the sound of her voice soothed me. I needed to see her, bad. That's why I asked her if she'd eaten breakfast. Once she said that she hadn't, I knew that this was my chance to see her.

When I got off the phone with her, I made a call to room service and ordered us some breakfast. After ordering damn near the whole menu, I rushed to take a shower and brush my teeth. When I was done, I threw on a wife beater, some basketball shorts, and some brand-new all-white Nikes.

I made sure that I looked and smelled good. Then I went across the hall to tell my boy Mark where I was headed and for him to keep an eye on the room. I went back in the room to make sure that everything was locked up and in order. Once I was sure that it was, I made my way to Mimi's room.

I made it to her door and waited five whole minutes before knocking on the door. There was something about this woman I really liked. I got myself together, and then knocked on the door. I swear what was probably only a minute felt like hours as I waited for her to open the door, and when she finally did, it felt like time stood still. A lump formed in my throat as I tried to swallow. I stared at her in a trance.

"Well, good morning to you too," she said, breaking me out of my thoughts.

"Good . . . morning," I stuttered, embarrassing myself.

"Come on in, I won't bite you," she said laughing and opening the door for me to enter.

I walked in and immediately noticed that she had about three large suitcases. I wondered how long she planned on staying here.

"Excuse the mess. Have a seat at the table while I take these to the room right quick," she said and walked over to her suitcases.

"It's cool, ma, you don't have to move them. I know you probably got in late and all. Oh, and here," I said, handing her a bottle of Tylenol.

"Thank you," she replied, taking it out of my hands. As she went to put her suitcases in the room, someone started knocking on the door.

"Yo, Mimi, somebody's at the door," I called out to her.

"Well, answer the dang door then, Jay," she replied.

Thinking it probably wasn't nobody but room service anyway, I went to open the door and was indeed greeted by room service. I hadn't realized that I ordered so much food. They had to enter the room with three carts. After they set the food down on the table, I tipped them, and they were out the door.

"Yo, ma, the food's here. Come eat before it gets cold," I said, calling out to her.

"All right, I'll be out in a minute."

I don't know what it was about this woman, because she had me open, and I'd just met her. What I do know is that I wanted her in the worst way, and I wasn't going to stop until I had her. I only had a couple of days left here, and I planned on spending every last one of them with her.

Mimi

To say that I was excited to see Jay would be an understatement. Words couldn't explain how I felt right now. I was really feeling this dude, even though I only met him a day ago. I wasn't really trying to jump headfirst into another relationship, but I was willing to see where this thing was heading. Besides, after all the things that Kay did to me, I don't think that I'd be able to trust another man ever again.

After putting my suitcases in the bedroom and spraying on some of my favorite perfume, I went back into the living room. When I got there, I saw Jay standing next to a table full of food. Shit, it looked like he ordered the whole breakfast menu. I mean, he had everything from grits and eggs, to sausage and bacon, cheese omelets, French toast, pancakes, steak, oatmeal, and home fries. He even had a side of fresh fruits with water, orange juice, and coffee. My mouth watered just by looking at it, but still, that was way too much food for the two of us to eat. I walked over to him, hugged, and kissed him, and then I sat down.

"Thank you, but are we expecting any company? Because there is *way* too much for here for us to eat."

"I didn't know what you like, so I ordered a little bit of everything," he replied.

"Well, thanks again."

"You're more than welcome."

"Let's eat then," I said, motioning toward the food.

After putting some food on our plates, we sat there in silence. I watched closely as he bowed his head and said grace, taking me by surprise. It was very rare that you'd find a man who actually appreciated God and gave Him thanks. After saying grace, we ate our food in silence. I was so scared to eat because he kept looking at me. So I kept taking little bites from time to time.

"So, are we going to go and get you a new phone or what?" he asked.

"I told you that I'd get my own phone," I replied, looking at him across the table.

"I know what you said, but I want to buy you a new one. Plus, I'll get to spend a little more time with you today," he said, staring back at me.

"Lemme find out you sprung already," I said, making him laugh.

For the first time, I noticed that he had dimples. Oh, how that shit was major cute to me.

He didn't say anything as he stared at me with those pretty, dreamy eyes. He moved closer to me and reached out his arm to touch me, but I moved backward. If I let him touch me, I know that I'd have gotten myself into some trouble. It's been weeks since I last slept with Kay, and I could clearly say that I was "fuckstrated." He smiled at me and then moved a bit closer. I laughed inside because we were playing a game of cat and mouse. We continued to play this game until I had no more space to run.

Staring down at me, he then asked me if I was scared. I shook my head no. Shit, I already came this far, I might as well finish. Plus, I haven't been getting any type of "act right" from Kaylin. My pussy needed some attention.

I wrapped my arms around his neck and kissed him. I continued to tease him for a minute or two until he couldn't take it anymore. With his hand on my waist, he started kissing me as our tongues played a dance with each other. From there, he started kissing me on my neck, making me wet instantly. That was my hot spot right there. I pulled his wife beater over his head and started kissing his chest. I then moved up and started kissing his lips, running my hands through his hair. I didn't miss a beat as he picked me up and carried me to the bedroom. Laying me down on the bed, he started to undress me.

"You sure you wanna do this, ma?" he asked between kisses.

Shit, I knew what I was about to do was wrong, but you see the way my body's set up, I needed some kind of release.

"Yeah, I'm sure," I responded.

That was all he needed to hear before he started ripping my clothes off. It didn't take long for him to finish. Next thing you know, I was lying there in my birthday suit.

"You have the most beautiful body that I've ever seen," he said, looking down at me.

He then took one of my breasts and started sucking on it. He took his time gently sucking and nibbling on each of my breasts. Minutes later, he started trailing kisses down my stomach. When he reached my pussy, he lightly blew on it and kissed in between my thighs. He made his way back toward my safe haven, where he grazed it with his tongue, making me gasp. Putting his whole mouth on it, he started licking and sucking me. Dude was eating the pussy like his life depended on it, and it was feeling so fucking good. His head game was so lethal that I busted all on his face within the first twenty minutes. He started eating me again; in and out, left and right his tongue went as I started grinding against his face. After my second nut, I was out of breath. Coming up for air, he smiled, and then kissed me.

"You sure you want this shit here, ma? Because I'm 'bout put it on you so good, you ain't gon' know what hit ya," he said, rubbing his head against my swollen lips.

"Damn, ma, your pussy is so wet."

"You sure do talk a lot of shit. Lemme see if you can back it up," I replied, and before I could finish what I was saying, he plunged deep inside of me. I swear I could feel that shit all in my guts.

He slowed down and started slower, and that shit was feeling good, but right now I wanted to be fucked.

"Umm, Jay, fuck me, baby," I whispered in his ear. I don't know why, but I thought being fucked rough was the shit.

"Yesssss, fuck me just like that," I moaned in his ear.

"Like this?" he asked, pumping fast and hard.

"Yeah, just like that. Fuck me just like *that*," I said, matching him, thrust for thrust. Throwing my legs over his shoulders, he started pounding away, hitting the bottom every time. Within no time, we came together . . . long and hard.

"Damn, Mimi, your pussy is the truth," he said, falling on the bed from exhaustion.

"You weren't so bad yourself," I replied, tired and all out of breath.

"Is that right?" he asked.

I said nothing, as I turned over with my back facing him.

We lay in the bed for a good fifteen minutes in silence. I really couldn't believe I just slept with a complete stranger. When I turned over, he was staring at me.

"What? Why are you staring at me?" I asked him, suddenly becoming shy.

"You, ma, you're so beautiful," he replied, stroking my hair.

"I'm about to take a shower. You want to come?" I quickly asked before we ended up staying in bed all day.

"Only if I get to wash you up," he responded.

"Deal."

I got up from the bed and walked into the bathroom, turned on the shower, and got in. It wasn't too long before Jayden joined me.

We took turns washing each other up. Then we got out of the shower and dried each other off.

"Thanks, I really needed all of this. Too much has been going on. Lately, I'm always stressed out," I said to him.

"No need to thank me. As long as I'm here, you'll be in good hands," he replied, and kissed me.

His hands traveled down to my already sore kitty, but I stopped him before he could touch me.

"You go get dressed. I know you didn't think that I forgot about my phone you owe me," I said, pushing him off of me before he started something again.

"All right, ma, I'll be back in a minute," he said, and then left the room.

Once I heard the door close, I proceeded to get dressed. I heard a message came through on my phone. I decided to get it once I was finished getting dressed. After I was fully dressed, I combed my hair into a high ponytail and went to get my phone. I picked up my phone and noticed that it was

Tyreek texting me. I already know that he was trying to start some shit . . . Shit that I didn't have time for.

Have you given any thought to what I said? I'm really trying to make some moves over here, the message read.

Tyreek, chill. You know that can't happen, I texted back.

Look, Mimi, I'm not playing with your ass this time. Either you do it or I will. Kayla kept asking about you. Tyreek's message sounded desperate, and I wasn't in the mood for it.

"Don't try to make this about Kayla, Reek. This is all you. You already know what up, though. Tell Kayla that I love her and that I'll try my best to see her soon," I spoke into the phone and hit SEND.

As I was setting my phone down, somebody started knocking on the door. I went to open it and found Jayden standing on the other side.

"Damn, ma. You look good enough to eat," he said.

"Let me grab my purse and keys. I'll be right there," I said, moving to the side so he could come in.

When I got back in the room, I grabbed my purse and keys, and then I picked up my phone. Looking at my phone, I noticed that Tyreek had texted me back.

Sooner than you think, the message said.

I brushed it off because he'd been saying the same thing lately. I don't know what the problem was.

I paid his ass enough money to stay away from me, but lately, he's been becoming too much to handle. All I know was that I already had a lot of shit on my plate right now. He'd just have to go on the back burner with all the rest of that shit.

Tyreek

Mimi must be out of her damn mind if she thought that I was going to wait on her ass another minute. If I kept waiting on her, that shit wouldn't ever happen, and Kayla was going to be ass out. The bitch done moved to Atlanta and forgot about what the fuck she left behind, but I was going to have to remind her ass of that.

Well, I have some news for her ass. As soon as I finished doing what I have to do for my mother, I was going to drive up there. I was going to tell her about my plans, but I decided to surprise her ass. I mean, what good would it have done if I had told her? She's not going to do anything but try to stop me. It's time for some action. I wasn't going to leave that bitch alone until Kaylin knew everything.

Mimi and I used to fuck around behind Kaylin's back. Yeah, I know that sounded foul, but Kay started fucking with my piece Stacy. He didn't give a fuck about me, so why would I give a fuck about him? Stacy and I were fucking around way before she started fucking with him, but all that changed when she started fucking with him. That nigga was supposed to be my nigga, but he started fucking my piece, and to make matters worse, they had a fucking child together. See, Stacy thought that no one knew about her and Kaylin's child, but I knew. I knew all about it.

After Mimi and I found out about them, we played a game of revenge. Shit, we were creeping real hard until Kay and I got knocked and went to jail. While I was in jail, Mimi came to see me. When she told me what she told me, it changed my life and my friendship with Kay. I waited until I got out so that I could talk to her, but by the time that I got out, she was long gone.

All I had left was a bank account in my name. She thought that all that money was going to keep me quiet, but it didn't. There was something way more important than that.

Shit, it was because of her that we even went to jail in the first place.

Kaylin

After the kids and I left IHOP, I took them to the park so they could play. I was filled with pride as I watched them play with each other on the swings. Suddenly, my phone started to ring. I looked at the caller ID and noticed that it was an unknown number.

"Yo," I answered the phone.

"'Sup, playboy? Long time no see," the voice on the other side of the phone replied. I looked at the phone because I couldn't believe it.

"Man, I *know* this ain't who I think it is," I said, not believing my ears. "Tyreek, nigga, is this you?"

"Yeah, this me, kid," he replied.

"Nigga, where the hell have you been? I haven't seen you in a long-ass time," I asked.

"I been around, still living in the boot. I'm just trying to stay out of trouble and make some money," he replied.

"Yo, word? You need to take a trip up here. There's a lot of money and lots of bitches," I responded. I was kind of happy to hear from my old friend.

"Shit, I don't know. Let me think about that, and I'll get back to you."

"That's cool, homie, do that," I responded.

"How's everything going with the family?"

"Everything is good. Kailay, Kaylon, and Kayson are a handful at times, but I wouldn't trade them for nothing in this world. As for Mimi, she's still Mimi, but a little feisty," I replied, with a light chuckle. *If only you knew what was up,* I thought to myself.

"Yeah, that's good to hear," he responded.

We chatted for a little while longer, basically catching each other up on what's happening in our lives.

"All right, homie, don't forget to get back to me about coming this way," I said.

"All right, man, for sure," he replied, then hung up the phone.

Tyreek was my best friend when I was in Louisiana. We did everything together. He was like my blood brother. I trusted that nigga with my life, and I knew that he would never betray me. Snapping out of my thoughts, I went to tell my kids that it was time to go. They put up a little fuss, but they complied when I promised to bring them back real soon.

On the drive home, I tried calling Mimi, but I still didn't get an answer. I didn't know how long I was going to allow this to go on. Mimi better get her fucking mind right before I got it right for her.

I arrived home, removed the kids from the car, and headed inside. Once inside the house, I instructed the kids to take a bath and brush their teeth. I was about to fix us a snack when my phone started ringing. I looked at the screen and saw that it was Stacy calling. I wasn't really in the mood for her right now, so I pressed IGNORE.

I gave the kids their snacks, got them settled, and then I went to take a shower. When I was done in the shower, I dried off and threw on my pajamas. As I was about to lie down, my phone started ringing again, indicating that I had a text message.

I walked over to my phone and noticed that it was a picture message, so I opened it.

I was instantly mad as I looked at a picture of Mimi holding hands with some nigga. Looking closer, I realized it was the same dude from the gas station the other day. Underneath the picture was a caption that said, I bet you won't think so highly of this bitch no more. I guess she's just like every other ho you fucking.

I was so fucking heated that I started pacing back and forth. I picked up my phone and tried to call her up, but I only got her voice mail again. I must've called that bitch about a hundred times within the hour with no answer. I started to call Ms. Emma to come get the kids, but she's lucky that I didn't want to wake them. That's okay, though. Mimi's going to have to show up sooner or later, and when she did, it wasn't going to be nothing nice.

Unknown

I sat outside of Kaylin's house plotting my next move. He had me fucked up if he thought the shit that we had was over. See, what them cheating-ass niggas failed to realize was that when they stick their dick in another bitch's pussy, there was a possibility of her catching feelings. Like why would you fuck me so good and I was only a fuck thing to you? If you knew we couldn't be anything more, than you shouldn't have fucked me that good.

Kaylin thinks that I'm 'bout to roll over and let him play me. He got me mistaken with them other bitches, because I don't roll over for anyone. I wasn't about to let him get off that easy. See, the mistake he made was when he started fucking me. Yeah, I know I went after him and all, but I ain't made him shove his dick in me. He did that shit on his own. If he knew it would've been all that, then he should've turned me down, but he didn't. I know it was supposed to be about business only, but who could only do business with a fine-ass nigga like him. Shit, I wanted to fuck him the first time that I saw him, but I waited until the right time, and when I did, boy, was it worth the wait.

The only real problem was getting him to leave his girl. That nigga wasn't thinking about that shit, and if I brought it up, he would flip out on me. I didn't know what she did to him or what kind of hold she had on him, but he was madly in love with her. Even though he cheated on her with me and every other bitch with a pussy, she was always number one, and he made that shit known from day one. I was just too stupid to take heed, and I ended up falling in love with a kept bitch's man. Kaylin was about to find out that if I couldn't have him . . . then nobody would.

Mimi

A Few Days Later

I'd be lying if I said that I wasn't feeling Jayden, because I was. I spent the last few days with him, getting to know him. I was sad about him leaving me today, but he promised me that he would be back real soon. I was already looking forward to his visit, and he hadn't even left yet.

As I sat in his room watching him pack, I thought about the last few days. My life was actually peaceful . . . That's one of the reasons why I was sad to see him go. I started smiling as I was thinking about him, and he caught me.

"What you over there smiling about?" he asked, putting the last of his clothes in his suitcase.

"You just don't know how happy I've been these past few days," I said, meaning every-fucking-word.

"Yes, I do! I was here too, remember?" he said, being funny.

I threw a pillow at him and laughed. That's another thing that I liked about him, he was always making me laugh. He always made me feel good. He never tried to hurt me.

"No, seriously, though. Before you came into my life, it was pure hell living with Kay. He was never home, and he stayed cheating on me. Whenever I get ready to leave him, he's always hollering about how he's going to kill me."

"You don't need to worry about all that, ma, I'm here now, and I don't plan on leaving anytime soon," he said, kissing my lips passionately.

I returned his kiss with just as much passion.

"You do know that I don't want you to leave, right?" I asked in between kisses.

"Ma, you know that I have to, but I already promised you that I'd be back soon," he assured me.

"Okay," was my only response as I pulled him onto the bed. I started kissing him as I removed his pants first, then his boxers.

"Me too," he said, as he removed his shirt.

He started kissing me as he pulled my dress up to see that I had nothing underneath. He instantly got excited.

"Oh, you came here ready, I see," he said, removing my dress completely.

"You think that I was going to let you leave without getting a snack first?" I murmured against his lips.

Next thing I knew, he started kissing all over my body. I can't lie . . . Just his lips on my body made me want to come. Leaving a trail of kisses, he made his way down south. I gasped because I knew what was next to come. Right when I was about to relax, he kissed my southern lips. From kissing, he went to sucking and licking my kitty. Spreading my legs wider, he dove headfirst into my pussy like it was his last meal. He was devouring me like he'd never see me again.

"Yes, that's it! Eat this pussy! Eat that shit, Jay, don't stop!" I screamed out loud. That shit must have turned him on more, because he started straight fucking my kitty with his tongue. I started grinding against his face when I felt my orgasm building up.

"Umm, I'm 'bout to come, Jay," I said, as I started coming.

"You taste so good, ma," he said, licking his lips. He then kissed me, letting me taste my own juices.

"Come on, ma, I'm just getting started," he said as he climbed on top of me. Entering me, he let out a low moan.

"Umm, baby, yes," I moaned, as he started pumping.

"You feel so good," he whispered in my ear.

"You do too, baby," I replied.

"This pussy is mine, right, Mimi?" he asked, fucking me long and hard.

"Yes, Daddy, this is your pussy. Fuck your pussy, baby," I replied, as he continued to slam in and out of my pussy, making me feel every hard inch.

"Oh, yes, like that. Do it like that," I moaned out in pure pleasure.

"Like this?" he asked, rotating his hips, stirring my juices. He then put my legs on his shoulders and started pumping faster and faster.

"Yes, baby, just like that. Do it just like that," I replied, meeting him thrust for thrust. My boy started pumping real fast and rolling his hips, and I was getting higher by the second. This nigga had me on a sex high that I was ready to come off of. Before I knew it, I was coming again, but I wasn't done with him.

I wrapped my legs around his waist, then I flipped him over on his back so that I was on top. I guided his tool back inside of me, and then I started riding him. Starting slow, I moved back and forth, kind of like a seesaw. I pulled out a few tricks and started out circling my hips in a figure eight, then I began bouncing on his dick.

"Mmm," he moaned, watching his dick going in and out of me. He put one of my titties in his mouth and started sucking.

"Yeah, ma, ride that shit," he said, slapping my ass cheeks. "Show Daddy how good you ride."

Closing his eyes, he threw his head back up and down. I rolled my hips like there was no tomorrow. I placed his hands on my waist, and he started pumping in and out of me fast, letting me know that he was about to come.

"Make me come, ma," he said.

I started riding him faster and faster, pulling out every trick that I knew. I wanted to send him home with something to remember me by. His dick was feeling hella good. Before I knew it, he was coming, and I was right behind him.

Falling forward out of breath, I lay my head on his chest, with his dick still inside of me. After a few minutes, he pulled out of me and laid me down beside him. I looked at him. I was becoming sad all over again. *Damn, I'm going to miss him,* I thought.

"Don't worry, ma. I promise that I'll be back before you know it," he said as if he could read my mind.

"I know. I'm going to miss you, that's all," I replied, but before he could say anything, his phone started ringing. I sat there staring at his fine ass while he was talking to whoever it was on the other end.

"Come on, ma. That was Mark. He over there bitching about me being late and all. So let's go take a shower before we leave," he said, carrying me to the bathroom.

After taking a shower, I walked them down to the front desk to check out. Once he was through, we headed outside to his car. I wanted to cry so bad right now, but I held it in as best as I could.

"Come here, ma," he said, pulling me in for a hug. "I promise you that I'll be back real soon."

"Hurry back," I replied, giving him a quick peck.

Shit, he was about to leave me. I wasn't trying to start something that I couldn't finish. I briefly said good-bye to Mark and turned back to Jay.

"See you soon," he said, getting into his car.

I watched until his car was no longer in sight. My baby was gone, and here I was going back to my fucked-up-ass life. Reality hit me too fucking quick. On my way back into the hotel, I bumped into the last person that I wanted to see.

"Oh, you ain't happy to see me?"

"What are you doing here, 'Reek?" I asked him with an attitude.

"You really thought that I was playing with you this time, Amina?"

"I told you that I was going to take care of it. Why you wanna try to start something? I already told you time and time again that we can't be together," I said walking off, but he pulled me by my arm. This nigga must be out of his mind!

"If I wait on you to do anything, then I'll be waiting on you forever. Besides, Kay invited me down here, and someone wanted to see you," he replied, stepping to the side.

"Hey, Mommy," I heard a soft voice say.

"Hey, Mama's baby, how are you?" I asked, stooping down so that I could look at her face-to-face.

"I'm fine, Mommy, but I want to come live with you," she replied sadly.

It broke my heart every time my daughter asked to come and stay with me, because I know that she couldn't. I love my daughter to death, but her father was a pain in the ass. If I knew this nigga was playing it like that, I would have never fucked with him in the first place.

***

When I Turned Eighteen . . .

I remember the day that I started fucking with Tyreek. It was my eighteenth birthday, and I was happy as I could be. I was supposed to be having this big birthday bash, followed by a walk on Canal Street. That day I was on cloud nine. You couldn't tell me that my shit was stinking, because I'd shoot you down with the quickest. That day was really my day . . . or so I thought.

I was sitting in the salon getting ready to get my hair and nails done when these busted bitches came strolling in. I paid them no mind as I read the magazine that I had in my hand. There was an article about the New Orleans Saints that I was trying to read, but I couldn't because them bitches were making too much noise. I was about to call them on that shit until I heard Kaylin's name come out of one of them bitches' mouth.

"Bitch, you going to the party with me, right?" the light-skinned one asked her friend.

"Girl, I already told ya ass that I was coming," she replied to her.

"Good, because I know Kaylin's going to be all in his bitch's face tonight. You know that's who he's throwing this party for, but if that bitch only knew," the light-skinned one replied, smacking her lips like she was chewing gum or some shit.

I wanted to go over there so bad, but I didn't. I mean, why the fuck would I worry about them hoes? He'd just bought me a brand-new car, and he moved me into a condo. Shit, I was over here getting myself all glamorous with his money, and that outfit that I was going to get from the mall, I was getting with his money. That party tonight? Oh, yeah, that's supposed to be for me. It was funded with . . . yet again—with *his* money. So I wasn't about to waste my time on these hoes. The only thing they got out of the deal was a wet ass. Bitches be lying on their backs and going home with empty-ass pockets. Bitch, please, and *they* wanted to feel sorry for *me*. Hell, I felt sorry for their stupid asses.

I let them talk that trash only because it was just that . . . trash. Those hoes couldn't touch me on my worst fucking day.

I had a surprise for them, though. I couldn't wait until I see them again. I was gonna make them hoes' head hurt. I was going to show them just who to feel sorry for, and, bitch, it wasn't Mimi.

I was happy when Cidney signaled for me to come on, because these hoes were too through for me. I did my nails and shit first, and then I ended up getting an updo with bangs to the front. When I was done, I paid for my hair and gave her a big fat tip. Then I threw on my shades and walked out like I owned the place. When I got to where those hoes were that were talking all that shit earlier, I took my shades off and looked at them.

"Yo, Cidney," I said to the woman who just finished getting me right.

"'Sup, Mimi, what's going on?" she replied, looking at me and then to them two birds.

"It's cool. Nothing is going on. I wanted to treat these ladies to whatever they were getting today," I said, pulling out two fresh and crisp hundred-dollar bills.

"Here, this should cover it."

"Okay," she replied, and took the money out of my hand.

"Thank you," I heard the light-skinned chick said.

"Yeah, thanks, girl," her sidekick responded.

"No problem, ladies, enjoy the rest of your evening," I replied.

I threw my shades on, flipped my hair on them silly hoes, and went to meet Troy and Stacy at the mall. I swear, after I did that shit, my ego was boosted up.

It didn't take long for me to make it to the mall. I quickly pulled up into a parking spot, got out, and went to meet my girls at the food court. Walking through the mall was a task itself. I received a million looks from the fellas and a billion glares from the hoes. If I wasn't on a timed schedule, I would've gave them hoes something extra to hate, but being as I had shit to do, I left that shit for another time. Right now, I had to find the perfect outfit for my party tonight. Otherwise, some of these hoes would've been going home with some sad faces—humph!

I made it to the food court and looked around for Troy and Stacy, but I didn't see them. The fuck these bitches rushed me for and they're not here their damn selves. I pulled out my phone and was about to call them when someone tapped me on the shoulder. When I turned to see who it was, I saw Troy standing there with Stacy.

"I was about to call and go off on you bitches," I said, hugging Troy.

"I bet you were, but you do remember that *you* was late and *not* us, right?" she laughed and hugged me back.

"What's up, girl?" I said, nodding my head at Stacy.

I wasn't into shady bitches, and Stacy was definitely one of them. Troy was the one who kept that ho around, because if it was up to me, that ho would've been cut the fuck off. You see, ever since I started talking to Kaylin, Stacy's been real salty. I mean, I don't know why, because she was fucking with his best friend Tyreek, and we were always double dating and shit. She don't think that I be peeping that out, but I do. Stacy was a hater on the low. That's why I chose to stay my distance from her. I mean, how could she hate and not like me and we supposed to be friends and shit? Where they do that at? Only in New Orleans, I guess.

"Nothing much. What's going on with you? How's it like living in Kenner?" she asked, with a slight attitude.

See, that's the shit I was talking about right there. She was always salty for no fucking reason. I wasn't even about to go there with her, but what I wanted to know was how did she know where I stayed at? I mean, the only two people that knew where I stayed were Troy and Kaylin. I know for a fact that Kaylin didn't tell her that shit, which left Troy. She knew that after that shit had happened to me, I didn't want anyone to know where I stayed.

"It's great. It's peaceful, and I don't have to worry about all the shit that I had to when I was staying in the ninth Ward," I replied, looking from her to Troy.

The look on Troy's face screamed, "Mimi, please, don't do this here."

That bitch looked like she was scared or something. I wanted to laugh in her face. Instead, I took the high road and left it alone.

"Well, that's good. How you and Kaylin been doing?" she asked, and I could've sworn that I saw a smirk plastered on that bitch's face a second ago.

"Look, are we going shopping, or do y'all want to sit here and talk? Because I don't have time for that shit. I have places to go and things to do," I said and looked at them.

I wasn't playing with these bitches today. Either they were shopping or not. It seemed like everyone wanted to play with Mimi today.

"Look, let's just go shopping. Today is supposed to be your day and all, so let's enjoy it. I would hate for something to go down and your day gets ruined," Troy said, but I was still focused on Stacy's ole salt-throwing ass.

I wanted to dog check that ho, but I didn't. Instead, I put my feelings aside, only because today was my day. If it wasn't, I would've done that ho in. See, people thought because I was quiet and shit that they could get over on me. I was not feeling that shit anymore. I was tired of that shit, and it wasn't going to happen again. Bitches used to say all kind of crazy shit to the old Mimi, and she didn't do anything. This here was the new Mimi, and I guarantee you that I wasn't letting that shit go down this time.

I was trying to be the bigger person, so I walked off, and I didn't care if them hoes chose to follow me or not. I was going shopping with or without they asses. Just to be sure, I looked back, and sure as hell, they were following me. See that shit wasn't hard; they should've done that shit from the jump. But, no, that bitch Stacy wanted to try me by coming at me sideways. As I recall, we all grew up struggling together, so none of us were better than the next.

It took four hours, six stores, and about twenty different outfits until I found the perfect one for my party. I was glad that I got there in time, because the lady was just putting them out. The other good thing about it was that it was one of a kind, so I didn't have to worry about somebody else showing up to my party wearing the same thing. I was a happy camper.

After leaving the mall, I went straight home. When I got in the door, I kicked off my shoes and tore my clothes off piece by piece, leaving a trail behind me. Walking into my room, I went straight to the bathroom, where I planned on soaking in a nice hot bath. I turned on the water and went to get me a glass of wine. When I came back, I popped in my Xscape CD and got in.

I started thinking about what had happened earlier in the salon. I wondered if Kaylin was really cheating on me. I mean, he didn't act nothing like it. He bought me all kinds of shit, he took me to all kind of different places, and he gave me plenty of money. So, when did he have the time to cheat? Or are all those things gifts because he knew for a fact that he's cheating, and he didn't want me to find out. I started thinking about Stacy and why, after all these years, she became salty with a nigga. I mean, I knew I didn't do anything to her. So why was she behaving that way?

Fuck it, if she didn't like me, then that's that. I didn't have time for all of that. I'd be graduating next month, and soon, I'd be leaving the NO altogether.

My mind started to drift to my mother, but before it could completely get there, my favorite song by Xscape came on. I sat up in the tub and started singing my ass off.

"Never should have kissed you, never made that call. I told myself," I sang along with "Tiny," LaTocha, Kandi, and Tamika as they took that song and its meaning to another level. Shit, after everything that happened today, I was starting to feel the same way "Tiny" did with Zebo's ass.

When I was done taking my bath, it was past eight. I had to move quickly because I still had a lot of shit to do. I had to get myself ready, pick up Troy, and go see the weed man. Shit, I was trying to get fucked up tonight.

I grabbed my bottle of oil from the dresser and went about the task of oiling my body. Squeezing a small amount onto my hands, I bent down to oil my legs. I was about to rise back up when I felt something hard pressed against my ass. I jumped and turned around. I stood face-to-face with Kaylin. Well, not face-to-face . . . sort of like face-to-chest, but you get my drift.

"Happy birthday, baby," he said in a tone that made my pussy jump.

"Thanks," I said, as I tried to turn from what I knew was about to happen.

"Nah, ma, don't try to run. I need some of that," he said as he started kissing my neck. That nigga knew just what he was doing; he knew that was my spot there.

"Nah, Kay, we gotta get ready for the parrrrrty," I tried to say, but that nigga was getting it.

"Fuck it. We gon' make a grand entrance in that mutha-fucker. Now, come on and get ya man right. All I need is a quickie . . . until later on," he said, and I couldn't do nothing but oblige.

I had a lot of time to make up for, because it took me a whole year after I got raped to have sex with him. He waited and was very patient with me. Now it was time for me to handle my business.

I turned around, stood on my tippy toes, and started to kiss him. It wasn't that fake-ass shit you'd see in the movies. My kisses spoke volumes. With each kiss that I gave him, it meant that I loved him. Leaving his lips alone, I start nibbling on his neck. Then I started trailing kisses down the side of his neck, coming all the way to the center of his chest. I pulled his shirt over his head and started kissing him in the center of his chest again, leading all the way down to his dick. I was scared as hell, because I never gave head before. I guess there was a first time for everything. No lie, this nigga had a pretty piece of meat, and the shit was so fucking thick.

I took his dick into my hands and gave it a couple of kisses. One was to say thank you for waiting for me, and another just because that shit was pretty. I slid it into my mouth and made sure that my mouth was sloppy wet as I started sucking up and down his shaft, mimicking the thrusting motion of penetration. Up and down, my head moved at a slow but pleasurable pace. I tried something that I had seen on them porn videos, but I had no idea if I was doing it right. Taking my time, I moved to his balls, gently sucking one at a time. After doing that for all of five minutes, I went back to his dick. Paying more attention to his head, I took it into my mouth. I placed as much of him in my mouth that I could take, and then I started sucking again. This time, I sped up the pace, making sure to keep that shit sloppy wet. If there was one thing that I knew, I knew for sure that a nigga never liked a dry mouth. That shit was such a turnoff, I'd heard. I wasn't too big on giving head because I didn't know what I was doing. I guess he knew that shit too, because it wasn't long before he decided to take control.

I was concerned about fucking him without a condom, but I let that shit ride for now. I lay back on the bed as he crawled on top of me. For some reason, my heart started beating superfast.

"Ease up, ma, all you gotta do is relax. I promise that I won't hurt you," he whispered in my ear.

"Oh . . . Okay," I replied, taking a deep breath, and then letting it out. I was trying to calm my nerves down.

Positioning his head at my slit, I took a deep breath as he entered me, giving me an inch at a time. When he was all the way in, he stayed there motionless, gazing in my eyes. After a minute, he started moving his hips in a circular motion. I tried not to think about what happened a year ago as I started to enjoy what my man was doing to me. Placing one of my legs in the crease of his arm, he started going in and out. He started off slow, and then he picked up speed. I started to move my hips, matching his thrust. He took my legs and placed them on his shoulders as he plugged in and out, hitting the bottom every time. It was a painful, but pleasurable experience and brought tears to my eyes. With each thrust that he took, those tears fell down my cheek. I finally knew what it felt like to be loved by a man, but he wasn't just any man . . . He was my man. I mean, we had sex before, here and there, but it was nothing like this. This time, it was special, like we were marking a new beginning for life—for us.

As time moved on, I ended up on all fours, taking the hit from the back. If I had to vote on any sex position so far, that'd be my favorite one, hands-down. That shit felt so good, and I enjoyed every bit of it. Before we knew it, what was supposed to be only a quickie, turned into an hour of lovemaking. When we were done, we just lay in bed, basking in the aftermath of our lovemaking.

"See, I told you that I wouldn't hurt you, ma," he said, kissing my face.

I smiled, because that was indeed true.

"How do you feel?"

"To be honest, I feel good. In fact, I feel so good that I don't want to go nowhere. I just want to stay here and enjoy the rest of my birthday, cuddled up with you," I said, looking up at him.

"Nah, ma. We got time for that later. Come on, let's get up and take a bath, so we can bounce," he replied, getting up.

Just like that, it was all gone, but I wasn't tripping, though, because we still had tonight and every other night that the good Lord continued to bless us with.

"A'ight," I said.

I got up and headed to the bathroom, where we ended up bathing together. When we were done, we dried off and got dressed. I ended up not putting on the outfit that I had picked out earlier and wore a simple, tight-fitted dress that hugged my curves, with some wedges and my accessories. When we were both ready, I locked the door, and we were on our way.

I had forgotten that I had to pick up Troy, so I called her as soon as I remembered.

"Yeah, bitch," she said, answering the phone. I knew she was mad at me, but I didn't say shit.

"Where you at? You still need a ride?" I asked her, totally ignoring her attitude.

"Nah, I called Stacy and Tyreek to come get me. We just got to the club. Where you at?"

"I'm on my way now. I'll be there in about five minutes."

"Tyreek asked if Kaylin was with you because he wasn't answering his phone," she said.

"Yeah, he's with me," I said, looking at Kaylin, who was smiling.

I reached over and locked my hand with his. Lord knows I was happy to have a man like him.

"Okay, I'll see you whenever you get here," she replied.

"A'ight, I'ma see ya."

"That was Troy. She said yo' boy Tyreek is looking for you," I turned to Kaylin and said.

"I bet he is."

***

We made it to the club no later than eleven, and when I tell you that that bitch was packed, it really was. There was a line that led from the front of the club and ended at the side. Everybody came out to show your girl some love on her birthday. Kay pulled his car to the entrance of the club, where he had one of his boys find a parking spot.

I spotted Troy, Tyreek, and Stacy waiting for us at the front door. As we made our way toward the club, I saw the two broads from the salon earlier. One of them even had the nerve to try to speak to Kay, but he shut that ass down fast as he could. They jaws dropped when they saw me.

"Ain't that the chick from the salon earlier?" I heard the dark-skinned one say to her friend.

"Oh, yeah, that was me. Hope y'all enjoyed y'all time at the salon earlier," I said waving at them. "Don't feel sorry for me, 'cause, bitch, I feel sorry for you," I said as I turned toward the light-skinned one with an "eat-shit" grin on my face.

That ho's face turned bloodshot red in two-point-five seconds. I flipped my hair on them hoes yet again and continued to walk in my party, with my man by my side.

When we made it to the front door, I noticed that Stacy had this disgusted look on her face. I wanted to check that ho so bad, but Troy seen it coming.

"Happy eighteenth birthday, Mimi," she said, handing me a squared black box.

"Thanks, girl," I said, ignoring Stacy.

"Hey, 'Reek, y'all come on."

The club was packed like a mutherfucka. We had a hard time getting to the VIP area, there were so many bitches and niggas all over the place. We eventually made it to the VIP area. The place was decked out kind of nice. I took a seat on the couch as Kaylin went to pour us glasses of champagne. He said a toast and thanked everyone for coming out. I was grateful too, but I wanted his ass to sit down, because there were way too many bitches trying to get his attention. I was about to walk over to him when my favorite song came on.

"Girl, you looks good, won't you back that azz up? You's a fine mutherfucker, won't you back that azz up?" The music blasted through the speakers in the club.

I grabbed Troy's hand and pulled her to the dance floor and started popping my ass and dropping it low. I was so into the song that I didn't notice a crowd had formed around us. I used that as my excuse to go all out on them. I started doing all the dances that I've seen the women on the videos doing. I was twerking so hard that I had to pull my dress down a couple of times. When the song finished, I headed to the bar to get me a bottle of water.

On my way over to the bar, a couple of dudes tried to holla at me, but I told them that I had a man and kept it moving. I took a seat on one of the bar stools and scoped out the scene. There were some fine-ass niggas in the club tonight. Too bad that I already had a man. Speaking of which, I wondered where he was at. I glanced over at the section of the club where our VIP was located and spotted Kaylin and Stacy having a heated argument. Hmm. I wondered what that was all about, I thought as I made my way over there. When I got there, they got hushed, so I asked what I wanted to know.

"What going on, Kay?" I said, looking from him to Stacy.

"Nothing, ma," he replied.

"Shit, it don't look like nothing. What was y'all so heated about just a minute ago?" I asked once again.

"I said it was nothing, now leave it the fuck alone," Kaylin said, getting mad.

"Nigga, I don't know who you think you talking to like that, but I'm *not* the one," I replied, getting in his face.

"Man, look, get the fuck out of my face. I said that it was nothing," he said, pushing me back.

"For real, though, Kay? You gon' push me over that bitch?" I asked, pointing to Stacy, who now had a smirk on her face.

"It ain't over no bitch. I told you that it was nothing, and yet, you still over here running ya mouth," he said.

"You know what, nigga? Fuck you," I said, storming off.

I went over to Tyreek and asked him to take me home. He looked at Kay, and then at me, and said that he would.

"Where you going?" Kaylin asked once he saw Tyreek getting up.

"I'm going home," I replied.

"Well, I'ma take you then," he said.

"No, nigga. I don't want you to do a fucking thing, but leave me the fuck alone," I said, moving away from him.

"Come on, 'Reek."

"Ma, why you doing this?" he asked.

"I ain't doing nothing. I'm going home," I said, walking off.

I waited for Tyreek, who was now talking to Kaylin. He looked over at me. I rolled my eyes and turned the other way. Five minutes later, Tyreek came and said that he was ready. I followed behind him as we exited the club.

When we got outside, I made eye contact with the hoes from earlier. The light-skinned one now had a smile on her face. I guess she had seen what happened, but I didn't care. Kay can play with whoever he felt like.

While we waited for Tyreek's car to come, I texted Troy and told her that I was leaving. She said all right and said that she and Stacy were catching a ride with Kaylin. I texted back okay and powered my phone off. Since I knew that he was leaving the club, he would most likely be calling me when he dropped them off. It took them niggas forever to bring Tyreek's car to the front.

When it pulled up, I got in and shut the door. On the ride to my house, Tyreek tried to make small talk, but I wasn't in the mood. I politely told him to leave me alone and sat back in my seat. I wasn't trying to be mean. I just didn't want to be bothered. The only time I did say something was when he asked where I lived. I told him where and left it at that. Twenty minutes later, we pulled up to my crib. I felt bad for how I was treating him and decided to apologize.

"Tyreek, I'm sorry for talking to you like that. It's just that Kay pissed me off, and I didn't want to be bothered."

"It's cool, I understand. Once a girl's pissed, she's pissed at everybody," he said, smiling.

"No, for real, though, I'm sorry. I didn't want to go off on you like that. Besides, you're always nice to me," I replied.

"I told you that it was cool. You straight. You just have to learn how to control your anger and shit," he said, still smiling.

"And that I do know. Thanks for the ride," I said, opening the door to get out.

"No problem. Aye, I don't want to come off the wrong way, but take my number down . . . in case you need me. I'm always a phone call away."

"Okay," I said, taking my phone out. I had to power it back on. I stored his number in my phone and thanked him again.

"Anytime," he said.

He didn't pull off right away like most people would've done. He waited until I was inside, then he left.

I kicked my shoes off by the door and made my way to my room. When I got there, I stripped down and headed to take a shower. When I got out of the shower, I threw on one of Kay's tee shirts and lay across the bed.

Kay's cologne smell was all over my room. I wanted to call him so bad and tell him to come over, but I didn't. I missed my man already, and we just had a fuss, not even an hour ago. Putting my feelings to the side, I got up, threw on some clothes, and made my way to his house.

The drive to his house usually took thirty minutes, but I made it there in fifteen. That's how much I was missing my man. I parked my car on the side of the street and got out. Then I pulled out my keys and searched for the one to his door. I found it and opened his door.

When I got inside, the house was pitch-black dark with the exception of his bedroom light. *See, my man missed me too,* I thought to myself. As I got closer to his room, I started to hear some funny noises. The closer I got, the louder the noises became. When I was only inches away from the door, I realized that what I thought was noises were actually moans coming from the other side of the door. I inched my way to the door as quietly as I could, grabbed the knob, and gently turned it. I couldn't see through that little-ass crack, so I opened it wider.

What I saw literally broke my heart. I stood there, watching my man plug his dick inside of a bitch that was supposed to be my friend. Tears came running down my cheeks. They were so into each other that they never realized that I was there.

"I knew something shady was going on between you two. I just fucking *knew* it," I screamed, letting my presence be known.

"Mimi, baby, let me explain," Kaylin said.

"Explain? What could you *possibly* have to tell me?" I asked, but he said nothing.

"That's what I thought, nigga."

"And you," I said, turning to Stacy. By that time, tears were streaming down my face.

"You was supposed to be my friend, and yet, I find you fucking my man. Bitch, we grew up together—we struggled to-fucking-gether."

"Bitch, please. You met this nigga and got brand new. From the first day that he dropped you off at school, you were a new person. I did this shit only so you could see that you wasn't no different. I've been fucking that nigga ever since you got raped," she said, looking at me with a smirk on her face.

I looked at Kaylin, shook my head, and then I charged that ho.

For everything that I've been through, I gave her a lick. For the shit that my mama did to me, I gave that ho a lick. For every day that I had to struggle, I gave that ho a lick. I took all of my anger out on her face. When I thought about me getting raped, I blacked out and went ham on that bitch. I didn't stop whooping her ass until Kaylin pulled me off of her.

"That's enough, yo," he said.

"Nigga, fuck you—*you* did this shit. I hope that ho was worth it, because we're done," I said and ran out of the house.

I jumped in my car and sped off. I didn't know where I was going. I just needed to get some fresh air.

I ended up in my old neighborhood, where I sat in my car, thinking about every little thing that I've been through. I cried for all of the days that I had no food. I cried for all the days that my mother abused me. I sat there crying for all the times that I was raped. I cried until I couldn't cry no more. *I have to get out of here,* I thought to myself.

I started my car and pulled off. I needed to be around someone who would comfort me. I pulled my phone out and called Troy, but she didn't answer. I started to ride by her house and wake her up, but I didn't. With no one to talk to, I decided to drive around the city. I threw in my Xscape CD and drove with no destination in mind.

I was about thirty minutes into my drive when Kaylin started calling me. I looked at the caller ID and hit the IGNORE button. I did not want to talk to him ever again. He ended up calling me again, but I kept ignoring him. By the thirteenth call, I was ready to go off on him, but it wasn't him. This time, it was Tyreek. I had forgotten about giving him my phone number.

"Hello," I said, as I lowered my radio.

"Yo, ma, where you at?" he asked me.

"I'm just riding around the city."

"Yo, Kaylin had been looking all over for you," he said.

"'Reek, I don't want to see or talk to Kaylin anymore. As a matter of fact, tell that nigga to go to hell," I said, meaning every word.

"What's going on this time?" he asked me.

I sat there and told him what happened from the time that he dropped me off, to the time that I went to Kaylin. Before I knew it, I was crying all over again.

"It's going to be all right, ma."

"No, it's not going to be all right. I gave that man all of me, only for him to do me like that," I said to him.

"I understand all that, but you can't be getting yourself all worked up. Yo, where you at?"

After I told him where I was, he invited me over to his house. I wanted to decline his offer, but I needed to be around somebody before I did something stupid.

I pulled into his driveway fifteen minutes later, and he was already waiting for me by the door.

"Come on inside, ma."

I went inside Tyreek's house and looked around. Dude had his shit laid out tight.

"You want something to drink?" he asked.

"Yeah, what do you have?" I asked, taking a seat on the sofa.

"Beer, water, soda, and wine," he replied.

"Do you have anything stronger?" I asked him.

"As a matter of fact, I do," he replied, getting up.

I looked around as he went into the kitchen. When he came back, he was carrying a bottle of vodka and two glasses. He set the bottle down on the table and poured us a glass.

"I thought I'd have a drink with you," he said, taking his drink to the head.

I followed suit and took my drink to the head also. When I was done, I asked for another one and repeated the process.

It was an hour later, and Tyreek and I drank through two bottles of vodka. I was feeling better, so I tried to go home.

"Nah, ma, you can sleep that shit off over here," he said.

"Okay," I replied, and lay down on the sofa. I was about to close my eyes when Tyreek handed me a pillow and a blanket.

"Here," he said.

I took the pillow and laid it down on the sofa. I handed him the blanket and got up. I then took off my shirt and my shorts and asked him for a shirt. I caught him staring, but I didn't pay it no mind.

"Sure, let me go get it."

I sat back down as Tyreek went to get a shirt for me. I waited for a good five minutes, and Tyreek still hadn't come with the shirt, so I went looking for him. When I made it to his room, he was lying on the bed. When I walked over and shook him, his eyes popped open, scaring the shit out of me.

"Hey, I thought you came in here to get me a shirt," I said, holding my chest.

"Oh, yeah! My bad," he said, getting up.

He walked over to the dresser, got a shirt out, walked back over to the bed, and handed it to me. When he handed me the shirt, our hands accidentally touched. I looked up at him, and he looked at me. I licked my lips as he stood there biting his. I couldn't front, dude was fine in his wife beater and basketball shorts.

Before I knew it, we were making out. I don't know if it was the liquor or the fact that I caught Kay with Stacy, but I wanted to fuck him, and I did. I fucked Kay's best friend, and I didn't give two fucks about it. The sex was so good that we started creeping on the low.

Of course, a couple of weeks later, I took Kaylin back. I mean, he was my first love and even though I was still fucking Tyreek, I still had love for him. It took a few months for Kay and me to get back to our normal selves. I was happy once again . . . or so I thought. Kay and 'Reek ended up going to jail behind Gorilla Zoe's ass, while I was stuck in the real world by myself. A few days later, I found out that I was pregnant, and the crazy thing was that I didn't know who I was pregnant by. Yup, life was always a bitch. But they say what goes on in the dark will come to the light.

That's how I ended up in this fucked-up situation that I was in now. My daughter Kayla was Kailay's twin sister. Yeah, I know you want to know how, huh? When I found out that Kaylin was cheating on me with Stacy, I started sleeping with Tyreek. At first, it was once a month, but the sex was so good, that we fucked twice a week. On the day that I got pregnant, I slept with Kaylin that evening and Tyreek that night. Thinking that I was pregnant, I went to the doctor, only to find out that I was indeed pregnant—with twins. When I found out, I told Tyreek that there was a possibility that the babies could be his. He told me that he'd be there for me, no matter what. On the day that I had my children, I thought no more of Tyreek being her father. Kailay came out chocolate like me, while Kayla came out a high yellow color, making me think that Kaylin was their father. I thought nothing of it, until the day we were supposed to leave. Kayla had gotten very sick and needed blood; blood that I couldn't give to her. By her being a twin, the doctor said that her sister would be able to donate her some. When they took Kailay to test her blood to see if she was a match, I was informed that she wasn't. I was confused because if they were twins, then that meant that they had the same blood. I thought that it was a problem on their end, so the doctor agreed to test both of my children's blood again. When the results came back, the doctor told me some very interesting news.

"What are you saying? I mean, I had these girls on the same day—shit, I was pregnant with them at the same damn time," I said to him.

"Ma'am, I understand all that, but what I'm saying is this: While these two girls are twins, and you being their mother is correct, they do not have the same exact DNA. Which means that they do not have the same father," he said, pointing to my daughters.

I knew right then that Tyreek was Kayla's father. The doctor said while I was ovulating, my eggs were released at once. When I had sex with Kay and 'Reek on the same day, the two eggs had been fertilized by two different sperm. Kayla even had some of Tyreek's facial features, but I've always thought that my mind was playing tricks on me. Shit, she could've easily passed for Kay's because of her skin color. Had it not been for her getting sick, I would've never known that Tyreek was indeed her father.

The day after I found out about Kayla, I went to see Tyreek's mother. She gave Kayla the blood that she needed, and I made her promise not to tell him about her. I wanted to be the one to tell him.

The day I left Louisiana, I dropped Kayla off at Tyreek's mother's house, and I never looked back. I knew what people might've thought of me, but I did what I had to do. I was in love with Kay at the time, but I was starting to regret all of that now.

Over the past five years, I kept in touch with her. I would send her money and gifts on her birthday. I even saw her one or two times per month, but what she wanted the most, I couldn't give. I promised her that I'd come to take her one day, but I never did; all that was about to change though. After I left Kay, I planned on taking all four of my kids and moving to another state, as soon as I could get all of my business in order.

"I promise that Mommy will get you real soon, baby," I said, as I used my hand to push her hair out of her face.

She had jet-black hair and an attitude just like her mother and her twin. She got her complexion and eye color from her father.

"Don't make promises you can't keep, Mimi. I'm not about to sit around and continue to let you break my daughter's heart," Tyreek said, stepping closer to me.

"Nigga, I said I was going to take care of it. Don't try to make a scene out here, especially not in front of my daughter."

"*Your* daughter? Tell me when was the last time you seen your daughter? What kind of woman, you know, would leave her child for somebody else to raise? Tell me what kind of a mother you know would only see her child occasionally. You think I want to hear this shit? You have three other kids, but you left your oldest daughter just because she wasn't for the nigga you were with. Explain that shit to me, Mimi, because obviously, I'm not getting the fucking point," he said, a little too loud for me and everybody else within earshot.

"Nigga, like I said before, I did what I had to do. You think that I really wanted to leave my child behind for you and your mother to raise? Like, I don't regret that shit? You actually think that I only wanted to see my child occasionally? You couldn't possibly think that I was happy all of these years, knowing that I had another child out there, who wasn't here with me. If you think that I was all right with leaving my child and not being able to see her every day, then you're dumber than I thought," I replied, with tears rolling down my face.

"Mommy," Kayla said, with tears in her eyes. This is why I told him not to do this. Kayla's my weakness. I know what I did was wrong. I've lived with that for eight years. I couldn't change that. I've lived with regrets, but not anymore, though. I ain't trying to make nobody besides my four kids happy.

"You see what the fuck you've done?" I said, getting in his face.

"I'm doing what I should've done a long time ago. You have until tonight to tell Kaylin about me and Kayla, and if you don't, I will," he replied, taking Kayla's hand and walking away.

"Tyreek, please," I started to say, but he raised his hand to stop me.

"I'm giving you until tonight, Mimi. No more, no less," he said, walking off.

"Tyreek, can I spend some time with her later today?" I asked him.

"You are her mother, right?" he asked.

I nodded.

"Well, call me when you're ready for her."

I watched as he walked into the hotel room with Kayla by his side. I waited a minute before I went back to my room. Once I was inside, I started packing up my suitcase to check out. I called down to let the front desk clerk know that I was checking out early and that I needed help with my bags.

Thirty minutes later, I was all checked out and on my way to one of my rental properties. After I dropped off my suitcases, I headed to check on my club, where I noticed Kay's car in the parking lot. I started to leave, but I decided to go in instead because I haven't been there in almost a week.

I walked up to the club and said hello to security and walked inside. Once inside, I looked for my manager Benny. After I located him, I instructed him to meet me in my office. As I walked up the stairs, I smelled him before I could see him. I walked inside and spotted Kay sitting in my chair behind my desk. Rolling my eyes at him, I said nothing. As I laid my purse on top of the desk, I took a seat on it.

"It would be nice if you'd leave my office," I said, turning my nose up as if I smelled something funny.

"Well, hello to you too. You don't miss me?" he asked, getting up from the chair. I rolled my eyes at him and moved to take my seat behind the desk.

"If I would've missed you, then I would've come home. So it's obvious that I don't," I said, with an attitude.

He walked over and sat on top of the desk where I was just sitting. Leaning forward, he looked me in my eyes and smiled.

"I see that little nigga got you feeling big and bad, huh?" he said, shaking his head.

"Don't nobody have me feeling shit. You just trying to start something, because I caught you cheating and ya mad. What you need to be worrying about is me leaving ya sad ass," I replied.

"I'm not mad at all, and I ain't worrying about you leaving, because you not. What you need to be worrying about is bringing ya ass home, because I want you there tonight," he responded.

"You must be out of ya mind if you think that I'll be listening to your ass. You don't scare nor own me," I said.

"You could play with me if you want to—" he started to say, but was cut off by someone knocking on the door.

"Come on in," I said, not taking my eyes off of him.

"What's up, boss lady?" Benny asked, walking in the room. "'Sup, Kay?"

"Hey, Benny. How's everything been going with the club?"

"Everything's been going great. The numbers have increased a whole lot, and you know we have the concert here tonight. Which is why I think we may need a little more security than we usually have," he responded.

"Okay, I'll make those arrangements and get back with you. I won't be staying long, because I have to head down to the salon," I said.

"Okay, boss lady. Will that be all?" he asked.

"For now, yes. Make sure that everyone comes in an hour early for work. You can leave now," I replied, sitting back down.

Once Benny was gone, Kaylin tried to speak, but I wasn't in the mood for him right now.

"Not right now, Kay. I'll think about coming home. Give me some space. Damn, I have a lot of things to do today. I'm not tryin'a go there with you," I said, grabbing my keys and purse to leave, but before I could make it to the door, he grabbed me.

"Mimi, I know that I've messed up, but you ain't leaving me," he said, trying to kiss me.

I pushed him and left, giving him my ass to kiss in the process. Fuck wrong with this nigga? He must've completely lost his mind. If he cheated on me all those years without worrying about me, what would make me think that he won't continue to do it? I was leaving his ass. I just had to come up with a plan. I was going—me and my kids, and we were getting up outta here. That included Kayla too.

I made it to the salon real fast. When I got there, I saw that it was packed with people. I walked in and said a quick hello to everybody and went into the back office. I really didn't have enough time to talk, because I wanted to spend some time with Kayla today.

I started going over the books to make sure the numbers were right. I also made sure I had enough supplies. I wasn't really worrying too much about the numbers, because Troy was in charge of everything while I was gone. As I was going over everything, someone knocked on the door.

"Come in," I said to whoever it was on the other side of the door.

"Well, hello to you too, ma'am," Troy said, stepping inside of the office.

"Hey, girl, what's up?" I asked, not looking up at her. I already knew why she was coming in here anyway.

"Bitch, I know you needed some time off, but you could've at least called a bitch to let her know that you was all right and shit. I started to send a search party out looking for your ass," she said, taking a seat in one of the chairs across from my desk.

"Girl, I've been trying to get myself together. You know that I was going to call you," I replied, sitting straight up in the chair.

"Uh-huh, I bet you was. I know that you was with Jayden," she said, rolling her eyes.

"Yes, I was," I replied, smiling.

"Lemme find out," she said, laughing.

"Don't do me like that. I'm sorry for not calling you, but I do have something to tell you," I replied, becoming serious.

"Oh, shit, what's going on now?" she asked, concerned.

"Guess who I ran into at the hotel when I was seeing Jayden off today?"

"Now you know I ain't good at guessing. So you might as well just tell me."

"Bitch, you ain't no fun, but I ran into Tyreek, and you won't believe who he had with him," I said to her.

"Oh, no. Please don't tell me that. Did he have Kayla with him?"

"Well, I won't tell you then," I replied, looking her dead in the eyes.

"Oh my God, what are you going to do?" she asked me.

"Girl, I don't know. He wants me to tell Kay about him and Kayla tonight. He said if I don't tell him, then he will."

Truth was, even though I planned on leaving Kay, I still didn't want to hurt him. Yeah, I know what I said, but I still didn't want to.

"Mimi, I don't know what you're going to do, but you know that I always have your back," she said, getting teary-eyed.

"I really don't know what I'm going to do myself. I plan on taking my kids and getting the hell away from here," I responded.

"Well, what are you going to do about your club, salons, and rental properties?" she asked.

"That's really what I need to talk to you about. While I was at the hotel, I called my lawyer and had him transfer everything into your name," I said. I went into my purse, took out a stack of papers, and handed it to her.

"All I need for you to do is sign them. I also have a phone that I need you to keep on you at all times," I said, handing her a pen and the phone.

"Once I'm settled in, I'll call you. When I do call you, I want you to put the club up for sale," I said, looking up at her. I had to make sure she's listening.

"After you sell the club, I want you to put both salons up for sale. I also want you to get another bank account so that you could put all of the money in it."

"What are you going to do about the rental properties?"

"For now, I want to keep them."

She was about to say something but was stopped by the screams that were coming from the front of the salon. We both rushed out of the office to see what was going on. When we got there, we saw one of our stylists fussing with some chick.

"What's going on, Candy?"

"This little rachet-ass chick came up in here trying to start something," she answered, pointing to the chick she was fussing with.

"Look, bitch, I'll fuck you up. Keep playing with me," the chick threatened her.

I stepped between them, trying to diffuse the situation.

"Hello, I'm Mimi, the owner. How can I help you?" I asked her.

"So, you're the infamous Mimi, huh?" she taunted, looking me up and down.

"Yes, that would be me. I'm sorry, but who are you again?" I asked, sizing her up.

"I didn't say who I was, but I'm Jade. You may or may not know me," she said, with a smirk.

I instantly knew who she was.

"Bitch, what the fuck do you want?" Troy asked from behind me.

"First of all, I ain't gon' be too many more bitches. I came to see little Ms. Mimi," she replied, looking at me.

"*See me?* What could you possibly want to see me for?" I asked, catching an attitude.

This ho had a lot of nerves to be coming at me, I thought.

"I came here to tell you that I'm pregnant with Kaylin's baby and that he and I are going to be together. So I'd appreciate it if you'd leave him alone," she replied, bold as fuck.

I couldn't do anything but laugh at this ho. I mean, if she seriously thought that I gave a fuck about her and Kaylin being together, then she must be a stupid dumb bitch.

"Bitch, if you think that I give a fuck about you or Kaylin's dog ass, then you must be out of your mind. I'm happy that you want him, because I don't . . . and if you think that I give a lovely fuck about that little bastard-ass baby, then you're for damn sure slipping. I could care less about whoever Kaylin's with, because it won't be me," I replied, loud enough to let this ho know I wasn't playing.

"Bitch, if you know like me, you would keep me and my child out of ya mouth. I just came to tell you what was going on, woman to woman," she responded, rolling her neck like the ghetto, low-life bitch she was.

I was about to go in on that ho, but Troy stopped me.

"Mimi, I got this. Go ahead and get Kayla and K2 and K3 and do what you have to do," she said.

I nodded that I understood. I then turned to Jade.

"Bitch, you got lucky today, because I assure you that you was about to get one hell of an ass whooping,"

"Don't let Troy beat her too bad. I don't want to have any more problems than I already have up in here. Just let her get enough so that it would make her think twice about coming here again," I whispered to Candy.

"I promise that I'll call you when everything's straight," I said to Troy, hugging her.

When I pulled back, she had tears in her eyes.

"I'll be fine, Troy. I promise."

"Bitch, *I'm* lucky? *You're* the lucky one," Jade said, but before she could say anything else, Troy started punching her dead in her mouth.

I didn't even stick around to see the ass whopping that I know Troy would've put on her. I walked to my office, collected my things, and I was out.

I got into my car and sat there thinking about Kaylin. If I had any thoughts in the back of my mind about staying with him, they were all gone. Right then and there, I decided that I didn't give two fucks about him finding out about Kayla or not. By the time he found out, the kids and I would be long gone.

Tyreek

I was surprised when I saw Mimi at the hotel where Kayla and I were staying. She looked more surprised to see us than we were to see her. I didn't give a fuck about her tears. She shouldn't have kept my daughter a secret. What woman you know would do that? Not one in her right mind, that's for damn sure. No matter what went down, she shouldn't have stayed away from her daughter—period.

Kayla was happy, though. She's been talking about her mother since she last saw her. I wasn't too thrilled, but as long as my daughter was happy, so was I. After getting the keys to our room, I took her out to get a bite to eat, then we went to the mall to get us some clothes because we didn't come here with any. As we were shopping, I got a call from Mimi asking me where we were. Once I told her that we were at the mall, she said that she would be there in a minute. Since we were already finished, we waited for her in the food court area. When she did show up, she had her other kids with her.

"Thanks for letting me spend some time with her," she said to me.

"No problem, but I see that you're finally taking me serious this time," I replied. I was talking about Kayla getting the chance to meet her brothers and sister.

She just waved my comment off. I turned to say good-bye to my daughter, then I left.

I went back to the hotel room and chilled for a minute. With nothing to do, I decided to call Kaylin.

"What's 'sup, playboy?" I said as he answered the phone.

"Ain't shit, I'm just living. What's up with you?"

"Ain't shit, man. I'm in yo' town right now," I said.

"Oh, yeah, man? Where you at?" he asked.

"I'm chillin' in my hotel room."

"All right, man, take down this address that I'm about to give you," he replied, reciting an address.

"Where I'm coming to, nigga?" I asked him.

"That's the address to Mimi's club. I'm over here getting everything ready for the concert at the club tonight," he replied.

"All right, homie, I'll be there in a minute."

"For sure. See you when you get here," he said.

"Bet."

I shook my head and sat there, smoking a blunt. Then I left my room and made my way to Mimi's club to meet Kaylin. This nigga really didn't know what's coming to him, I thought.

Mimi

After I left the salon, I went to pick up my kids before I went to get Kayla. Once I had them, I called Tyreek to see where they were. When he informed me that they were at the mall, I made my way to go and get her. I was excited and nervous at the same time, because I didn't know how my kids were going to react when they see their sister. I really hoped that this would go as smooth as I thought it would; either way, I wasn't turning back now.

After finding a parking space, I got my kids and headed inside to get Kayla. They were sitting in the food court waiting for me. With every step that I took, my heart pounded an extra two beats. My plans were to introduce Kayla to her brothers and sister, take them shopping, then hit the road and never look back.

Only the Lord knows that I hate having to fool with Tyreek. He made me sick every time I looked at him. Like now, all I said was thanks for letting me spend some time with her, and here he was saying something smart. All he had to do was say you're welcome, but he didn't, which was why I ignored his ass and went about my damn business.

I waited for him to leave so that I could get this over with. I sat in the food court and watched as my kids stared at each other. K3 was looking at Kayla like, "Bitch, who you is?" but don't get it wrong, she was mugging them back. I just smiled because all of my kids had my attitude.

"Come here," I said to my kids.

"You too, Kayla."

"Kayson and Kaylon, this is your sister Kayla," I said to them.

They said nothing as they stared her down closely. Out of the corner of my eyes, I saw Kailay watching her. So I went over to talk to her.

"Kailay, baby, this is your sister Kayla. She's your twin sister," I said to her. I waited to talk to her last, because this was a big deal to everybody, especially her.

"Twin? You mean, like Kaylon and Kayson?" she asked me, looking confused as hell.

"Yes, baby, like your brothers, you and Kayla are twins," I responded to her. She looked back at Kayla, and then me.

"Come here, Kayla," I said, motioning for her to come over to us.

"Baby, I know this might be a little weird for you all, but this is your twin. You and Kayla were in my tummy at the same time and were born on the same day," I said to my daughter Kailay.

"If she's my twin, then why we don't look alike, like Kaylon and Kayson?" she asked me. I swear, for an eight-year-old, my daughter caught on to everything.

"It's real complicated. I promise to explain it to you one day. But let's get through this first, okay?"

I watched as Kailay walked over to Kayla.

"Hi, I'm Kailay, and I'm your twin sister. Nice to meet you," she said to her, extending her hand.

"I know, and I'm so excited to meet you. I never knew that I had a twin sister," she replied.

She then reached over and hugged Kailay. Kailay hesitated a little, but she hugged her back. At the sight of their sister hugging Kayla, the boys ran over and joined in.

"Hi, I'm Kayson, and this is Kaylon," he said, as he started hugging and kissing on her, while Kaylon was talking nonstop about his toys and whatnot.

"Nice to meet y'all. I'm your sister, Kayla," she replied, smiling.

"We know," they both said together, causing everybody to laugh.

"Mom, can we go shopping now?" Kailay and Kayla asked at the same time.

I laughed because they'd just met, and it's like they were never apart.

"Yes, we can go shopping now," I responded to them.

That went smoother than I thought it would go. After getting acquainted with each other, I took them shopping. Every store that we went to, the girls picked out the same clothes, but in different colors. I guess they were trying to make up for lost time. The boys reminded me so much of their father. They picked out the same kind of clothes and shoes they saw him in and kept on talking about they got swag or whatever.

After we were finished shopping, I took the kids to get something to eat, and after that, we left. On my way home, I called Troy to tell her that I was leaving. I informed her that if anybody came by looking for me, she was to tell them that she hadn't seen or heard from me. She informed me that Kaylin and Tyreek came by the shop together. Hearing that made me speed up a little. I was not trying to run into them because I already know that Tyreek was going to try to start some shit. I told her that I would call her once we were on the highway, then I hung up the phone, and threw it out the window.

I arrived at my house, quickly parked, and got the kids out. Once we were inside, I instructed them to go to their rooms and get one thing that they really wanted. After I told them what to do, I then headed to my room. I wasn't trying to pack anything. I would get all new stuff once I arrived at my destination. I walked into my closet and grabbed my safe. I opened it and removed four yellow envelopes, which contained our birth certificates, Social Security cards, passports, and other important documents. I then removed my bank statements and deeds to my properties.

I took one last look around and then headed to get the kids so we could leave. We headed down the stairs, but before we could get to the door, someone entered, stopping me dead in my tracks.

"Well, well, well. I hope I'm not interrupting anything. You going somewhere? You look like you're in a hurry," I heard a voice said.

"What are you doing here, Stacy?" I asked her.

"I came here looking for Kaylin. Is he here?" she asked with a smirk on her face.

"Obviously, you can see that he's not here. So you're gonna have to come back when he is," I replied, trying to move past her.

"Not so fast. You see, I came here to introduce somebody, with the intention that Kay would be here too, but since he isn't, I'm going to do it anyway," she said.

"Introduce who? As you can see, I don't have time for your bullshit right now. I'm busy."

"We'll see," she said, stepping to the side. A little boy was standing behind her.

"Meet the fifth member of Kaylin's crew, Kaylin Jr."

I stood there shocked. I mean, obviously he was Kaylin's child, because he looked just like him. If I didn't know any better, I'd think he was Kayson or Kaylon, only taller. That's how much he looked like them, and they looked like Kay.

"Kaylin Jr., say hi to Mimi and your sister and brothers," she said to him, pointing behind me to where the kids were standing.

"Hi," he said to the kids.

"Oh, and little Ms. Kayla's here too, I see. I take it Kaylin knows about you and Tyreek then?"

"How old is he?" I asked, ignoring her last statement.

"He's nine years old. Only a year older than Kayla and Kailay," she replied.

"How do you know about Kayla?" I asked her.

"Well, I've known about Kayla for a year. You see, my plan actually was to come and tell you about Kaylin Jr., and to tell Kaylin Sr. about you, Tyreek, and Kayla," she replied.

"What could you possibly gain by telling him about Kayla?" I asked her.

"Everything that I'm entitled to. I've played the back end to you for too long. Now it's time that I finally get what I deserve, and that's my family, which includes Kaylin and his kids," she said, drawing a gun from behind her back.

"Bitch, I could give zero fucks about you or Kaylin. I don't want him, and the only way that you'll be able to take my kids is over my dead body," I told her.

"That can be arranged," she said, pointing her gun toward me, but before she could pull the trigger, we heard Kaylin's voice.

"Mimi, where you at, and why is the door wide open?" I heard him ask, but I didn't answer him.

Once I entered the living room, my eyes landed on Kaylin and Tyreek. I watched as he looked at me then Stacy holding a gun.

"Mimi, what's going on? And, Stacy, why the fuck are you here?"

"As you can see, I got tired of you hiding me and keeping my son a secret. So I came here to finally tell Mimi. But when I got here, little Miss Mimi was leaving, and imagine my surprise when I saw little Miss Kailay together with her twin sister Kayla," she said to him, pointing toward Kailay and Kayla.

"Twin sister? Bitch, what the fuck are you talking about? Kailay's not a twin," he said to her, then looked at me.

"Why don't you ask Mimi what I'm talking about."

Just then, Kayla ran over to Tyreek.

"Daddy, what's going on? Why do that lady has a gun pointed at Mommy?" she asked him. I looked at him and then looked at Kaylin, who looked like he was getting madder by the second.

"*Daddy?* 'Reek, I thought you said that you didn't have any kids, and, Mimi, why is this little girl calling you Mommy?" he asked me and Tyreek.

Again, I said nothing as I watched them.

"Well, I lied. This here is Mimi's and my daughter Kayla. She also happens to be Kailay's twin sister," Tyreek said to Kaylin.

"Yo, Mimi, what the fuck is going on?" he asked me again. All I did was look from Kayla to the rest of my children.

"Cat got your tongue, bitch?" Stacy said, a little too loud for me.

"Bitch, you better say something. Explain this shit right now!" Kaylin screamed.

I was so busy looking at Stacy that I didn't see him pulling a gun from his waist.

"Don't have a lot to say now, do you, Mimi?" she taunted.

"I guess Kaylin will finally get to see you for the real ho that you are."

"Fuck that, I've had enough of both of you. Bitch, you came in here trying to start something over a nigga who will never be for you," I said to Stacy, shutting her up.

"And you, I've had just about all I can take from you. First, you cheat on me with these random, microwaveable bitches, and then you go ahead and cheat on me with a bitch that was supposed to be my friend. Not to mention that you have a baby with her," I said to him, pointing to Stacy.

"Now you want to bitch about me. Nigga, I should've been left yo' ass, but I played a game of catch back and started fucking your friend. I pulled one of your moves on you."

"Bitch, and you proud to say that, ho?" he said, inching toward me.

"What, nigga, you mad or nah?" I asked him.

"You want to know something else? On the day that y'all got knocked by the police, I fucked both of y'all and got pregnant with Kayla and Kailay. When I found out that Kayla wasn't yours, I decided to move, but you were supposed to stay behind. Instead, you followed me, and I had to leave Kayla with Tyreek's mother. But don't think that I've completely abandoned her. That ten thousand that I would get from you each month went to Tyreek for Kayla. Remember the 'monthly meetings' I'd have to take? Well, it wasn't actually a business meeting. I went to see Kayla.

"You want to be so high and mighty like you're so innocent, but you're not. Kayla and Kailay are eight, if I can recall right. Didn't you say Kaylin Jr. is nine years old? So you do the math, but that's not all. I ran into Jade today at the salon, and she told me that you all are expecting," I spat.

"Bitch, and you think you got something special," I said to Stacy.

I then walked over to my kids and prepared to leave.

"Bitch, I don't care what the fuck I did. You were fucking my friend, my best friend at that, and you got pregnant. Not only did you get pregnant with one baby, but you got pregnant with twins, by two different niggas," he said.

"And you, nigga, you was supposed to be my boy, but you go behind my back and fuck *my* bitch and got her pregnant," he said, pointing his gun at Tyreek.

"Kayla, go to your mother," Tyreek said to the child.

She then ran over to me crying. I instructed my kids to go upstairs to their room. They all started crying but went anyway.

"Nigga, you fucked my bitch, so why you mad? I think we even," Tyreek responded, moving closer to Kaylin.

All of a sudden, things started going in slow motion. I watched as Kaylin raised his gun and shot Tyreek in the head, killing him instantly. I heard screaming and crying, but I couldn't move for nothing. Kaylin then pointed his gun at me. The look on his face was one that I've never seen before.

"I told you that I'd kill you if you tried to leave me," he said, walking toward me.

I tried to run, but I didn't get too far before I felt four hot slugs in my back. I heard more crying and screaming as my life started flashing before my eyes. The last thing I remembered was Stacy standing over me with a smirk on her face. Then everything went black.

Troy

I've been calling Mimi's phone since I left the salon, but she wasn't answering. She was supposed to call me once she was on the road, but she never did. I started to worry as I hopped in my car and headed to her house.

I pulled onto her block and noticed a lot of police cars and two ambulances. I wondered what was going on. I drove down farther and noticed that they were at Mimi's and Kaylin's house. I hurriedly parked my car, and then ran over to the house.

"Hey, you can't go in there," I heard someone say from behind me, but I wasn't trying to hear none of that.

Once I made it inside the house, I saw blood and a body bag by the door. I broke down crying as I continued to walk farther inside of the house.

"Hey, you can't be in here," an officer said, walking over to me.

"This is my sister's house. Can you tell me what's going on?" I asked him.

"What's your sister's name?"

"Amina Washington."

He then walked over to some old black dude and said something to him. The man then looked at me and walked over to where I was standing.

"Hello, I'm Detective Webber. What's your name and relation to the home owner?"

"My name is Katherine Miller, and I'm Amina Washington's sister. We moved here a couple of years ago from Louisiana. Can somebody please tell me what's going on?"

"Well, Ms. Miller, we received a 911 call saying that there were shots fired at this address. When we got here, we found two bodies; a male and a female. One, as you could see, is over there by the door, and the other one is over by the stairs.

"Witnesses said that they saw a man leaving the scene in an all-red 2013 Yukon Denali, and a female with a little boy leaving the scene in a 2011 gray Toyota Camry."

"Can you tell me whose body it is that you've found?" I asked him, hoping Mimi wasn't one of them.

"Well, we need someone to identify both bodies. Will you be able to do that?" he asked me. I nodded, saying a silent prayer in the process.

"Right this way," he said, leading me over to the body by the door. He then instructed the coroner to open the bag. Once he opened the bag and I saw the body, I gasped loudly.

"Th—that's Tyreek Carter," I said to him.

"Tyreek Carter, and what is Mr. Carter's relationship to the home owners?" he asked.

"He's the father of one of Mimi's, I mean, Amina's, twin daughters, and a friend of Kaylin Williams," I replied, and he looked at me like, "Bitch, what did you say?"

"Kaylin Williams, is that the other home owner's name?"

"Yes."

"And where is Mr. Williams now?"

"I don't know. The last time I seen him, they were together," I said, pointing to Tyreek's dead body.

"Okay," he replied, writing something down on his notepad.

"Follow me this way," he said, walking farther into the house.

With each step that he took, it felt like my oxygen was being cut off. I mean, there was blood and shell cases everywhere. We walked toward the stairs where another body was covered by a white blanket. Once we were there, he instructed the coroner to lift up the blanket so that I could see who was underneath it.

When the blanket was finally pulled away, I dropped to my knees. I started boo-hooing at the sight before me. I looked at my best friend of eight years lying there lifeless on that cold-ass floor. I screamed and cursed out loud, not caring who could see or hear me. My best friend was gone. She wasn't coming back, and it was all Kaylin's fault. I was so emotional that I had to be removed.

"No, Mimi. Please get up. Baby, please get up. It can't be you down there," I screamed, trying to break away from the people who were holding me back. A little while later, I was calm enough to talk to the detective.

"Kaylin did this. I know he did," I said to him.

"And how do you know that?" he asked.

"Because Mimi found out that he was cheating on her again. She was going to leave him today. She was also taking her kids with her. They were going to leave Atlanta for good, but he told her that if she left him, then he would kill her, and he did. He killed my best friend," I replied as I started to cry again.

"Okay," he said, as he walked off to talk to another officer. Once he was done, he then walked back over to me.

"I've got officers out looking for Mr. Williams. I also put an APB out on his car."

"The kids, where are the kids?" I asked him.

"Kids? When we arrived here, there was only one child here. A female. She says her name is Kayla," he said to me.

"No, no, no. Mimi and Kaylin have three children. An eight-year-old girl named Kailay Williams, who happens to be Kayla's twin sister, and two four-year-old twin boys named Kaylon and Kayson Williams. Oh my God, he took them. Please don't tell me that he took the kids with him," I said.

"Ma'am, when we arrived here, there was only one child. Now, if you say that there are three more kids, then I have to assume that Mr. Williams has indeed taken them with him."

"Please, you have to find them. Mimi would want them with me, not him. Please find them. Please," I pleaded.

"Excuse me," he said.

He walked over to some lady, whispered something, and they walked over to me.

"Hi, I'm Mrs. Holmes from DFACS. I understand that you said that there are three children missing."

"Yes, Mimi and Kaylin's eight-year-old daughter and their four-year-old twin boys."

"Okay, do you have any recent photos of the children?"

"Not on me, but there are some inside."

"Umm . . . Detective, we're going to need recent photos of the children so that we can send out an Amber Alert in the immediate and surrounding areas. Could you please escort Ms. Miller into the house, so that she can retrieve them?"

"Yes, right this way."

Once I got the photos out of the house, I went back over to the woman from DFACS.

"Excuse me, but what's going to happen to Kayla?"

"For now, we'll be taking her down to the station until we can locate her family," she replied.

"She doesn't have any family. We moved here from Louisiana years ago. I'm all she has left. Can I take her?"

"Once we verify who you are, then you'll be able to take her. But until then, Kayla has to stay in our care," she replied.

"So she'll be spending the night at the station?"

"Most likely," she replied.

"Mrs. Holmes, I'm her aunt. This child has been through enough tonight. Please let me take her," I begged.

"Ms. Miller, I can't do that," she replied.

"Please, I'm begging you. I'm all she has left," I said to her.

She looked at me, and then at Kayla, who was crying silently in the backseat of the car.

"Okay, I'm not supposed to be doing this, but I'll let you take her."

"Thank you," I said and sighed in relief.

"I'm going to need your full name, address, and phone number. If everything checks out, then maybe you'll be able to keep her." She handed me a pen and paper.

I quickly wrote down everything that she needed, and then handed it back to her. Once she had my info, she opened up the back door to let Kayla out.

"Auntie Troy," she said, running to me, crying.

"Come on, baby. Let's get out of here," I said to her.

I took one last look at the house and walked away. God, please give me the strength to do this, I said to myself.

Arriving at my car, I secured her and went around to the driver's side. When I got in the car, she was still crying. I reached over and kissed her forehead.

"It's going to be all right, baby," I said to her.

"Auntie Troy, are Mommy and Daddy going to be okay?" she asked me.

"I don't know, baby," I replied. I couldn't tell her the truth.

"Well, where are my sister and brothers? That man and woman took them. They had a little boy with them, and they said he was my brother too," she said to me.

"What woman, Kayla? What little boy? Honey, what you are talking about?"

"When we went over to Mommy's house, she told us to get something that we wanted to take with us. I didn't have anything to take, so my sister gave me something of hers to take. When we were leaving, a woman came inside. She said her name was Stacy or something. She told Mommy something, then she introduced some boy name Kaylin Jr., and said that he was our brother."

"Kayla, baby, what else happened?" I asked her.

"Well, after that, her and Mommy started fussing, and she pointed a gun at Mommy. That's when my daddy and a man who looked like Kayson and Kaylon walked in. He started fussing with the woman, but she turned him against Mommy. He started calling Mommy all kind of nasty words and was asking about me and my dad. He pointed a gun at my dad, and that's when my dad told me to go by Mommy. When I got to Mommy, I was crying. She told me, my sister, and my brothers to go upstairs to the room. While we were in the room, we heard a lot of fussing and cussing. That's when we heard gunshots, so we hid in the closet. We heard screaming and crying, then three or four more shots. Then everything went silent."

"Well, where are your sister and brothers?" I asked her.

"After everything went silent, the man came upstairs and took them. He left me there. I waited a little while before I went downstairs, and I saw my mommy and daddy lying on the ground in a lot of blood. I was going to go check on them, but when I was going, the police came inside. They took me outside and started questioning me, but I couldn't say nothing. I was still worried about my mommy and daddy," she replied.

I sat there in silence wondering what the fuck was up with Kaylin and why Stacy was there.

"After a while, some lady came and sat me in a car. That's when you showed up."

"Okay, baby, you don't have to say no more," I told her.

"Auntie Troy, I'm scared. I just met my sister and brothers, and I want my mommy and daddy," she said, crying. I rocked her in my arms and let her cry.

"It's okay, baby. Everything is going to be all right," I said, rocking her back and forth. It took a minute for her to calm down, but when she finally did, she had fallen asleep. I laid her back in the seat and prepared to leave.

I turned the car on and pulled off. I didn't know how I was going to get through this, but I had one thing on my mind as I rode down the lonely Atlanta highway, and that was to make both Kaylin and Stacy pay for what they did to Mimi. I didn't have a lot of time, but I was going to come up with a foolproof plan. No matter where they went, I was going to find them and kill them both. Slowly.

Stacy

Yes, finally, I've gotten what I wanted for years. I won't ever have to play second to Mimi's ass ever again. My son can finally have an actual family, with both of his parents and his siblings. I just couldn't believe that Kaylin actually killed Mimi. I mean, I was happy that she's dead and all, but I didn't think that he would actually do it. I was also shocked when he killed Tyreek. That wasn't a part of my plans. I didn't know that he would even be there. I guess Tyreek was in the right place, but at the wrong time.

When I went to Mimi's house, my intentions were to tell her about Kaylin Jr. and to tell Kaylin Sr. about Mimi, Kayla, and Tyreek. I didn't think that he would leave her, let alone kill her, and I was kind of bittersweet about the whole thing. I mean, if he could do that to a woman he claimed that he was madly in love with, then what would he do to me?

After leaving Mimi's house, Kaylin ended up taking his three kids with him. I was mad because he left little Kayla there all by herself, but what was I supposed to do? He instructed me to go home and pack a few bags for Kaylin and me so that we could leave Atlanta ASAP. While we went to pack, Kaylin said that he had a few things that he needed to take care of, something important. So he and his kids ended up leaving right away.

I packed as many bags as I could and placed them by my bedroom door. I then went to my closet and removed all of Kaylin Jr.'s and my important documents. After I made sure that I had everything, I went to check on my son. I walked into his room, where he was sitting on the bed looking all sad.

"K.J., what's wrong with you, and why haven't you started packing yet?" I asked, walking over to him.

"Because, Mom, why do we have to leave? I like it here, and besides, I just met my sisters and brothers. I don't want to leave," he said, whining.

"Kaylin, right now, I don't have time for your shit. I'ma need for you to get your suitcases out of the closet and start packing before your father comes back here."

"Why do we have to leave? Is it because Dad shot them people? If so, then why do we have to go with him?" he asked, all in one breath. His little ass was trying to be too grown, and I really didn't have time for him right now.

"Kaylin, I don't have time for your shit right now. So get your ass off of that fucking bed and pack them bags. Now!" I said, pointing my finger at him.

I watched as he took his sweet little time getting off of the bed. He then went over to his dresser and started pulling clothes out. One piece at a time. He was actually moving like a damn turtle, so I went ahead and started to help him. By the time we were finished, Kaylin still hadn't made it back. I wondered where that nigga was.

I brought all of our things downstairs, then I went ahead and fixed us something to eat. We both sat there and ate in silence as I thought about the events that took place earlier tonight. When we were done eating, we sat down in the living room to watch a little TV and wait on Kaylin. When I looked at the clock, it was late as hell. I had no idea where that nigga was at, but I know he better hurry the fuck up.

Kaylin

I didn't want to shoot Mimi, but I had no choice. I had to. She was trying to leave me, and I already told her that if she left me, that I would kill her, so I did. What really pissed me off was finding out that her and Tyreek were fucking. Well, they used to or were, but that wasn't the point. The point was that they did it, and for her to try to clown about it was fucked up. Then they had the nerves to have a child together and shit. The kicker is, she's my daughter's twin sister. Now where they do that at? Bitch must've thought I was stupid or something. Fuck, my nerves just all over the place, but I know I had to get my ass out of Atlanta. Fast!

After getting my kids and leaving the house, I told Stacy to go ahead and pack her some clothes for her and Kaylin Jr. I had some shit to do before leaving, so I had to leave, but I took my kids with me. I mean, yeah, she was my other son's mother, but I didn't trust that bitch around my kids. I was only taking her ass because of Kaylin. Otherwise, she would've stayed her ass in Atlanta.

After I left Stacy's house, I went to my apartment that I kept. It was right by my strip clubs. I needed to get all my things outta the safe, because more than likely, I won't be returning to Atlanta anytime soon. I parked my car, and I got the kids from out of the backseat and headed inside of the building. I was almost to the door when I was stopped by a voice coming from behind me.

"Kaylin," she said in a sad voice.

"Jade, what the hell are you doing here?" I asked her.

"I need to speak with you. I tried calling, but you won't answer, so I decided to see if you was up here," she replied, walking over to me.

I took a step back. Obviously, this lonely bitch didn't get the fucking memo.

"You must be out of your mind. I didn't answer the phone, because I didn't want to talk to you. You played the fuck out of me, and what you did earlier at Mimi's shop was foul as fuck. If you're indeed pregnant, then I know that baby ain't mine. I always wore a condom, bitch, remember? You're better off getting another abortion, and you know it. Ain't no way a ho could raise a boy or girl," I said turning to open the apartment door. This bitch was tripping. Lemme just get the fuck in here and get my shit so I could be out. *There's nothing in Atlanta for me anymore,* I thought to myself.

"Kaylin, you can't do this to me. I know that this baby is yours. Remember, the last time we had sex? You didn't wear a condom," she replied, crying.

I shook my head. I looked at her and closed the door. That shit only made her crazy ass spazz out more.

"Kaylin, open the door. You can't do me like this. I'm pregnant with your baby. We're supposed to be a family," she screamed, kicking and beating on the door.

"Kaylin, please. We're supposed to be together, as a family, as one. I promise I'll do whatever you want. All I want to do is be with you," she hollered, continuing to make an ass out of herself.

The crazy bitch continued beating on the door like she was about to break it down. My kids started crying, and that shit angered me.

I walked to the door as I made sure that I had my gun on me. I mean, who knew what this crazy bitch was capable of. Removing the locks from the door, I opened it fast. This bitch was still standing there, looking a mess with snot and makeup running all over her face. I removed my gun and pointed it at her.

"Bitch, I asked you nicely to leave, but you want to act an ass. I told you that I don't want you, and yet, you're out here making a complete fool of yourself. Bitch, get this through your head. I don't want you, and that baby ain't mine," I spat through gritted teeth.

"Kay, please," she sobbed.

"I'm giving you five minutes to move the fuck up out of here before I dead that ass once and for all." I backed up a little, so she could move, but she just stood there staring.

"Bitch, do we have a muthafucking problem?" I asked while I cocked my gun.

The sound of that made her eyes pop out.

"No, we don't have a problem," she said, shaking her head as she began to back up.

I watched as she backed up all the way to the door and left the building. Once I was sure that she was gone, I went back inside to tend to my children.

"Daddy, I want my mommy," my son Kaylon said, crying.

"Yeah, Daddy, I want Mommy too," Kayson said. He was also crying.

"Mommy's not coming, because Daddy and that lady killed her," Kailay said sadly.

I looked at her shocked. I mean, I knew that I killed her mother, but I didn't think that she would know.

"Kailay, I didn't shoot Mommy. She had an accident," I lied to her.

She looked at me and rolled her eyes. "If she had an accident, then why we aren't at the hospital, and why isn't Kayla with us?" she asked with an attitude.

I stared at her. My baby girl who loved me so much was showing me a side that I've never seen from her before.

"It's complicated," I replied, walking to the back room.

"It's not complicated, Daddy. You killed Mommy and left my sister. You also shot that man, and now I hate you!" she screamed at me.

I decided not to say anything to her about it. We all needed some time to cool down.

Once I entered the room, I went straight to the closet. I opened the safe, grabbed a duffel bag, and started throwing all of my things in it. When I was finished, I grabbed the duffel and another empty bag from out of the closet, and went into the second and third room and removed everything out of each of the safes that I had in the closets. I probably had almost three million in cash and jewelry altogether. Along with the product that I had, I was going to be straight for a minute. I know once word got out that I was nowhere to be found, I'd be the prime suspect. Not to mention, they had an eight-year-old witness that I'd left behind. Which is why I had to leave right away. If I wanted a chance to get out of Atlanta, then I had to leave now.

After dragging all the bags into the living room, I double-checked to make sure that I didn't leave anything behind that could link me to the apartment. Once I was sure that everything was straight, I grabbed the bags and the kids and headed out the door. I decided to take the minivan since they would probably be looking for all of my cars. The van was in Stacy's name, so I know that we'd be straight. I threw the bags in the back, then buckled the kids up and headed to pick up Stacy and Kaylin Jr.

I made it to Stacy's house in no time. I parked in the driveway and blew the horn. She opened the door and walked over to the van.

"Shit, Stacy, come on. Where's Kaylin?" I asked her.

"Shit, you took so long that he fell asleep," she snapped.

"Well, come on then. We gotta go."

"I mean, you could come help me with the bags."

"Not right now, Stacy. I don't have time for your shit," I said, getting out of the van.

"Come on."

I made it inside and grabbed the bags as Stacy went to grab Kaylin. She then went into the kitchen and came back out with a big brown bag.

"What's that?" I asked.

"While you were gone, I made some snacks and sandwiches for the kids. I don't know where we're going, but I know that they're going to be hungry," she replied.

"All right, come on so we can get out of here," I responded.

Once we were outside, she closed and locked the door. I opened the back of the van so that I could put their bags inside while Stacy strapped Kaylin into the van with his sister and brothers. I looked to see if anybody was watching. I didn't see anybody, but that didn't mean that they weren't there. The streets were always watching.

I jumped in the car and sat there, trying to catch a breath. A lot happened within the past few hours. I looked in the rearview mirror at my kids. All of them had tired looks on their faces.

"Where exactly are we going, Kaylin?" Stacy asked me as I backed out of the driveway.

"I don't know," I replied, shaking my head.

I really didn't know. If somebody would've told me twenty-four hours ago that my life would be like this, I probably would've laughed right in their faces. But right now, I couldn't, because my life was fucked up because of me, and I knew that from this point on, it won't be getting any better.

Jayden

I've been trying to get in touch with Mimi for hours now, but she hadn't answered any of my calls. The last time that I'd talked to her, she said that she was taking her kids and they were leaving Kaylin and Atlanta for good. I mean, I knew that she had plans to leave him, but I didn't think that she would leave him this soon. If I would've known that, then I wouldn't have left. I would've stayed there until she got her things and the kids, and they were all out of harm's way.

I was able to get her to decide to come to West Virginia, where I lived. She was supposed to call me and let me know that everything was okay with her and the kids. I was really worried, because she told me that ole boy had threatened to kill her if she'd leave him. I wanted to go back down there when she told me that, but she begged me not to and promised that she would be okay. Hell, this nigga had me ready to bring it to him behind a female, and she wasn't even my woman. Like I said before, though, Mimi had me like that. She's the kind of woman that you would want to make your first and your last. I'd be devastated if I lost her.

As I walked around pacing back and forth, trying to get in touch with her, my phone started ringing. I looked at it hoping that it would be Mimi, but it wasn't. It was my boy Mark calling me. I really wasn't trying to hang out tonight. Well, not without seeing or making sure that Mimi and her kids were okay.

"Yo, what's up with ya, man?" I asked, answering the phone.

"Shit, I can't call it. You done heard from ya girl yet?" he asked, referring to Mimi.

"Nah, man, she hasn't returned my calls, and I've been trying to get in touch with her for hours," I replied.

"Yo, my man, you might need to check that out. Something is definitely not right," he said.

"Man, I'm trying, but she's not answering. I know that punk-ass nigga had better not touch her, though." I was getting heated again.

"Yo, man, let me call ole girl and see if she know something. I mean, they are friends and shit," he said.

"Oh, yeah, they're friends. Shit, man, I didn't know you was still talking to her."

"Yeah, bruh. We be kicking it on the phone every now and then. Lemme call her and see what's up with ya girl. I'll call you back in a minute," he said.

"Yeah, you do that, while I try to call her again," I replied, hanging up the phone.

After talking with Mark, I tried calling Mimi once again, but I still didn't get an answer. Just as I was about to call her once more, my phone started to ring. I looked to see that it was an Atlanta number calling. Thinking that it was Mimi calling from a different phone, I answered in a hurry.

"Mimi, hey, ma, what's up? Why you haven't been answering the phone?" I asked.

"Hello, I'm Detective Webber with the Atlanta Police Department. I've seen that you've called Ms. Washington's phone a countless number of times. May I ask who you are," I heard a deep voice say.

"I-I'm Jayden. I'm a friend of Ms. Washington. Can you tell me what's going on, and why do you have her phone?" I asked him.

"Well, it seems that Ms. Washington has been in an accident," he responded, making my heart rate speed up.

"An accident? Can you tell me what happened?"

"I'm sorry, but I'm not at liberty to say," he replied.

"Well, how am I supposed to find out what's going on?"

"You could come down to the station if you like."

"I live in another state."

"Well, I'm sorry, but like I said, I'm not at liberty to discuss the situation over the phone."

"Okay. Thank you anyway," I said, hanging up the phone.

I went to my room to pack some clothes. I was going back to Atlanta to find out what was going on with Mimi. When I was done packing, I tried to call Mark to see if he'd heard anything from Troy, but like everybody else, he wasn't answering the phone. *Fuck it,* I thought as I grabbed my bags and headed for the door, where I ran straight into Mark. I realized that he had a bag on his shoulder and a suitcase in his hand.

"What's up, man? I just called you, and what's up with the bags?"

"I know, but I was so busy packing for our trip down to Atlanta, that I didn't hear the phone. Besides, I wanted to tell you what I had to, face-to-face. Let's go back inside right quick, though."

"All right," I said, as I followed him back into the house and went into the living room in silence.

"Yo, man, what's up? Why you so quiet?" I asked him once we were seated on the sofa. He said nothing as he just stared into space.

"Yo, my nigga, what's up? Why you so quiet?" I asked him again, nervously.

"Not too long ago, I got off the phone with Troy," he replied, sitting back on the sofa.

"Yeah? Some detective just called me and said something about Mimi being in an accident. Did she say how bad it was?" I asked him, but he said nothing.

"Yo, man, what she said?" I asked again, not sure I really wanted to hear what he was about to say.

"She's dead," he replied.

I sat there stuck. A lump formed in my throat, and I tried so desperately to swallow, but it wasn't budging.

"Dead? What happened?" I asked, not believing him.

"Man, she said ole girl planned to leave her man today. They got in a fuss earlier at her club, but she brushed it off because she had made plans to take her kids and leave Atlanta tonight. She went to pick up her kids from school early, and they went to the mall to get a few things. After they left the mall, she called to let her know that she was on her way over to the house and that she was leaving after. Before they hung up the phone, she promised her that she would call her once she was on the road to wherever she was going. Hours went by, and ya girl never called, so she called her, but she never answered. So she decided to drive by her house. When she made it to Mimi's, there were cops and two ambulances there. When she got inside, there were blood and shell cases everywhere, but ya girl Mimi was nowhere in sight," he said, stopping to catch his breath.

"She asked the cops what was going on, but they asked her for her identification and shit. Once she gave them her info and shit, they asked her to identify two bodies. She said the first body was some dude named Tyreek, but the second body was Mimi's. She said homeboy shot her like three or four times. He must have taken the kids and left before the police got there, because when they got there, he was nowhere in sight. She also said something about a chick named Stacy being there or something like that." He got up and walked over to the duffel bag that he'd brought in. He picked up the bag, then came and sat down.

"I know it's hard, being that you just met her and all, but I also know that you'd want to go back down there. Which is why I packed these," he said, showing me a variety of guns. "I also packed myself a bag, because you know I wasn't going to let you go alone."

I sat there for a minute, trying to get myself together. I mean, like he said, I just met her, but I couldn't let him get away with it. I felt something for her, and for that, this nigga was going to pay. I had planned on making a future with her, but I couldn't now.

"All right, man, thanks. I know that I can always depend on you, because you always have my back," I said, giving him a dap and brotherly hug.

"Fo' sure. man, you already know that you my nigga," he replied, returning the love. When we were done, we just stood around until I broke the silence.

"All right, man, let's go bring some of the West Virginia heat to the A," I said, picking up my bags and heading for the door.

"Shit, I know they ain't ready for this here," he replied, as he followed me out the door.

Atlanta PD better get ready, because I'm not leaving until I find that nigga. And when I do find him, there's going to be a lot of flower bringing and sad song singing, I thought as I locked up the door and headed to my car. All I know is, if they ain't ready, they better get ready.

Mimi

Opening my eyes, I looked to see that I was standing in my living room. As I looked on, I noticed there was blood all over the place. I began to walk around to see what was going on. As I was walking around, I saw Troy bent over by the door. I walked over to her so that I could see what she was doing. Looking down, I noticed Tyreek's lifeless body in a body bag. My head immediately started to spin as I tried to figure out what was going on.

Turning toward Troy, I asked, "What's going on, Troy? What happened to Tyreek?"

Troy said nothing to me as she continued to talk to a detective. I watched her mouth Tyreek's name as the detective wrote something down on his notepad. He said something to her and motioned for her to follow him to the back of the house. I walked to the back of the house too, where I saw more blood and shell cases everywhere. Stooping by the stairs, I saw another body there. The detective waved for the coroner to remove the cover, and when he did, I almost passed out.

I started shaking as I looked at myself lying there in a body bag. I then realized that I was wearing a long white gown, and my skin had a glow to it. Looking around, I noticed that everyone was moving past me and around me, and not one of them could see or hear me.

"Where am I?" I asked out loud.

"You're between the lines of the living and the dead," I heard a voice say. Turning around, I saw my grandma standing there.

"Oh my God, Grandma," I said, walking over to her, not believing my eyes.

"Yes, baby, it's me," she replied, taking my hand into hers.

"Well, if you're here, then that means that I'm—" I paused, not wanting to finish my own statement.

"No, baby, you're not dead. It seems that your soul is not yet ready to cross over," she responded to my statement.

"How did I get here, and where are my children?" I asked her.

"Your kids are fine for now, and if you'd turn around, I can show you how you got here," she said, waving her hands for me to turn around.

Turning around, I watched as I pulled up to the house and got my kids from out of the car. We then went inside, where I instructed them to get one thing that they really wanted.

"Do you remember how you got here now, Amina?"

Shaking my head, I said, "No."

"Well, let's continue on with this, shall we?" she asked, as I nodded my head for her to continue.

I then watched as I ran upstairs to my bedroom. Once I was in the room, I went into the closet and removed a couple of envelopes from the safe. After getting whatever it was that I needed, I hurriedly ran out of the room, into the kids' rooms. Once we were all finished, we were prepared to leave.

"Do you remember what happened next?" I heard my grandma ask, stopping yet again. I closed my eyes and tried so hard to remember, but I came up with nothing.

"It's okay, baby, don't try so hard to remember. You'll get it, and if you don't, then I'll show you," she replied, moving along.

I watched as Stacy entered the door, stopping us from leaving. What the hell she was doing there? I thought to myself. She said something to me, and all I did was look at her. She then pointed to my daughter Kayla, and I watched as she moved to the side, to reveal a little boy who looked just like Kaylin. She said something and pulled a gun from behind her back and pointed it at me. Tears started to fill my eyes as she said something about Kaylin, and right after, he and Tyreek walked through the door.

"Mimi, where you at, and why is the door wide open?" I heard him ask. I said nothing as I watched him walk into the living room, where Stacy and I were.

"Mimi, what's going on and why you are here, Stacy?" he asked, looking from me to Stacy. A lump formed in my throat as I tried so desperately to remember what happened next.

"I came here to introduce Kaylin Jr. to his sister and brothers, but I was shocked when he actually got to see *both* of his twin sisters together. I also caught little Ms. Mimi about to leave," she said to him.

"Twin sisters? What are you talking about? Kailay's not a twin," he replied, looking at me, then to Kailay and Kayla holding hands.

"Daddy," I heard my daughter Kayla said, running to Tyreek.

"*Daddy?* 'Reek, I thought you said that you didn't have any kids."

"Well, I lied. This here is my and Mimi's daughter Kayla. She also happens to be your daughter Kailay's twin sister," he responded.

I instantly broke down as the events from tonight flashed before me and I remembered exactly how I got here.

I cried as I remembered Stacy saying that she and Kaylin had a nine-year-old son and how Kaylin moved her up here. I also remembered her telling Kaylin about Kayla. Still crying, I remembered Kaylin and Tyreek having a few words and fighting, then Kaylin killing Tyreek with gunshots to the head. He then turned his gun on me and started shooting. I was going in and out of consciousness as he walked over to me and said something, and then everything went completely black.

"Oh my God! Kaylin did this to me?" I asked my grandma through tears.

"Yes, but it looks like it's not your time to go yet," she responded.

"Why? I'm getting so tired of living with secrets and regrets. I just want to stay here with you and be in peace," I said to her.

"Chile, your secrets aren't really secrets anymore, and besides, you have some important business to tend to. Now, go ahead and get out of here. When it's your time, you'll be seeing me again," she said as she started to back up. She then turned and was walking toward a bright light. But before she could leave, she said something else.

"Pay attention, Mimi. You have a lot at stake here. Your kids need you, but before you go looking for them, you must pay a visit to your mother first."

"Wait! Why do I have to go see her?" I asked, but before I knew it, she was gone, and I felt my soul being pulled . . . and just like before, everything went black.

When I came to, I was being wheeled down a long hallway. I looked around frantically to see a bunch of people in white coats and blue scrubs, running. Entering what I assumed to be an operating room, I heard a lot of shouting and then felt my clothes being cut off. I felt a cold sensation as the medication was entering my IV, making me sleepy as hell.

I tried my best to fight it, but it was getting the best of me. I watched as the nurse came over and injected something else into my IV. As I lay there falling asleep, I remembered thinking, "I can't believe Kaylin would do me like that . . . After all of the shit that I've been through with his ass." Then I fell into a deep sleep.

Mimi

I stood on the end of a curb in some unknown neighborhood as I watched the cars that were zooming by.

"Mommy," I heard a voice say, but I didn't see anyone.

"Look, Mommy, look," the voice said again. Turning around I was now facing an apartment building. As I looked farther, I noticed that this was indeed my old neighborhood.

"Mommy," I heard the voice say again, and that's when I noticed that there was a little boy standing beside me.

"Where's your mother, baby?" I asked the child, but he didn't answer. He kept his head down and covered his face.

"It's okay, baby, don't be shy. I won't hurt you," I said, but again he didn't answer. Stooping down to his level, I asked, "Can you show me where your mother is?"

Shaking his head, he pointed at me.

"Me?" I asked in disbelief. Shaking my head, I said to him, "No, not me. I can't be your mother, baby, because I don't have any kids."

"Yes, you are. You're my mommy," he replied, still pointing at me. Then he took off running, "Follow me, Mommy."

I stood there stuck. I knew for a fact I didn't have any kids. *So why is this child calling me Mommy?* I asked myself, confused.

"Hurry, Mommy, hurry," he said, turning around. Even though I was convinced that I was indeed not this child's mother, I followed him anyway.

"Where are we going?" I asked as I struggled to keep up with him. He was running like his little life depended on it.

"Hurry, Mommy, you have to save me," he replied. "Hurry, hurry, before it's too late."

"Save you? What am I supposed to save you from?" I asked, but he said nothing as he kept running.

When I caught up to him, I asked, "What am I supposed to be saving you from?"

He said nothing as he pointed to a closed door. He then said, "In there."

I was scared, because I didn't know this child, and here he was calling me mommy. Not to mention that I'm supposed to be saving him from whatever it is that was on the other side of the door.

"Hurry, Mommy, you don't have much time," he said as he gave me a little push. Curiosity got the best of me as I wondered what this child could possibly need saving from.

Walking toward the door, I could hear a lot of screaming and crying, followed by a bunch of other noises. When I got closer, I could hear the sounds of someone getting slapped, which had me frozen in fear.

"Mommy, you have to hurry or else you won't be able to save me," the boy said from behind me.

Moving at a slow pace, I reached for the doorknob. My heart began to beat rapidly as I started turning the knob. When I finally opened the door, I froze as I watched some big, ugly, black dude roughing up some chick.

"Oh my God!" I said as I looked while he raped her. Shorty put up a struggle, but dude was obviously stronger than she was, so she surrendered. I felt bad because I couldn't imagine being raped by anyone.

"Mommy, save me," the little boy said again, pointing in the room. Turning back toward the room, I could see the man getting off the woman.

"Baby, you gotta tell me what I'm saving you from," I replied, turning around to see that he was now on his knees, holding his stomach as if it was hurting. Running toward him, I dropped to my knees to aid him.

"It's too late, Mommy, you didn't save me," he said, crying a hurtful cry.

"What's too late? Late for what?" I asked him, rubbing his back as I tried hard to soothe his pain.

"That," he replied, pointing toward the room. Looking back, I could now see that the woman was crying and there was blood all over the place. When the man left the room, she got up off the bed in a zombielike state. I covered my mouth with my hand as shock came over me.

"That can't be!" I yelled as tears stung my eyes. I was in utter disbelief as I watched what looked to be a younger version of myself. "But I don't remember getting raped!"

"You was supposed to save me, Mommy!"

"But I didn't know," I said crying, "I really didn't know."

When I looked down, my heart nearly jumped out of my skin, because the child that I had cradled in my arms didn't have a face at all. He had a head, but there were no eyes, nose, or lips—just a blurred face. My heart felt broken for the child that was taken from me, and yet, I didn't remember any of this.

"I'm sorry, baby," I said, rocking him in my arms. "I'm so sorry," I said crying.

I was awakened out of my sleep suddenly. Opening my eyes, I frantically looked around as I tried to figure out where I was. The beeping sounds of monitors, white walls, and the stale smell led me to believe that I was in a hospital.

What am I doing in here? Where are my kids? How long have I been here? Where's Kaylin? Those were all of the questions that were flowing through my mind. The million-dollar question that I needed an answer to ASAP was, *How did I get in here in the first place?* I said to myself, wiping my face. I tried to go back in my memory bank to recall my last memory, but I came up empty. *What the fuck is going on?* I thought to myself.

Deciding not to dwell on the issue, I reached to my left and hit the call button to summon the nurse. "I really hope they hurry up," I said.

While waiting on the nurse, I decided to inspect my body to survey the extent of my injuries. Bringing my right hand up to my face, I tried touching it, only to experience a sharp pain.

"What the fuck!" I said aloud. I couldn't see it, but I could tell that my face was swollen and bruised up.

Moving on, my hand then traveled from my face down to my chest. "Oh my God!" I gasped as I pulled back the cover and then lifted my gown. "Why am I bandaged so heavily?" I said aloud. That's when I noticed that I had bloodstains in several spots. With my fingers, I tapped the spot closest to it. I immediately regretted doing that, because a pain like no other hit me so hard, it brought tears to my eyes.

Just the mere thought of me going through something painful had me in an uproar. Grabbing my chest, the pain and the fact that I had started hallucinating made it hard for me to breathe. With my hand on my throat, I tried desperately to suck as much oxygen in my lungs as possible, while I was repeatedly hitting the call button for the nurse. With each second, it felt more like minutes that my call was being unanswered.

Seeing as though help was taking far too long to come, I started yanking every cord or wire that I had attached to me, which made all the machines in the room start beeping. Not giving a fuck, I got out of the bed. Well, at least I tried to . . . until my legs started giving out on me. I was almost to the door when my legs failed me completely. I damn near broke my back when I hit that cold-ass floor. The last thing I remembered was a nurse rushing to my aid before everything went black.

Troy

Three Weeks Ago . . .

If there was one thing that I hated the most for sure, it was a bitch-ass nigga. A nigga who walked, talked, and looked like a man, but was actually a bitch. One who did bitch things, but wants to be known to the world as a man. Get the fuck outta here with that shit, giving people nothing but bitchassness.

After leaving Mimi's house, I went home so that Kayla could get some rest. I knew she was tired because of what the poor child has been through these past hours. Between just meeting her siblings and reuniting with her mother, then to have to see both of her parents lying dead in the living room . . . Shit, I know that had to be hard on her. I mean, even though both of my parents are basically dead to me, I still can't relate to that. Then, by her only being eight, shit, I know that's a hard pill to swallow there. This is going to be so hard for her to come back from, and to be totally honest, she might not be straight after this.

I wonder where that li'l pussy-ass nigga Kaylin done ran off to. I done called all over looking for his bitch ass, and no one seems to know where he's at. Either they're lying for him, or he done up and left that damn fast. Kaylin's a bitch nigga to me for two reasons. One reason is that he cheated on Mimi countless times, and she still took him back with no problems, and here he wants to trip when he found out that she done pulled his shit on him. The second reason is that he wasn't man enough to walk away from the shit. He did his dirt, and she did hers. She ain't killed his ass, so why he had to go and kill her? I mean, take ya lick like a fucking man and keep it pushing—but, no, he just *had* to go there. He had to play the bitch role and kill her, then he want to take her kids and leave. Again—bitchassness.

I sat in total darkness as I thought about Mimi. To me, my girl was one of the realest to ever bless this cold-ass world. She was a strong and caring woman who would give you the shirt off her back if you needed it. She wasn't selfish. She was always putting everyone and their needs and happiness before hers. No matter what, she never once turned anybody down for anything. She had a heart of gold and like Boosie Badazz once said, "One day, this heart going to get me zipped up in a body bag." My bitch was laid up in a body bag, in a morgue, cold as ice, and I ain't do shit to help her. *If only I would've went with her, then she would probably still be here*, I thought as I brought the bottle of Peach Cîroc that I was drinking up to my lips. I've been drinking and sitting in the dark all night. I can't help it, though. Every time I try to close my eyes, I kept picturing Mimi lying dead on her living-room floor. Shit still had me in a fucked-up state of mind.

Getting up from the sofa, I walked into the kitchen to get me another bottle to drink. My mind was all fucked up, and drinking was the only way I was able to put my mind at ease. I went into the cabinet where I kept my liquor and grabbed a bottle of Patròn. I needed something a whole lot stronger right now. As I was about to open the bottle, my phone started ringing. I knew it was Mark, because Verse Simmonds's song "Boo Thang" started playing, and that was his ring tone. Both he and Jayden were supposed to be coming back down here, but I didn't think that they'd be here this quickly, because I'd just talked to them about four hours ago. *It takes damn near seven hours to get from West Virginia to Atlanta, so why is he calling me?* I thought as I walked back into the living room.

"Hello," I said answering the phone and slurring a bit.

"Yo, ma, what's up?" Mark asked.

"Ain't shit up, I'm sitting over here trying to drink myself into a fucking coma," I replied, opening the bottle that I had in my hand. I grabbed the glass to pour my drink, but then the thought occurred to me, *Fuck that glass, I might as well drink straight from the bottle.*

"Ma, you need to chill on that. I know that it's going to be hard to deal with, but I'm pretty sure Mimi wouldn't want you to do that," he said, pissing me off. Right now was not the time to be telling me what Mimi would've wanted me to do and shit.

"Well, tell me what I'm supposed to do, huh? You just tell me what I should do, Mark, because you don't get it. You really don't. I lost my best friend, my family. She was the only one there for me when nobody else was. Whenever I had needed anything, I could always count on her. I didn't just lose my best friend, I lost my sister. That nigga killed my fucking sister, and I ain't do shit to help her," I replied as I started crying again. No matter what they say, this shit will not be easy.

"I understand all that, ma. I been through that before. I can tell you that drinking ain't going to make it better, and it won't bring her back. You just have to take it one day at a time. Time heals all wounds, baby. You're going to be all right. You're not alone. Remember that I'm always here if you need me." He sounded more like a father instead of a friend, but it made me feel a little better to know that he was here for me.

I would be lying if I said that I wasn't falling for him, because surely but slowly—I was—falling for him, that is. He's been there for me in my time of need. He could've been like any other man and taken advantage of me. Hell, he could've said to hell with me and left me on my own, but he didn't. He was a great friend, and I appreciated him for that.

"Okay," I murmured.

"Aye, what's your address again?" he asked. I quickly gave him the address and told him that I'd call him back once I straightened up.

After hanging up the phone with Mark, I went to check on Kayla. Peeking in the room, I noticed that she was still sleeping, so that gave me some time to clean up, take a shower, and cook us some breakfast. I started with the living room. There wasn't a whole lot that I had to do, so it didn't take me long at all. After that, I then went to the kitchen. Everything else was already clean. After finishing that, I went into the bathroom and prepared to take a shower. I wish that I could soak in the tub, but I knew that Kayla would be up soon, and I wanted her to have something to eat. I wanted to make her stay here as cozy as possible for the time being.

When I was done, I threw on my bathrobe and went into my room to put some clothes on. Walking over to the dresser, I looked at the picture of Mimi and me when we graduated from high school. I wanted to cry, but as Mark said, I know she wouldn't want me to cry. No matter where you looked, my whole room had some kind of memory of her. Picking up the picture, I kissed it and set it back down. "Mimi, I'm so sorry, I know that I promised to always be there for you, and I failed miserably," I said as a lonely tear fell down my cheek. As I was about to wipe it, I heard somebody enter the room. Turning around I noticed that it was Kayla. I quickly wiped my face as I walked over and hugged her.

"Auntie Troy," she said, wiping her eyes.

"Yes, baby," I replied.

"Are you crying?" she asked.

"Uhhh, no, baby, Auntie had something in her eyes," I replied, saying the first thing that came to my mind.

"It's okay, Auntie Troy. She's with the angels in the sky now," Kayla replied. As much as I tried to hold them in, tears came running down my cheeks. Here I was, twenty-six. She was only eight years old, and there she was, holding up better than I was.

"Auntie is fine Kay Kay. I just miss her, that's all." I replied as I stood up. "Come on, let's go cook us some breakfast."

Before leaving my room, I took one last look at the many pictures of Mimi and me. That's when I decided that after the funeral, I'd be putting this place back on the market. There was no way that I'd be able to continue to stay here and not think of Mimi. I just had to get the fuck out of here. There were just too many memories of her everywhere. In all honesty, I realized that my life as I knew it was going to be over, and since my best friend wasn't here to get revenge on the people who did this shit to her, then I'd do it for her. I was not stopping until both Kaylin and Stacy felt my muthafucking pain, and that's a bet!

Walking into the living room, I sat Kayla down on the sofa and went to turn on the TV. After changing the channel to cartoons, I went into the kitchen to cook us some breakfast. Just as I was about to put the skillet on the stove, I heard Kayla scream.

"What's wrong, Kayla?" I asked, running into the living room. She didn't say anything. She just pointed at the TV. Looking at the television, I saw a picture of Kaylin, with a banner at the bottom that said, *"Wanted for questioning."* I knew she was probably scared that he might come back, so I decided to change the channel, but a picture of Kailay, Kayson, and Kaylon popped up, with an Amber Alert at the bottom. I hurriedly tried to change the channel so that Kayla wouldn't see it, but she saw it anyway.

"Auntie, is that my sister and brothers?" she said, getting up.

"Yes, Kayla, that's them," I replied, turning the television off.

"Why are they on TV?" she asked, looking sad. "Did they get hurt too? When are they coming back?"

"No, Kayla, they're not hurt. The reason why they are on the TV is that they were reported missing, and they need people's help to find them, so that they can bring them home," I explained to her as best as I could. Looking at her sad little face had me feeling sad for her.

"Okay," she said in a soft voice.

"It's going to be okay, sweetie. Auntie Troy's here for you," I said, hugging her. I promised myself that I'll do my best and be there for her.

"Now, why don't we go and get you dressed? Then we can go out and eat breakfast," I said, deciding to change the subject to something else.

"Okay," she replied, giving me a small smile.

"Come on, I should have something of Kailay's in my closet. I'm sure you'll be able to fit in it. You look like you're about the same size as her," I said, walking in the other bedroom.

Looking through the closet, I found a little yellow and white sundress. Thank God she and Kailay were twins, and they could actually fit the same shoes and clothes, because I happened to find a brand-new pair of white sandals too. That reminds me that I'll have to take her shopping, so we might as well add that to our agenda for the day.

After getting Kayla dressed, I pinned her hair up into a messy bun and added a yellow ribbon. When she was done, I let her look at herself in my full-length mirror. She twirled around and smiled. She looked so much like Tyreek and Mimi that it brought tears to my eyes.

"Okay, little lady, let's go," I said to her. I grabbed my purse and keys, and we headed out the door. The day was beautiful and under normal circumstances, it would've been the perfect time for parents to take their kids to the park to play. After everything that's happened, I didn't really feel like doing anything. The only thing I was going to do today is to check on Mimi's salons, club, and then spend some time with Kayla. Tomorrow, I'll make the necessary arrangements for the funeral. Lord knows how much I'm not ready for that, but it has to be done.

Before going to eat breakfast, I stopped by the main salon to check up on a few things. When I pulled up on the street that the salon was located on, I noticed that there was an assload of cops out there. When I got closer, I realized that they were at the salon and not just on the street. Bringing the car to a complete stop, I hopped out and grabbed Kayla from the back. I spotted Candy by the front door, and as I grabbed Kayla's hand, I hurried over to her to find out what was going on.

"'Sup, Candy, what's going on?" I asked, once I made it to where she was.

"I don't know. When we got here this morning, there were cops all over the place. We tried to ask them what was going on, but they said that they could only give out information to the owner, and Mimi hasn't been answering the phone," she said, looking worried. At the mere mention of Mimi's name, my eyes started to get misty.

"Candy, have you seen the news lately?" I asked, choking up. I then looked away and quickly wiped the tears that had escaped my eyes.

"No, I'm not the type of chick who watches the news. Why? What happened that I don't know about?" she asked, looking like a concerned parent.

"First, let's get to the bottom of this and I'll fill you in on the rest of that later," I said, quickly trying to change the subject.

Taking a quick look around, I spotted the first officer in uniform and walked over to him. "Excuse me, can you tell me what's going on?" I asked as I approached him.

"And might I ask who you are?" he said with a hint of an attitude. I had to catch myself before I blew, because knowing me as well as I did, I'd tell his doughnut-eating ass off in a heartbeat, but right now was not the time or the place.

"Well, who might I be? I might be the owner," I retorted. Fuck, it was too hot, and my best friend was dead. I ain't got time to fuck with these flashlight-toting motherfuckers. Shit, I had better and more important things to be doing instead of looking in this pig's face. I guess since I'm black, he wanna look down on me and shit, but what he don't know is that just like white folks could get big and rich and shit, us black folks could do the same thing. "As a matter of fact, point me to the person who's in charge," I said in a disgusted tone.

Rolling his eyes, he pointed toward an elderly black man who was standing by a parking meter talking on his phone. Rolling *my* eyes, I walked off toward the head nigga in charge.

"Excuse me, sir," I said, trying to get his attention.

"Hold on," he said to whoever he was on the phone with. "Yes, ma'am, how can I help you?" he asked.

"Umm, I'm the owner of this salon right here, and I'm trying to find out what is going on."

"Okay, give me a minute," he said and went back to his call. I stood off to the side, trying to give him some privacy. When he was done with his call, he came walking over to me.

"Sorry about that, but what is your name, miss?"

"My name is Troy Miller."

"Well, I was under the impression that . . . uhmmm," he paused, trying to find something on his notepad. "Ms. Amina Washington was the owner of this shop," he said, looking back at me.

"Yes, she was the previous owner, but I'm the new owner," I said, reaching into my purse and pulling out the document that Mimi had me sign. "Oh, and I'm Amina's sister too."

Looking over the document, he sighed. "Oh, okay. Well, this looks legit."

"Yeah, so it seems," I replied in a sarcastic tone. I guess he was mad because I was making his job a little harder to do today. "Now can you tell me what's going on here?"

"Well, it seems that this shop was broken into and vandalized this morning," he said, removing his glasses from his eyes as he wiped the sweat from his forehead.

"Broken into and vandalized?" I asked for confirmation.

"Yes, it's pretty bad in there," he said, looking back at the shop.

"Can I have a look around?" I asked. I wanted to see the damages for myself.

"Sure, right this way," he said, leading the way.

My heart rate started speeding up as we walked closer to the front door. There was already so much shit going on, I didn't need this shit right now. I mean, how much more could I take? Fuck!

Walking through the frame where the door was supposed to be, I stepped on a pile of broken glass. Grabbing Kayla's hand tightly, I pulled her closer. I didn't want her to slip or fall and hurt herself. Walking farther into the salon, I felt like I was about to pass the fuck out. I had to grab hold of one of the chairs on my way—well, the one that wasn't fucked up. My head began to hurt as I looked at all the hard work that my girl had put into this shop—all fucked up. Every station was fucked up, the mirrors and countertops were all broken, the chairs were ripped, the white walls had red paint on them, and the drapes were all finished. The couches in the sitting area had paint on them, and they were ripped. The floors were completely flooded. Every painting that they had on the walls was ripped into pieces and thrown all over. All of Mimi's certifications were fucked up. They had the nerve to open every hair product, rinse, perm, hair spray, and poured that shit all over the place. "I can't stay here. I can't see no more of this shit," I said out loud. Grabbing Kayla, I made my way toward the exit.

"Excuse me, ma'am, but you can't leave. We're going to need you here while we write the incident report," the officer said.

"I'm not going anywhere. I just can't be in here. I just can't take seeing all of my girl's hard work gone down the drain. I can't believe someone could be this fucking bold to do some shit like this. Please, by all means, do what you have to do. I'll be waiting outside when you're done," I replied, turning on my heels. Hell, I didn't give the poor man a chance to respond. I just needed to clear my head, because too much shit was happening all at once.

When I got outside, I spotted Candy and a couple of the other stylists hanging by the curb. I tried not to show how frustrated I was, but people already knew I'm not good at hiding my feelings.

"How bad is it?" Candy asked as I neared her.

"It's fucked up, yo. It's completely fucked. They ain't leave shit untouched. They fucked the spot completely up. Had shit all over the fucking place. There ain't shit in there we could save. We gonna have to pack up what little we can and move everyone down to the other salon." I choked up as tears streamed down my face. Shit, I didn't care who saw me crying. This shit was just too much for me, man. Every time I think that I'm getting a break, something else pops up.

"Don't worry, Mimi, we'll fix it," she replied, trying to console me.

Pulling away from her, I looked directly into her eyes so she would understand what I was about to say. "That's the fucking point, Candy. Mimi can't fix anything when she's lying on someone's morgue all cold and shit. So tell me how she's gonna fix this shit. Unless you're able to bring someone back from the dead, then that shit there ain't going to be happening at all."

She said nothing. I guess she was letting what I said sink in her head. Not waiting for her to respond, I continued, "Have someone come and board the shop up until I'm able to come and clean this shit up. In the meantime, tell everyone that they all have the next few days off. If they don't know that Mimi's dead, then fill them in, because I want everyone that works for her at the funeral. Right now, I have so much on my plate, and without Mimi being here, I don't even know how I'm going to make it."

Shaking her head, she replied, "Will do, and I'm sorry for your loss."

"Yeah, me too; I'm going to holla at y'all later," I said to her. Taking Kayla's hand, I began walking to my car. Placing Kayla in the backseat, I was about to get in my car when someone called out my name.

"Troy, wait."

"What now?" I huffed.

Turning around, I noticed that it was the dude who owned the barbershop next door.

"Yeah, what's up?" I asked with an attitude. I wasn't feeling any small talk right now. I just wanted to get as far away from this place as possible.

"I know you've been through a lot in the past few days, but I wanted to say that I heard about Mimi, and I'm sorry to hear that. She was a real cool chick."

"Yeah, she was, and thank you," I said, turning to get in my car.

"Wait!" he hollered, stopping me in my tracks again.

"What!" I snarled, full of attitude because dude was really getting on my nerves. Fuck, if he had something to say, I wish he'd hurry the hell up and say the shit already, because I had places to be and things to do.

"Hey, hey, don't bite my head off," he replied, throwing his hands up as if he surrendered. "I only came to tell you that I seen a chick by the shop this morning when the cops first came here, and she said for me to give this to you," he said, pulling a white envelope out of his back pocket. "It has your name on it. I was going to give this to the police, but since I know this shit is prolly personal, I decided to give this to you instead. Take care and stay out of trouble." He handed it to me and walked off.

I stood there holding the envelope in my hand like it was a disease or something. *What the fuck is this shit?* I thought as I began to open it.

My mouth fell open as I read the contents of the letter. Looking up, I called out to him and asked, "Can you describe the chick who gave you this?"

"Hmmm, she was about five foot five maybe, caramel complexion with short hair. Hell, she looked crazy as fuck, as if she ain't slept in days or some shit."

I stood there speechless. Hell, I didn't know anyone that fitted that description. I quickly looked around to see if anyone stood out of place, but everyone out here was basically the people who worked at the salon, a couple of clients, and a shitload of policemen. There was not one person who stood out to me or remotely fit that description.

"Fuck," I screamed aloud as I passed a hand through my hair. This shit was beginning to take a toll on me. I started pacing back and forth as I tried to think about my next move.

"Uhh, shorty, are you all right?" dude asked, looking concerned.

"Shit, I forgot you was right there, but, yeah, I'm straight."

"All right, cool," he said as he turned to leave.

"Hold up, do you see the chick who gave you this?" I asked, waving the note back and forth in the air. "Could you possibly describe her to me again?"

"Well, I don't remember much about her. All I could really tell you is that shorty was about five foot five, caramel complexion, big doelike eyes, with a beauty mark on the right side of her upper lip. Umm, she was kind of skinny, with a bad weave that needed a major touch-up. That's why I thought she left you that letter and shit, but by the look on your face, I can tell that my assumption was wrong, and there was nothing nice written on that note."

"Oh, okay, cool. Thank you so much, but I have to go," I sighed, turning to get in my car, totally ignoring what he said about the note.

"Ma, hold up," he yelled out.

I turned to see what he wanted this time. "Yes?"

"Look, ma, I don't know what's going on, and I don't care to know, because that's your business, not mine. But what I do know is that you and Mimi were some really cool chicks. So be careful, ma. There are some grimy-ass people out here. Female or not, they wouldn't hesitate to body anyone. I know Mimi is gone and shit, but you're always welcome to stop by if you need anything," he murmured as he walked away.

I took a minute to collect my thoughts as I sat there in the car. Hell, the description he gave me wasn't helpful at all. I had no idea who had left that note for me. For all I know, this could be any bitch living in Atlanta. Who knows how many bitches we came across that was hating for no reason. Hell, who knows how many bitches Kaylin done fucked, ducked, and misled.

Then a thought came to my mind. It could be either Star or that crazy bitch Jade. I mean, who else could have a score to settle with us? We did whoop both of their asses—well, Mimi never touched ole crazy-ass Jade—she was about to, and she let the shit go down. So why wouldn't they come for us? I know one thing . . . If that was us who had gotten our asses whooped, we wouldn't stop until we settled the score. We would've made it our business to get back at whoever it was, but those bitches weren't that bold . . . or were they? Nah, they wasn't made like that. Why wait until after all this time to come for us, when the shit done died? Shit, but we always did say, "Beef don't die . . . That shit just die down for a while." Best believe you was gonna get dealt with when you least expected it. Nah, these hoes are green as fuck. They ain't 'bout that life. Them hoes ain't built for that shit, because if they was, they would've handled that shit the same fucking night.

Pushing that thought to the back of my mind, I started my car and pulled off. I didn't care if I was supposed to remain at the scene. Occasionally, I would steal a couple of glances at Kayla, who was busy playing with my iPad in the backseat. Poor child just didn't know the shit that was going on around her.

I was about to say something to her when this black Altima caught my attention as we were leaving. Any other time I wouldn't have noticed it, but with everything that's been going on, I've been on high alert. There was something about this car that totally creeped me out. Shit, it was just sitting there with the engine still running. It was parked just a few blocks down from the salon. I knew for a fact that there was someone sitting inside, because one of the windows was cracked, and there was a cloud coming from out of it. If they were trying to be incognito, it wasn't working very well.

I slowed down as I tried to get a peek at the person inside, but the heavy tint on the windows prevented me from doing so. I wanted to turn around, but I didn't want to make it obvious. I'm pretty damn sure that I'll be seeing this car again real soon. Only time will tell who was sitting in that car, spying.

Speeding up, I headed in the direction of the mall. I wasn't about to let no one intimidate me or spoil my day. If they really wanted me, they were going to have to work real hard to get me, because I ain't the bitch they think I am. I'm going to give them a taste of their own medicine. What they don't know is that I was born and raised in New Orleans. I don't scare easily. It's going to have to take a bunch of hardcore shit to scare a bitch like me. Being from NOLA had taught me one thing . . . I'm a bitch who knows how to hold her own—with or without a nigga's help.

Kaylin

We've been on the road all night trying to put as much distance between Atlanta and us as fast as possible. To be honest, I really didn't have a destination in mind. I just knew that I had to get the fuck up out of Georgia, and fast. I wasn't trying to get caught. I had more than enough money to live my life on the run before I'd spend the rest of my life in a four-by-four prison cell. Besides, I needed to be there for my kids since I knew for sure that Mimi wasn't going to be there for them. There was no way I was going to let anybody else raise my kids, and I damn sure wasn't about to let the state get ahold of them. I heard about how people in those foster homes be doing those children wrong. I'd never let that happen to one of mine.

"Kaylin, you're going to have to find a rest stop soon. We're almost out of gas, and the kids have to use the restroom," Stacy said, pulling me from my thoughts. I'd been tuning her ass out the whole ride. I don't know what in my right mind would make me bring her ass with me in the first place. I should've left her ass to fend for herself. Only reason I took her was that she had my son. If it weren't for him, I would've been got ghost on her ass.

"Kaylin," she yelled, "yo' ass over there daydreaming and shit. I know you hear me talking to you!"

"Bruh, why the fuck you gotta be so fucking loud? I can hear yo' stupid ass just fine!" I yelled back. This bitch was touching my nigga nerve.

"Because you over there acting like you can't hear me, and I know you can. I ain't stupid. You've been ignoring me this whole fucking time."

"Bruh, look, go 'head with all that dumb shit. Right now is not the time for you to be fuckin' trippin' and shit. I got other things to worry about!" I waved her off.

"What other things could you possibly have to worry about, huh? The new chick that's supposed to be having ya baby? That's what you over there worrying about?" she yelled, a little too loud for me.

I was really starting to regret the mistake I made by killing Mimi and taking this bitch. Hell, I could've charged it to the game, but no, I let my anger get the best of me. Now I've lost the only girl I've ever really loved, and I'm stuck with this nagging bitch. I really didn't want to leave her behind, because I didn't wanna leave no witnesses. Yeah, I know I left behind Kailay's supposed-to-be twin sister, but that was a child. Believe it or not, I'm not a monster. I didn't kill her because she was a part of Mimi, and I'd already killed her parents. I didn't want to kill her too. Hell, it was me who started this whole fucking thing. If I hadn't fucked with Stacy's ass from the beginning, we mighta been married right now. I would've had my family and great life—but I don't—and I have no one to blame but myself.

"Oh, so you don't have anything to say now, huh?" she asked, getting even more ignorant.

"Bruh, I'm telling you to chill out and leave me the fuck alone. I already told you, right now ain't the fucking time for your bullshit!" I growled. I spotted a service station to my right and decided to pull in to get some gas and a couple of things out of the store. I also wanted the kids to get out and stretch their legs. They've been cramped in this van for hours. I know they need a good stretch.

"Oh, so now you want me to chill, huh? Well, guess what? I don't want to chill. Mimi was right. I started shit over a nigga who was and never will be for me. I should call Atlanta's police department and turn ya red ass in."

I hurriedly threw the van in park and turned toward her. With my right hand, I grabbed her by her throat and spoke through gritted teeth. "Bitch, let me tell you one thing. Yo' mouth will get you in a world of trouble because you don't know how to shut it. If you ever threaten my freedom again, I'll leave ya ghetto ass stinking with the rats, and I won't think twice about it. I told you to shut the fuck up, but, no, your ho ass don't know how to do that. You just wanna keep fuckin'

with me and shit, like I give a fuck about you. Bitch, I told yo'
ass once before that you will *never* be my woman. You ain't
shit—all you will ever be is a piece of pussy to me—nothing
more, nothing less!"

She desperately clawed at my hand, trying to get me to let
her go. I wasn't feeling none of this shit. I was in a zone. I
told her ass to leave me alone, but she didn't. She was only
seconds away from passing out when the kids started crying,
which made me let her go. I watched as she desperately tried
to fill her lungs up with as much air as possible.

"Bitch, I bet the next time I ask yo' stupid ass to shut the
fuck up, you will. Now, get the kids and take them to the
bathroom," I ordered and got out. I didn't try to see if that ho
was all right, I just needed to get away from her before I killed
that bitch and added another thing I gotta worry about.

Getting out of the car, I made my way to the store. I wasn't
too worried about people seeing me because we were in
Mississippi, and I know the shit hadn't made it that far yet, so
I was cool. Making my way into the store, I paid for the gas,
and then went to the bathroom.

Walking into the bathroom, I went straight to the sink.
Looking into the mirror, I looked like a maniac who'd aged ten
years in the last couple of hours. My eyes were bloodshot red
and had bags under them. Turning on the faucet, I splashed
water on my face and sighed. Saying a silent prayer to the
Lord for forgiveness, I made my way back into the gas station.

When I walked out of the bathroom, I spotted Stacy and
the kids checking out by the counter. Walking over to
them, I noticed a boy in blue entering through the front door.
Turning my back so he wouldn't see me, I grabbed her by her
arm. "Y'all almost done?" I asked her.

"Yeah, we were just about to pay for our stuff when you
walked over here," she replied. "Why you looking like you
done seen a ghost and shit?"

I said nothing as I went into my pocket, pulled out three
twenty-dollar bills, and handed them to her. I was about to
say something when I noticed the blue boy standing behind
us. She noticed him too and shot me an *Oh, yeah, motherfucker, I see why you acting all spooked and shit.* I shot her
back a glare that said, *Bitch, play with me if you want to.*

"That should be enough for whatever you need. I'll be waiting in the car," I snarled and walked off. Once I made it out the door, I picked up my stroll. I wanted to hurry up and pump the gas so as soon Stacy and the kids finished up in there, we could get the fuck away from here. I was already having a bad day. A run-in with the cops was not what I needed right now.

I started pumping the gas when I noticed a second patrol car pulling up to the gas station. I instantly got a bad feeling in the pit of my stomach as I watched two more uniformed officers walk into the gas station. I pulled my phone out of my pocket to call Stacy when I spotted her still standing by the counter talking to the first officer that was in there. My mind instantly went into panic mode as I put the pump back in its place and hopped in the car, started it, and waited, trying to figure out my next move. The minute I see a police officer walking this way, though, I'm gone. I'm not going to jail, and I most definitely don't want to lose my kids, but if I get knocked by the police, I can kiss any chance of that good-bye.

I tapped on the steering wheel as I thought about my next move. If Stacy was indeed ratting on a nigga, it was going to be hard as hell to get away from five-o. "Fuck it," I screamed and threw the car in drive, prepared to leave them right here.

Just as I was about to pull off, I spotted them coming out of the store. Placing the car in park, I waited for them to get in.

"Hurry up and get in," I nervously said as Stacy opened the door for the kids to enter. Once they were all in the car, I hurriedly pulled off, leaving smoke behind.

"What took you so long?" I asked the minute we were back on the road, away from the gas station.

"Kailay had to go to the bathroom, and Kayson and Kaylon forgot to get their chips."

"Well, why did I see you talking to them boys in blue, though?" I asked.

"They were just making conversation, that's all. Wasn't nothing funny going on."

"Uh-huh. It better not be," I said and turned the radio up. I didn't want to hear shit else she had to say. All I wanted was to make sure she didn't give me up to the people. Now that I know she hadn't, I wanna find a place where we could chill out for the time being. As soon as the dust settled, I'm taking my kids and sending her on her merry way.

I didn't have time to settle down with no bitch. I had made plans to do that with Amina, but unfortunately, things turned out differently. Now I'm rocking solo. I'm going to be a bachelor for the rest of my life. If I couldn't have Mimi, I didn't want nobody else.

Stacy

Kaylin's been acting funny ever since we left the A. I needed to know what he was thinking, because I didn't come this far to turn back around now. All the shit I've been through these past few years is going to count for something. I spent a whole year keeping Mimi's secret, only because I had to. I know people been wondering why I ain't come out and tell Kaylin the minute he moved me and Jr. up here, but I had no choice in the matter. The shit was out of my control, but now that Mimi's out of the picture, I wondered what his next plan was.

I sat there wondering how I let my life get this way. I'd come from having great friends to being forced to hate them. I'd never really told anyone the truth, but I really had considered Mimi as being one of my best friends. She was always the type to have a nigga's back, but when I found out our family secret, the shit made me start hating her. Had she'd been for anyone else, we'd have been the best of friends, but she wasn't, and I couldn't stand her ass.

I sat back for years watching her get the better end of the deal. Even when she was poor and ain't had shit, she still was living a better life than the one I was living. She was always surrounded by people who loved her, and I never had that. When she met Kaylin, I instantly got jealous of her. I secretly envied her, until one day we thought of a plot to take everything away from her. Only thing is that my plan didn't fully work. She still had Kaylin by her side, but that's all over now. Hopefully, I won't have to deal with the devil himself for much longer. I wanted to enjoy my life, and now that my one and only competition is out of the way, it should be much easier to. I was even willing to accept three kids that didn't belong to me.

I was still a little heated after the episode at the gas station with Kaylin choking me, but I was willing to overlook it. Yeah, I know what y'all might be thinking, but I truly loved Kaylin, and that's why I spent all this time trying to get him to be mine. I went to great lengths to get Amina out of the picture. I did shit one wouldn't imagine me doing to someone close to me, and I ain't ashamed of it. I'd do it all over again in a heartbeat for the man that I love. One might wonder why I would trust a nigga who would kill his own girl. My answer to them is simple—I don't know. Love makes you do some crazy-ass things. Love would make you turn ya back on your own mother and never see her again. Trust me, I know, but what I want Kaylin and everyone else to know is that if I can't have him . . . then no one will. I'll do the same thing to him that he did to Mimi.

Looking back at the kids, I turned to Kaylin and said, "Kay, I think we need to find somewhere to rest at. These poor children look like they all worn out and shit. We're far enough away from Atlanta to take a quick break from driving to wherever we're supposed to be going."

"Yeah, all right," he responded, playing with his phone. This nigga is really starting to test me and shit.

"Kaylin," I yelled.

"Look, ma, I said all right, now chill. Don't make me fuck yo' ass up again," he said, finally taking his eyes away from the phone.

Rolling my eyes, I sat back and pulled my phone out of my purse. Scrolling through my text messages, I located the name Mister and prepared to send him a text.

Me: In case you don't know, everything is all said and done.

Mister: Good, we still got one more thing left to handle. Then you get paid, and I'll go my own way and leave you alone.

Me: Hold up, all you said I had to do was get Mimi's casket ready and I'd be able to have Kaylin. You ain't said shit else about whatever it is you're trying to do. I didn't agree to shit else.

Mister: Doesn't matter what you agreed to do. You're going to do whatever I tell you to do.

Me: I don't have to do a damn thing else. I already did what you asked me to do.

Mister: You're right, you don't have to, but you will. Or do you want me to tell Kaylin about what you did that landed them in jail? Or how, in fact, you sent Tyreek down there to stir up trouble? I'll be in contact shortly, just be ready when I do. Talk to you later.

Throwing my phone in my purse, I sat back and wondered what the hell I'd gotten myself into. This ain't what I signed up for. All I agreed to do was to take Mimi out of the picture. I ain't agreed to do shit else, and I ain't about to. Fuck that. He done been my puppet master for too long. It's time for me to start playing right along with him.

Jayden

It's funny how you can go from living a dream to living a fucking nightmare, all in a matter of hours. I don't normally pray, but today, I asked God to hold my hand and guide me through this whole process. My mind has been clouded with thoughts of Mimi. From the first time that I saw her, to the first time that we kissed, I just couldn't stop thinking about her. I still remember how sweet she tasted and how real she was. Yeah, I know I just met her a couple of weeks ago, but there was something about her that made me want to give her my all. Man, I'll never see her again! Fuck! This bitch-ass nigga just don't know how bad I'm going to do him in when I see him.

The drive from West Virginia to Atlanta is normally about seven hours or so, but my boy Mark got us there in like five. He damn near broke every traffic law known to man. Shit, it was a good thing that we didn't get stopped or else we would've been in a whole world of trouble—trouble that I didn't have time for right now.

I was basically quiet the whole way down. Shit, I really didn't have much to say. All I wanted to do was pay my final respects to Mimi, get my hands on that bitch-ass nigga Kaylin, and do him something grimy, then head my ass back to West Virginia. That nigga robbed me of my future wife and shit. I don't know the whole story, but I plan on asking that girl Troy as soon as I see her. Shit, this shit is way too deep, and some things just ain't adding up.

I was deep in my thoughts until Mark started calling my name.

"Jay, nigga, you ain't hear me calling ya name just now?" he asked.

"Nah, man, I didn't hear you," I replied, looking at him.

"Well, we here, nigga. What you wanna do now?"

"Man, just find me a Motel 6, so I can lay low," I replied, staring out the window. All I needed was a little spot where I could come and go without someone seeing me. I wanted to be incognito so that I could do my dirt and get the fuck on. Atlanta doesn't have shit for me down here anymore. Oh, but please believe, they may not see me, but these bitches will feel me.

Pulling into the parking lot of the motel, I quickly pushed all thoughts of killing to the back of my mind, for now anyway. I knew how I could be at times, and if I'm not levelheaded, I'll do shit without thinking. My nigga Mark found us a motel with the quickness. I mean, even though it's cheap and shit, it doesn't look it. I told him to get a room all the way in the back. It was kind of empty and shit, but like I said, I wanted to be felt, not seen.

After getting the keys to our rooms, we unloaded the car and settled in. I wasn't in the mood to do anything, so my plans were to smoke and chill. Besides, I didn't come down here on a vacation. I came down here on a mission.

I was just about to get in the shower when someone came knocking at the door. I already knew that it was Mark, because he was the only one who knew we were here, so I answered the door.

"I know you prolly wanna chill and get ya mind right, so I brought a few things over to do so," he said, holding up a bottle of Peach Cîroc and a Ziploc bag full of loud.

"You know me too well," I replied, stepping aside so that he could come in. "I'm about to hop in the shower right quick, though."

"All right, cool, you do that and I'ma go get us something to eat from the McDonald's up the road." He placed the contents that he had in his hands on the little nightstand by the bed.

"All right, then, but remember to stay out of sight for now. Don't let anyone see you," I reminded him.

"Yeah, I know, man. I ain't new to this. I'm true to this," he replied, walking to the door.

"Bet."

After Mark left, I proceeded to the bathroom to shower. I was stressed out and tense as a motherfucker. Stepping into the shower, I allowed the hot water to caress my skin. I could actually feel the tension leaving my body as the water beat against it. I used this time to clear my mind, because only God knows how heavy the shit really is. Between the beef at home and the shit that's done gone down with Mimi, I'm just too beat. At times, it feels like I got the weight of the world on my shoulders, and all I wanna do is say fuck it, because there's only so much a person could really take. I know they say a man ain't supposed to wear his emotions on his sleeve, but by now, people should know I'm not like most men. I actually have a heart, and I'm one of the few men left who honestly gives a fuck. Putting all my issues in West Virginia in the back of my mind, I decided to focus on the issue in Atlanta.

After almost an hour of just standing under the water, I grabbed the soap and washcloth and scrubbed my body clean. By that time, the water was damn near cold, so I quickly rinsed off and got out. Walking into the front of the room, I grabbed a wife beater, some sweatpants, a pair of socks, and my red and white Jordans. When I was done getting dressed, I grabbed the Ziploc bag and the box of cigars to start rolling up, but a knock at the door stopped me once again. Grabbing my gun from the nightstand drawer, I went to open it. Looking through the peephole, I saw that it was Mark.

"Man, why you ain't take one of them keys off the night-stand?" I asked as I opened the door.

"Man, I forgot, and I'm glad, 'cause you prolly would've started shooting or some shit if I just walked in the door like that," he replied. Motioning to the gun in my hand, he stated, "You better be careful with that."

"Yeah, nigga, you prolly right. Besides, we can't be too careful, especially when we came down here to get our hands dirty in the first place," I warned as I took a seat on the bed and resumed what I was doing before he came knocking.

"Yeah, true that," he replied, placing the McDonald's bag on the desk by the wall.

"We're about to have a fucking smoke session in this bitch," I exclaimed as I tried to spark up a conversation. The silence was too uncomfortable for me.

"Yeah, I could use me a nice high right about now," he replied from across the room.

We sat in silence as we both were lost in our thoughts. My mind was on Amina and this situation at hand. I still hadn't come up with a plan, but I planned to drop by Troy's house later on today. I needed her to give me the 411 on that fool and all his hangout spots.

"So did you come up with a plan yet?" Mark asked once we put the joint in rotation.

"Nah, man, I plan on going to see Troy later today, but right now, all I wanna do is chill."

"Cool, but you do know ya can't sit on this too long. The longer you wait, the farther you're letting him get away."

"Yeah, man, I know. That's why I wanna talk with ya girl. After I get the whole backstory, I'm going to come up with a plan then."

"Yeah, that would be a good choice," he agreed, passing me the blunt. "Yo, when is the funeral, though? You know we need to go shopping and shit."

"Man, I have no idea, but fuck it. Let's roll to the mall then," I replied, passing back the blunt to him.

"For sure, but lemme go hop in the shower right quick. I know you ain't think I was going somewhere without getting fresh, huh?" he laughed.

"Nah, nigga, I know you. You're a pretty boy. Ain't no way you was going to leave without getting fresh on me, man," I replied, laughing because I knew what I said was true. No matter where we went, his pretty ass was always trying to get fresh. I guess since he was poor all his life. Now that he's got something, he wanna floss it, and I don't blame him, 'cause I'm the same way. It was hard growing up without having enough of this or that, and now that we have it, it's too hard not to want to showcase our newfound wealth. Don't get me wrong . . . We're not the kind of niggas who think they're too much for the next one, because we ain't. Just like we got it, the next person could get it. We don't mind giving back to our community or those in need, because like I said, we were once poor ourselves.

"All right, man, just holla at me when you're done then."

"All right, man," he said, dapping me off. After he left, I sat back on the bed to think about my life. Hell, if it ain't one thing, it's another. Whenever I'd try to get my life in a more positive position, trouble would always come and find me. But this time, I planned to come out on top instead of being defeated and at the bottom.

Troy

Instead of going straight to the mall, I decided to stop by McDonald's on the way. We never got the chance to go and eat out like we had planned to, thanks to that episode at the salon earlier. I decided that something quick would do. Besides, I have to stop by the funeral home later on. I had put the task off for a whole week, but now it was time that I laid my girl to rest peacefully. I wish this shit was all one big-ass dream, but it isn't, and I'm willing to accept the fact that she's gone and she ain't coming back. Pushing all that other shit to the side until later, I decided to focus on Kayla right now.

"Kayla, baby, what do you want to eat?" I asked, turning to her.

"I want some chicken nuggets, fries, and some juice," she replied, with her eyes still focused on whatever she was doing on that iPad.

"Is that all?" I asked her, but she wasn't paying me no mind. She was more interested in what was on the screen than what I had to say.

"Kayla, baby, is that all you want?" I asked, repeating myself.

"Yes, Auntie Troy," she quickly replied, finally.

I chuckled a bit, and then placed our order. We decided that we were going to eat in, so we went ahead and found us a table to sit at. Once Kayla was seated, I went to fill up our cups.

Returning to the table, I placed both drinks on it and went to retrieve our food. After getting our meals, I went back to the table and sat down.

I was taking the food out of the bag when my phone started ringing. I already knew that it was Mark, because the ringtone that I had assigned for him was playing.

"Hey, could you hold on right quick?" I asked when I answered.

"Okay," he replied.

I set the phone down and fished the rest of Kayla's meal out of the bag, leaving everything except my fries inside. I began eating them as I said, "Hello," bringing the phone up to my ear.

"Yeah, I thought you had done forgot about me," Mark replied, with a light chuckle.

"No, baby, it ain't even like that. I was getting Kayla's food out of the bag," I replied laughing.

"Kayla? Who's Kayla?"

"Kayla is Mimi's oldest daughter."

"But I thought you said that ole boy took all of his kids when he killed ya girl that night," he stated, obviously confused.

"Yeah, that's exactly what I told you," I said in an annoyed tone. I wanted him to drop the shit; I really don't know why he trying to elaborate and rehash this shit. *I told you what I told you. End of story*, I thought to myself.

"Well, why shorty over there with you, if she had supposedly left with dude then? Shit, I'm not getting this. It don't make no sense."

"Can you hold on for a minute please?" I asked in an irritated tone. "Kayla, baby, Auntie's gonna step away from the table right quick. I'll be right back, okay?"

"Okay," she replied, still playing with that damn iPad.

"And put that iPad away so you can eat your food," I demanded before I got up. Getting up from the table, I moved to a spot right outside the door, but close enough where I could still keep a close eye on Kayla.

"Hello," I said, bringing the phone back to my ear.

"Yeah, ma, I'm still here."

"Remember when I told you that Mimi had four kids? Two sets of twins, one was a set of girls and the other one a set of boys?"

"Yeah."

"Well, three of the four kids belong to Kaylin, the twin boys and one of the twin girls."

"But wait, that shit don't make no sense. How could she have two sets of twins, but only three of the kids are for ole boy? That shit just ain't possible!"

I said nothing as he tried to figure the shit out. I wasn't trying to air out all of my girl's dirty laundry. Hell, that was her business. I mean, I already been through the shit before and I was just like he was, but DNA proved that shit to me. I didn't think it's my place to try to prove that shit to nobody. It's Mimi's, and now that she is dead, her secret should be too. Hell, I ain't want to tell his ass that much, but he kept asking, and I already regret telling him the shit. I didn't want anyone judging my girl, because everyone makes mistakes, and she's already paid for her mistakes with her life.

Then as if a lightbulb went off in his head, he exclaimed, "Hold up, you mean to tell me that—"

I quickly interrupted him. "No, please don't. Don't do that, don't judge her," I said. I could feel my eyes watering up. "She already paid for her mistakes. She don't need anyone else judging her. So can you just drop it?" I pleaded, just as a tear rolled down my cheek. Wiping it away with my free hand, I silently counted to ten, trying to get myself together.

We sat on the phone in silence, listening to each other breathe.

"Ma, are you all right?" he asked with his voice full of concern.

"Umm, yeah, I'm fine. Could you maybe not mention our conversation to Jayden? I don't want him getting the wrong idea about my girl, without him finding out the whole story. Since she's not here to tell him, he will never know the whole story, so I don't want him to know that part either."

"Okay, I understand. I won't tell him anything."

"Good. Where are you guys anyway?"

"Well, we 'bout to leave the hotel and head to the mall right quick."

"Oh, well, that's where Kayla and I were headed after we left here. After that, I have to stop by the funeral home. Maybe we could meet you guys at the mall," I mentioned, taking a peek at Kayla. She was still playing with that damn iPad, but I wasn't tripping, because she had eaten most of her food.

"All right, just call me when y'all make it there, so we can meet y'all in the parking lot."

"Okay, I'll see you when I get there," I said in a sexy tone.

"Bet."

After we hung up the phone, I stayed outside a moment longer to catch a little fresh air. I can't lie and say this shit isn't getting to me, because it is. Never in a million years did I imagine that my life would be like this. I've always imagined my life with Mimi in it. Not one time did I imagine her being dead. Shit still don't seem real to me.

Sighing, I was about to walk back inside when my phone started to ring again. Looking at the caller ID, I noticed that it was the people from the funeral home.

"Shit, I wonder what the hell they ass want," I said softly. *I hope they ain't calling me to remind me about my appointment. Hell, I know that I'm supposed to see them later.*

That reminds me that I have to call the detective that is working her case and find out why they ain't showing her murder investigation on the news anymore. I mean, it has only been a week, and they completely cut her shit off. I don't hear shit else about it. It's like they done either quit trying to find Kaylin, or they're trying to keep all of this one big-ass secret. Whatever the reason may be, I'm going to find out.

"Hello," I said, answering the phone.

"Umm, good afternoon. May I speak with Ms. Troy Miller, please?" I heard a male voice say.

"This is she. How can I help you?"

"Well, I'm Ralph from Davis and Weber's Funeral Home," he said, then paused.

"Okay, Ralph. Again, how can I help you?" I snapped. Hell, I knew who the hell he was. I spoke with his ass the other damn day. I wanted to know why he was calling me when I was due to pay them a visit later on today.

"Umm . . . I know that you were supposed to come pay us a visit later on today, but something has come up, and I'm going to need you to come in a little earlier than expected."

"Well, how early and what is the problem, if you don't mind me asking?"

"Umm . . . Can you come in right now?" he asked, ignoring my other question.

Looking at my phone, I checked the time. It was almost one o'clock in the afternoon. Hell, I was supposed to stop by at

2:00 p.m. to confirm Mimi's funeral services. It was only an hour away. Why couldn't he just wait to tell me whatever he had to tell me then?

"Well, can you just tell me the issue over the phone?" I asked in a sarcastic tone.

"Umm . . . Well, I'd rather tell you in person, ma'am."

Blowing air out in frustration, I replied, "Okay, I'll be there in a minute." Then I hung up on his ass.

What the hell is so damn urgent that he can't tell me over the fucking phone? I wondered. His ass was supposed to have Mimi's body ready, and I was supposed to be delivering the rest of the payment today. What is he going tell me—that somehow she miraculously lived? Yeah, right, I fuckin' wish.

I was deep in thought when my phone started to ring yet again. Seeing as though it was a private caller, I let the call roll to voice mail. I didn't have time to be entertaining that petty shit right now. Someone had been calling me from a private number for the past couple of days. Hell, I even answered the call a couple of times, but all I kept hearing was shallow breathing. I could also hear what sounded like beeping sounds. I tried to get them to say hello, but they never said anything. Even on the answering machine, all I heard was them breathing, and the shit was really starting to creep me the out. I have no idea as to who this person could be, but I really hope that they'll leave me the hell alone. Right now was not the time for me to be entertaining all of that petty shit. I had more important shit to be doing other than answering private calls from people who don't want to be known.

When I was done, I went back inside. I wasn't even hungry anymore, so I just sat at the table while Kayla finished up the rest of her food. I know dude from the funeral said he needed me there right now, but I wasn't about to put anybody's needs before hers. Mimi wouldn't have wanted it any other way. I'll just go whenever she finishes.

After another fifteen minutes, she was all finished. She went back to her iPad activities, while I took on the task of cleaning up the table. When I was done, Kayla and I headed out to my car.

I wasn't in the car two seconds when my phone started ringing again. Looking at the caller ID this time, I saw that it was my messy-ass cousin Asia. Not wanting to be bothered with her messy ass right now, I hit IGNORE, sending her call to voice mail. I'd call her back after I left the funeral home. I already had a lot of shit going on, and knowing her messy ass, she had nothing but drama coming from over her way. I mean, the bitch was so messy that her own mother didn't want to fool with her. She'd give you up in a fucking heartbeat. She put the true meaning in the saying, "Blood makes you related, loyalty makes you family." I never considered that ho my family. She was like everyone else . . . a fucking associate. That ho wasn't good for no-fucking-body, not even herself.

Starting up the car, I looked up, and I could've sworn I saw that same black car that was parked down the street from the salon. It was leaving the parking lot. Shaking my head, I murmured to myself, "Bitch, you tripping. You better get it together." I said a silent prayer asking the Lord for guidance through this hard time, threw the car in drive, and made my way to the funeral home.

It took me all of fifteen minutes to get to the funeral home from where I was. Just the sight of this place gave me the chills. A funny feeling developed in the pit of my stomach, and I just wanted to leave, but I knew that I couldn't leave without doing what I came here to do. *You only have a couple of days left. After that, you won't have to see this place anymore*, I kept repeating silently to myself.

After finding a parking place, I turned the car off and just sat there so I could get myself together. A few minutes later, my stomach had finally calmed down a bit. Pulling the keys out of the ignition, I reached over and unlocked the glove compartment so I could get the documents that I needed pertaining to Mimi's funeral service.

Once inside the glove compartment, I searched for the envelope that I was looking for when a red flashing light caught my attention. It was coming from the phone that Mimi gave me when she was about to leave town a few weeks ago.

I glanced at the phone like it was some type of disease or something. This was the last physical thing that my friend had given me before she died. Lord, I could feel the tears welling up in my eyes yet again. I dabbed at my eyes and silently swore, *You can do this, Troy.* I then took a glance in the backseat at Kayla, who was quietly sitting there, still playing with the iPad. Hell, she's been a trooper through this whole ordeal. This child has lost both of her parents, and she's holding up better than me. If she could do it, then I could do it too.

Pushing the phone to the side, I grabbed the envelope that I was looking for and closed the compartment door. Then I grabbed Kayla, and we got out. Kayla looked from me to the building, then back at me. Taking her hand into mine, I got down so that I was eye level with her.

"Kay, Auntie is going to run in here right quick to handle some grown folk's business, then after that, we'll go to the mall. Okay?"

"Okay," she nodded.

"Good girl," I said and planted a gentle kiss on her forehead. "Come on."

Grabbing her hand, we made our way to the front of the building. The minute we entered, the smell of death and stale air immediately met our noses. As soon as I walked in there, I wanted to walk right back out. This shit ain't for me. I hate being around death. The shit was creepy and spooky as fuck. I didn't want to be anywhere around it.

Taking a deep breath, I walked up to the front desk and proceeded to ring the bell. While waiting, I took a slight look around. Bruh, this place is really creepy. I mean, this is already a funeral home. Why the lights gotta be all dimmed and shit? Hell, even the paint on the wall is black—now them people know they wrong for that.

"Excuse me, how can I help you?" I heard a sweet little voice say. When I turned, I noticed this short lady who was about four foot nine. Hell, Kayla was almost as tall as she was.

"My name is Troy Miller. I'm here to meet with Mr. Ralph, please."

"Okay, let me go ahead and get him for you. You can have a seat over there," she said as she pointed to two chairs in a corner to the right.

"Okay, thank you."

"You're welcome. Would you all like anything to drink?" she asked, turning around.

"No, ma'am, we're good."

"Okay, let me go and get Ralph for you. I'll be right back, dear," she said and disappeared around the corner.

What were only minutes felt like hours as we waited for Ralph. I still had a funny feeling in my stomach, but I ignored it. I looked up in time to see the little old lady that I had seen before and a tall, old, bald-looking dude, walking down the hallway. I stood up and went to meet them halfway.

"Hello, I'm Ralph. You must be Troy," he said, reaching his hand out for me to shake.

"Yes, that would be me," I said as I shook his hand.

"Thanks for coming."

"I already had to come here anyway, which leads to me the issue. Why did you need me to come in early today?" I asked him.

"Well, if you would just hold on right quick, I'd be more than happy to explain it to you in my office."

"Okay. Come on, Kayla," I replied.

"Umm . . . If you don't mind, could you please leave her here with Betty? She'll be in good hands with her."

I looked at him as if he was crazy. *I don't know either of them. Why would I leave Kayla here with her?* I asked myself.

"I see that you may have some doubts. You may even have some worries, but I promise you that Betty won't let anything happen to her," he said, sensing my hesitation.

I looked from them to Kayla, and back to them again. I then turned to Kayla and asked, "Kayla, would you be okay out here with this lady until I come back?"

She looked from me to Ralph to Betty, and then to me again.

"She'll take good care of you, pretty lady. You'll be in good hands with her," Ralph added.

"Okay," she said in a low tone.

"Are you sure?" I asked her. I wasn't trying to make her stay if she didn't want to.

"Yes," she replied as she looked at Betty again. She then took the iPad out of its case and took a seat back in the chairs we had just been sitting in.

"All right, follow me; this way, please." Ralph led me down a short hallway. He then took a right and led me down another hall. His office was located on the right-hand side of the hallway. Opening the door, he let me go in first and followed behind me.

"You may have a seat in one of those chairs," he said, pointing to the two chairs sitting in front of his desk.

"Okay," I said taking a seat.

"Can I get you anything? A bottle of water, a soda maybe?" he asked as he started playing with his tie. He was acting as if he was nervous about something. Shit, he had me wondering why the hell I came back here alone.

"Uhhh, no, thank you. Can we just get to the reason why I came here?" I placed the envelope down on his desk. "I have a funeral planned for Amina Washington this Saturday."

"Well, that's the thing—I know that you hired us to take care of Ms. Washington's body and funeral service, but there's a problem—we can't seem to find Ms. Washington's body."

I didn't hear nothing else after that. It was like what he said was on repeat in my brain. *There's a problem, we can't seem to find Ms. Washington's body,"* echoed in my head over and over. The shit was like a broken record. I was sitting here in shock and disbelief.

"Ms. Miller, are you okay? Did you hear what I just said?" he asked. The look on his face said, *"Lord, I hope she don't act a fool over this shit."* He just don't know that his prayer wasn't going to be enough.

I sat there with my fingers intertwined, trying my hardest not to let the first words that come out of my mouth be a whole lot of cuss words. I silently counted to ten in my head twice as I took a couple of deep breaths to calm my nerves.

"What you mean, y'all can't seem to find her body?"

"Umm, uhh, as I said before, we're unable to locate Ms. Washington's body. When we went to pick her body up from the hospital morgue, it wasn't there."

"Well, where the hell could it be, and how could y'all lose a whole fucking body? I mean, where they do that at?" I yelled.

"Ma'am, will you please calm down?"

"Calm down? You want me to calm down? How the fuck am I supposed to calm down when I'm only days away from burying my best friend and y'all can't find her fucking body? Hell, what the fuck am I supposed to do?"

"Ma'am, I understand that you're upset, but will you please calm down a bit?" he implored.

"I ain't about to do a damn thing until y'all find my friend's body!" Fuck he think this is—how the fuck you call me to rush over here—tell me that y'all can't find her body—then tell me to calm down? Nigga, please, I'm from New Orleans. We don't know what calm is. Hell, no wonder his ass needed me to come in early. I bet he wish that he would've told me this shit over the phone now.

"Ma'am, if you don't calm down, I'm going to have to call security," he pleaded, which pissed me off more.

"Call 'em. You think I'd give a lovely fuck? How you gonna call ya fake-ass flashlight cops on me when you should've called the police when y'all couldn't find Mimi's fucking body? Man, please!" I said, waving my hand as if I was dismissing him. "Better yet, I'll do you a favor."

Pulling out my phone, I scrolled through my call list looking for a number. When I found the number that I was looking for, I hit the SEND button and waited for the call to connect. I looked over at Ralph who was watching my every move. Rolling my eyes, I stepped away from his desk.

"Hello, may I speak with Detective Webber, please?" I tapped my foot as I waited for an answer.

"Detective Webber isn't here right now. May I take a message?" she asked.

"Does he have a cell phone or something?" I asked. I didn't need this bitch to take no message for me right now, I needed to talk to Detective Webber before I went to jail.

"He's not in, and I don't have his cell number. If you tell me what the problem is, I'd be happy to relay the message to him when he gets here."

"Yeah, yeah, yeah. Tell him that Troy Miller called, and it would be in his best interest to call me back ASAP."

Looking at Ralph, I growled, "Y'all got two days to find Amina's body . . . or else."

Walking back to his desk, I grabbed my purse and headed for the door. I stopped right before I put my hand on the doorknob and looked back. "Oh, and it would be in your best interest to have my money back into my bank account today," I ordered, slamming the door on my way out. I don't give a fuck who he is and what he do. He better have my money back in my shit today, or I'ma pay his ass a personal visit. I'm tired of playing nice to every-fuckin'-body. Playing nice don't get ya ass nowhere in this world anymore. Fuck, this was only extra shit for me to add to my list of drama. *How could these people really lose a whole fucking body, bruh?* I kept repeating the same question in my head.

Walking into the hallway, I instantly froze in my tracks. *Shit, I forgot that I don't know how to get the fuck up out of here,* I thought.

Walking back to Ralph's office, I opened the door to see him leaning on the desk with his head in his hands. "Yo, come help me get out of here." He jumped as if I'd scared his ass. Hell, he works in a funeral home. His ass shouldn't be scared of anything.

"Okay, could you give me a second please?" he asked. Fuck if I care about his issues. All I wanted right now was to get away from his ass and out of this creepy-ass building.

"Okay," I said. Walking back into the office, I took a seat and waited for him to do whatever the fuck he asked me to give him a second to do. While I was waiting, I sent a text to Mark and asked where he was. I looked up just in time to see Ralph staring at me. Shit, this nigga is really starting to creep me the fuck out.

"Look, are you going to stare at me or are you going to show me the way out of here?" I snapped. He didn't say anything. He just placed his hand under his chin and continued to stare.

"Look, it's bad enough that y'all ain't got my girl's body and shit, but you staring at me and not saying shit isn't doing shit for me other than creeping me out!" I screamed, getting up from the chair that I was seated in. "Fuck this! I'm about to find my own fucking way outta this bitch."

"Ma'am, please," he begged, but I ignored his ass. I didn't have time to be sitting there, and neither did his ass when he needed to be calling around looking for answers as to what the fuck happened to Mimi's body. I left his ass in that creepy-ass room hollering as I made my way to the front of the building.

I made it to where Kayla was sitting when he came up right behind me speed walking. "Ma'am, uh, Ms. Miller, please," he begged once again.

"What? What could you possibly have to say to me that would make me feel better right now, huh?" I asked, stopping to turn around. He just stood there with this dumb look on his face. "I thought so. Kayla, come on, let's go."

"Is everything all right, sir?" the little lady asked when she saw me frantically trying to leave.

"Yes, Betty, everything is fine," he said raising his hand up to her.

I ain't gave a fuck about him or Betty. All I wanted to do was get the hell out of there before I caught a case in this bitch. After getting Kayla, I hurriedly made my way out of the building. I was planning to head straight to the police station to see Detective Webber. Somebody was about to give me some fucking answers, and I meant right damn now.

I was putting Kayla in the car when Ralph came walking my way. I hurriedly shut her door and moved to the driver's door.

"Hold on, wait, Ms. Miller. There's something I need to tell you," he implored, attempting to stop me.

"You've said all that you could possibly say. What could you have left to tell me?" I asked, not bothering to turn around.

"It's about Ms. Washington," he replied, stopping me in my tracks. Turning around, I gave him a stone-faced look.

"Look, I don't know what type of games you trying to play, but I ain't playing them with you."

"This isn't a game. What I'm about to tell you is serious."

"Shoot."

"Wha . . . What?" he stammered as he stood there with his hands raised in the air, looking pitiful.

"It means start talking," I explained, shaking my head. "I wasn't really going to shoot you."

"Oh, okay," he sighed with relief, messing with the tie around his neck. He stood there staring at me once again.

"Umm, today would be nice." I threw my hands up, exasperated.

"Well, when you came to me and ask me to take care of your sister's body, I agreed to do it. I went to pick up the body, but the people at the hospital morgue said that the body was unavailable. I asked them where the body was, and why it wasn't available for pickup. They told me to take that up with the lead detective on the case, a Detective Webber. That same day, I went to his office down at the police station to ask him what was going on, and he told me basically the same thing."

Ralph took a deep breath, exhaled, and then continued. "He also told me that if anyone was to ask about the body, I had to pretend I had the body and that when you came to see about her, to tell you that the body was cremated. I told him I couldn't lie to the people I service because I have a reputation to uphold, so he told me to say that the body was lost and whatnot. When you came in, I was supposed to suggest that you have a closed casket funeral for Ms. Washington."

"Hold up. So you mean to tell me that the whole time, you *never* had the body and that Detective Webber is doing some type of cover-up thingy?" I asked in disbelief.

"Yes, uhh, yes, ma'am, that's what I'm saying," he replied, playing with his tie again.

"Uh-huh, and he didn't tell you what happened to the body either?" I asked, making sure that he was telling the truth.

"No, ma'am, I never got close to her body because it wasn't there when I went to pick it up."

"Okay, thank you for telling me that," I said, completely blown away.

"You're welcome," he replied, looking relieved, and then he walked off.

I was about to get in my car when a white piece of paper caught my attention. Walking to the front of the car, I removed the paper from the windshield wiper and opened it. Once again, someone was leaving me notes and shit. *Who has time to be following people around and shit?* Taking a quick glance around, I didn't see anyone. Putting the note in my pocket, I hopped in my car and headed straight for the gas station. I was about to pay Detective Webber a visit. It was time for someone to give me some answers.

I made it to the police station in record time. I was lucky that I didn't get a ticket or have an accident, because I broke all types of traffic laws. Truthfully, being stopped by the police was the last thing on my mind. I needed to see Detective Webber now.

Pulling into the parking lot, I quickly found a parking space and got out. My nerves were so bad that I almost forgot about Kayla in the car until she started knocking on the window.

"Aww, baby, Auntie's so sorry. You okay?" I asked, kissing her on her forehead.

"Yeah, I'm fine, Auntie Troy."

"Okay, well, come on, then." We started walking to the front of the building, and I'm sure I looked like a madwoman, the way I was walking. I wasn't playing, though. Someone was about to give me some damn answers, or else I would be going to jail. Fuck all that other shit.

I literally made it to the door in seconds, that's how fast I was walking. Poor Kayla was struggling to try to keep up with me. Once I made it through the door, I went straight to the front desk. "Umm, good afternoon. Is Detective Webber in?" I asked the woman sitting behind the desk. "It's really important."

"I'm not sure. Can you have a seat while I check for you?"

"Yeah, sure, okay," I responded, grabbed Kayla by the hand, and went to look for a chair. The police station seemed packed today.

I sat there with my legs shaking, nervous as fuck, as I waited for this fat bitch to find out if Detective Webber was here. My nerves were too bad for this shit. I took my phone out of my purse and called Mark.

"Hey, ma, I was just about to call you. Where y'all at? We're here waiting on y'all," his voice boomed through the phone.

"I don't think that I'm going to be able to make it to the mall. I'm at the police station right now. I'm going to need y'all to meet me here ASAP," I hoarsely whispered.

"What's wrong? What are you doing at the police station?" he asked, sounding all worried.

"It's a long-ass story, but I'll tell you once you get here." I blew air out in frustration.

"Well well well, what do we have here?" I heard a voice say from my left. Turning, I spotted the same bitch whose ass I kicked the same day Mimi died.

"Hold on right quick, Mark." Getting up, I walked over to her.

"Bitch, what the fuck do you want, huh? Right now is not the time for you to be playing with me," I hissed at her. If she knew better, she'd see that right now wasn't a good idea to come fucking with me. I already had a lot of frustration and anger built up in me, and if she wasn't careful, she'd be foolish enough to make me whoop her ass in the police station.

"I still owe you one, bitch. Don't think the shit is over, because it's far from being over. I can't get your bitch-ass friend since she's maggot food, but I sure as hell can get you," Jade laughed like the shit was funny.

When she said that, I blacked out. Taking the phone that I had in my hand, I punched her dead in her face with it, drawing blood instantly. I ain't gave a fuck if we was in the police station or not, that ho was asking for it, so I was about to give it to her.

"Ho, I told you that right now was not the time for you to be fucking with me, but, no, you wanted to take it there," I snarled, giving that ho a two-piece combo to the side of her face. She tried pulling my hair, but I wasn't about to have that. I snatched her by her fucked-up weave and swung her into a row of chairs. Walking over to her, I began to stomp that bitch all in her face, her stomach, her back—shit, all over. I was trying to paint the floor with that bitch's blood. I was in pain, and I wanted someone else to feel just how much pain I was in. I went to kick her again, but some big dude suddenly picked me up.

"Fuck that shit, put me down. I told that ho not to come fucking with me, but she asked for the shit," I screamed as I tried to get loose.

"Ma'am, you're going to have to calm down," he said firmly, holding me tighter.

"I ain't gotta do shit, but stay black and die. Now let me go," I yelled, but he refused to loosen his tight hold on me.

"I'll let you go when you calm down."

"Okay, I'm calm then," I said as I stopped fighting and let my body go limp.

"Okay, I'm about to let you go, so don't try anything."

"Yeah, all right, I ain't gonna do nothing. Just let me go," I said softly. He was putting me down when this bitch screamed across the room at me.

"Y'all let that bitch attack me, and I'm pregnant. Bitch, on my momma I'ma fuck you up, I swear to God I'm going to fuck you up," she yelled. I broke away from dude's loosened grip and tried to charge her ass, but I didn't get far before he grabbed me again.

I hollered, "Fuck you! I'd love to see you try, ho. I'm going to fuck yo' slow ass up, just like I did the last two times." They restrained me again, but this time, they took me to one of those interrogation rooms to cool down.

"Ma'am, you're going to have to be still," the man who was holding me said.

"Why I gotta be still? I ain't said two words to that bitch. She came over there, fucking with me. So I gave her the ass whooping she was asking for." I squirmed, sitting on the steel chair.

"Uh-huh," was all he said as he closed the door, leaving me to think about what had just happened.

"Fuck," I said, realizing what I had just done. I had completely forgotten just that fast that I had Kayla with me, but that's how I get when I black out. I tend to forget shit. I sat there with my legs shaking as I waited for someone to come into the room. *How could I be so stupid? If I go to jail, Kayla won't have nobody. It's bad enough that she done lost both her parents. I don't want her to have to live in a foster home because of me.*

I was about to get up when someone came walking through the door. "Okay, young lady, are you calm enough to talk?" he asked, taking a seat in the chair across from me.

"Yeah, I'm good now," I said, still shaking my legs.

"Well, okay. What's your name?" he asked

"My name is Troy Miller," I replied.

"Well, Mrs. Miller—"

"No, it's *Ms.* Miller. I'm not married."

"Okay, Ms. Miller. Are you aware that you were fighting in the middle of a police station?" He leaned back, folding his arms across his chest.

"Well, like I said earlier, she came at me. I tried to tell her to leave me alone, because I know that we were indeed in the middle of the police station, but she didn't. She touched my nigga nerve, and I whooped her ass." I folded my arms across my chest, mimicking what he just did. "Now, if I'm going to be arrested, just arrest me. If not, can I please get out of here and go see about my niece? I'm sure she's out there looking for me."

"Today is your lucky day, Ms. Miller. Since we are, in fact, very busy, and a lot of folks stated that you didn't, in fact, start the altercation, you will not be arrested," he said, uncrossing his arms. It felt like a huge weight lifted off my shoulders, not because I was afraid, but because I was relieved. I knew Kayla didn't have anyone down here, which probably would've led to her being in DCFS services. I didn't need that right now.

"But next time, Ms. Miller, think before you decide to start fighting someone right in the middle of the police station."

"Okay, thank you. Am I free to go now?" I asked, ready to get the hell up out of here. It was evident that Detective Webber wasn't in his office either. I wasn't tripping, because I was bound to see his ass one way or another.

"Yes, you may go," he said, getting up from his chair. Opening the door, I could see Kayla waiting on me with Mark and Jayden. I walked over to her and noticed that she had tearstains on her face. I kneeled down in from of her and pulled her close to me.

"Kayla, baby, Auntie Troy is really sorry. I didn't mean to leave you like that, but it was out of my control," I said, apologizing to her. She didn't say anything; all she did was nod her head and hugged me back. I felt so bad for putting her in this position. I knew that times were hard on her, and here I go, making the shit worse.

"Come on, let's get out of here," I exhaled, grabbing her hand.

"'Sup, ma," Jayden said to me. He then turned and looked back and forth at Kayla and me. I'm pretty sure he was thinking that she looked like Mimi.

"Is this Mimi's—" he began to say.

"Yes, this is Mimi's daughter, Kayla," I finished his sentence.

"Yeah, but—" he started to say, but I ended up cutting him off again.

"I'll explain later," I replied, because I could already see the wheels spinning in his head.

"Okay." His eyes were still fixed on Kayla.

"Hey, handsome," I said, placing a kiss on Mark's lips.

"Hey, beautiful, I see you're around here being bad as usual," he chuckled, placing his arms around my waist.

"I didn't go looking for trouble this time. It found me," I corrected him.

"Yeah, I know. Shorty here told us a little something about what happened," he said, nodding toward Kayla.

"Is that right?" I asked, looking at her. Nodding her head, she flashed me an innocent smile.

"All right, y'all come on," Mark said, leading the way for us.

On my way out, I stopped by the front desk and left a message for Detective Webber. When I was done, I caught up with Mark, Jayden, and Kayla, who were waiting for me by the door.

"Okay, now we can leave," I said to them. Walking outside, I realized that it had gotten dark and there was a slight breeze. It was definitely cooler than earlier.

"Where y'all parked at?" I asked as soon as we made it to the parking lot.

"We're over here," Jayden replied, pointing to the opposite direction of the parking lot.

"Okay, cool, I'm over here. I'm going to just go and get my car and meet y'all over there," I said to them.

"All right, that's cool," Jayden said, and then they walked off. I took my time as I began walking to my car. I needed that breath of fresh air to clear my mind. Lord knows I was having a really bad day, and I hoped this day wouldn't get any worse.

Once I made it to my car, I fished around in my pocket for my keys, but instead of finding them, I found the note left on my car earlier today at the funeral home. I completely forgot about that note until now. Come to think about it, I still got the other note sitting in my purse. Sighing heavily, I remembered the keys were in my purse, so I dug them up from the bottom.

Opening the door, I waited until Kayla got in before I plopped down in the driver's seat. I feel like the weight of the world is on my shoulders, and there's no way to relieve the shit.

Pulling my phone out of my purse, I scrolled through my phone for a name and number that I vowed to never contact again. I sat there stuck, tossing around the thought, *Should I call him or not?* I kept going back and forth with myself until I finally said fuck it and just hit the TALK button.

My heart damn near jumped out of my chest as I waited for someone to answer the phone. I just wanted to hang up, but I know that I couldn't, because I needed the help. I already know that Mark and Jayden have their hands full trying to find Kaylin, with no luck. I can't bring this to them too. That's too much shit to pile on their plates. All I need is his help this one last time, and then I promised myself that I wouldn't contact him anymore.

"Hello," a chick said. I pulled the phone away from my ear to see if I had dialed the right number, because I knew Weedy wouldn't have no chick answering his phone. When I indeed realized that I had, in fact, dialed the right number, I placed the phone back to my ear.

"Hello," she repeated again.

"Umm, hello, can I speak to Weedy, please?" I asked in a nice tone.

"Uhhh, who is this, and what do you want with Weedy?" she asked with a slight attitude.

"Who I am shouldn't matter to you, because I didn't call your phone nor did I call to talk to you. I called to talk to Weedy," I replied with just as much attitude. "Now, can you please give Weedy *his* phone?"

"Hold up, boo, you tripping. Who you are does, in fact, matter to me, because Weedy is *my* man."

She sounded stupid. I know this chick had to be dumb as fuck, because I never knew Weedy to wife no chick. Hell, he ain't even wifed me, and I had his heart, so I know this bitch was lying.

"So, I'ma ask you again. Who are you, and what do you want with Weedy?"

"Look, trick, right now is not the time for you to be trying to play all these childish-ass games. I don't care if Weedy's your man or not, just put the nigga on the phone," I screamed. I was getting heated with this bitch and her twenty damn questions.

"Look, bitch, in case you didn't get the message when I said it the first time, you ain't speaking to Wendell. Now you can state what you want or hang the phone up. It's your choice, but just know you ain't speaking to Weedy."

"Bitch, look, I don't know why yo' simple ass over there playing Madame Secretary on a nigga's phone for, but I can tell you that, if I was within miles of you, I'd come and show you a thing or two. It's obvious that you have some doubts about yo' nigga, but let me tell you something right quick. I don't want Weedy—"

This bitch ass interrupted me midsentence. "Good, because you wasn't going to get him!" She sounded like a fuckin' fourteen-year-old who was about to get into a fight over her high school boyfriend.

"Boo, if only you knew about the history that Weedy and I have, you wouldn't be coming out of your mouth like that. I done been there and done that shit already. I don't want nothing like Weedy. Trust me if I wanted him, you'd be gone. All I gotta tell him is that I'm coming back home, and yo' ass is done for," I said with confidence. "Trust me, you can have that nigga to yourself, but then again, no, ya can't. He's a liar, a cheater, and he can never keep his dick in his pants. Why the fuck you think I left home? I ain't had time for a nigga thinking he could do all kinds of shit like I didn't have any feelings. He's selfish and only thinks about himself and his own happiness."

I sucked my teeth at this silly ho and finished schooling her. "Yeah, you might be sleeping over at his house, riding shotgun sometimes, and getting a li'l change, but know this, boo. Weedy is going to be Weedy, regardless. That shit there is basic. Any bitch with a pussy can do that. Lemme ask you something, though. Do he still stay out all times of the night? Got you fighting bitches in public like you done lost ya mind? Do he leave you in the middle of the night to go only God knows where? Have random hoes popping up at his house?

Does his phone stay ringing so much that he has to cut it off?"
I asked that ho, recalling some of the shit that I went through
with his ass. When she didn't answer me, I knew what type of
day it was.

"I thought so. Trust me, you can have that headache, because
I for damn sure don't want or need it," I said, setting her
straight. "Now when Wendell comes back or when you bring
him back his phone that you're going through, tell him that
Troy called looking for him."

I hung up the phone; I had no energy left in me to fuss with
her ass no more. I already proved my point to that simple
ho, and I knew damn well that she was snooping through
his phone. Weedy ain't going to change for nobody, not even
himself. He's gonna forever be the same low-down, selfish,
dirty nigga he was when I left his ass. Throwing my phone
and purse on the passenger's seat, I started the car and went
to meet Jayden and Mark on the other side of the parking lot.

If only if Mimi was here, none of this would be happening,
I thought as I made it to where the guys were parked.

"Damn, 'bout time. I thought you got lost or something, ma,"
Mark said as I pulled up right beside them.

"Nah, I was just on the phone," I replied, putting the car in
park.

"Well, that explains why you wasn't answering the phone
either," he said, being sarcastic.

"Look, you guys should follow me home. There are a few
things that we have to discuss before the funeral next week," I
said, ignoring his last remark. I looked at Mark and rolled my
eyes. Now was not the time for that shit. Besides, I had too
much shit on my plate already.

"All right, cool," Jayden replied, looking from me to Mark.

"All right, follow me then," I said, raising the window up. I
pulled out of the parking space and hit the main road, prepar-
ing to drive the twenty-five minutes it took to get to my house.

On my way home, I decided to call my cousin Asia back
in Louisiana. I was tripping about the time, because they
was already an hour behind us. Shit, her ass was prolly up
anyways. She's like an owl; she sleeps all day so that she'll
have enough energy to walk the streets and party at night, so
I know her ass was up.

"Hello," she said, answering the phone.

"'Sup, girl, you called?" I asked in the fakest happy voice I could summon up.

"Oh, yeah, I called earlier."

"I knew. What's up? You found anything out yet?" I asked.

"I don't have much of nothing yet. The only thing I can tell you is that it was true when people said that Kaylin and Stacy had a nine-year-old son. Y'all didn't know because he sent her and the child somewhere, but she came back the minute Mimi left town. He had her staying in one of his properties and everything, but he ended up moving her to Atlanta when she threatened to tell Mimi about them and their son. Some shit was going around about how he wanted her closer to him so that he can keep an eye on her and shit."

"Damn, so the shit was true. Kaylin really did have another child this whole time, and he hid that shit from her. I wonder how he managed to do that, considering all them money-hungry bitches New Orleans got." I wondered how he hid her for so long. "I know somebody had to have known about that shit."

"That's because he didn't have her out here in New Orleans. He had her hiding out in the country in some little-ass town called Edgard. Bitch, there ain't shit out there but sugarcane fields and stuff. They don't even have a real fucking store out there. So I don't know how she managed to make it."

"Well, did you find out where they are now?" I asked, wanting to know how good her source was.

"Hell, nobody has seen them down here. They even went looking in Edgard for them, but the house was all boarded up and shit like they hadn't been there in years," she replied, smacking her lips.

"All right, thank you," I said, trying to rush her off the phone.

"Thank you, nothing. What happened to the money that I was supposed to be getting from this whole ordeal?" she asked like the true bitch I knew that she was. She ain't gave a fuck if we were family or not. She'd try to con her own damn mother or give her up for money. That ho wasn't no good for no-damn-body, not even herself.

"Girl, I'm going to send you the money," I lied through my teeth. I wasn't about to send that ho a dime of my money. "Girl, I'll send your money in the morning. Make sure you call me."

"Uh-huh, all right. I'll call you in the morning," she said and hung up.

I looked at my phone like I was crazy, because I know that ho ain't just hang up on me. That's why her ass was going to wait for me to send her that money, and the way I'm set up, she'll be waiting forever for it. Placing my phone on the seat, I continued to drive in the direction of my house.

"Kayla," I called out to her, but she didn't answer. I looked in the rearview mirror to see that she was knocked out on the backseat. Poor baby, I know she had to be tired. She done had yet another hard day.

On my way home, I happened to pass by the gas station where Mimi caught Kaylin cheating. That was the same day that Mimi and I whooped Kaylin's side piece's ass, and also the same day that Mimi met Jayden, and I met Mark. Even though it was sad to find Kaylin cheating yet again, faith had brought her Jayden. Her happiness didn't last long enough before Kaylin decided to kill her, though.

I thought, *Life can be a total bitch at times.*

Pulling up on my street, I noticed the same black car that was parked down by the salon now parked on my street. Driving past my house, I decided to circle the block. Pulling my phone out, I dialed Mark's number.

"What's wrong, ma? Why are you circling the block?" he asked, noticing I was passing up my building.

"Did y'all see that black car that was parked down the street?" I asked in a low tone, as if the person could hear me.

"Ma, why are you talking so low? What black car? You talking 'bout that black Altima?"

"Yeah, that car."

"What about it?"

"Well, today, I received a threatening note when I went by the salon and found it broken into. While I was on my way to head out to the mall, that same car was parked a few blocks down from the salon, and—"

"So what? You think whoever is in that car is stalking you?" he asked, cutting me off.

"I'm not finished. I stopped by McDonald's on my way to the mall, and when I was leaving out of the parking lot, I happened to see that same car again. To make matters worse, when I came from the funeral home earlier, I received another note. So you tell me if you think I'm being stalked or not," I replied, getting a little worried. Three times in one day . . . Whoever that is ain't playing no games.

"All right, sit back, we're going to handle it."

"What do you mean?"

"Like I said, we're going to handle it."

"But I wanna come too. I need to know who that is and why they stalking me."

"Fall back, ma." He hung up the phone.

I sat there as I watched them pass by me on some detective shit. I wanted so badly to follow them, but I remembered that Kayla was in the backseat, so I just parked my car on the side of the road.

"Oh, yeah," I exclaimed, snapping my fingers. I popped the trunk of my car and got out to retrieve my pink case. I had completely forgotten about my piece I had in the trunk. Grabbing the case, I got back inside of my car, closed the door, and locked it. Once I was inside comfortably, I opened the case and ran my hand up and down my pink and black 9 mm. Mimi had a purple and black one just like it.

I still remember when Mimi and I got our guns about two years ago. It was closing time at the salon, and we were the only two left. We were just about to head to our cars when someone came walking up behind us. Being as though it was nighttime and we were in the back of the salon, no one was able to see us.

"Put y'all hands up," the man said from behind. Not wanting to piss him off, we did like we were told and put our hands in the air.

"You, give me your purse," he said to Mimi.

"Look, I ain't got shit on me, so you're wasting your time," she replied, giving up her purse.

"Uh-huh. Gimme that bracelet, watch, and them earrings too," he gestured, taking all of her jewelry.

"You ain't getting my jewelry, so you can go head 'bout ya business," she protested, folding her hands across her chest. I looked at her like she was crazy.

"Girl, you better give that man that shit before he kills us," I said, turning to her with my hands still raised above my head.

"Yeah, you better listen to your friend before I blow y'all brains out all over this alley," he said, with his shit-smelling breath.

"I ain't giving you shit, and what you need to do is throw a Tic Tac in ya mouth," Mimi replied, scrunching her nose up in disgust.

"Bitch, I ain't playing with yo' ass. I'm fixing to kill yo' ass, fo' real."

"Wait, wait, wait," I called out, trying to turn around.

"Bitch, if you turn around, I'll blow her brains out," he said, stopping me. I hurriedly turned back to my original position and threw my hands back up.

"Mimi, just give the man the jewelry," I cried out. I was more than a little scared.

"All right," she said, finally giving in. She removed her jewelry and gave it to him.

"Yours too," he said to me. I quickly removed my things and gave them to him.

"Now, I'm going to back away. When I count to ten, y'all can turn around. If y'all try to turn around sooner than that, I will shoot y'all," he warned, backing up.

We nodded our heads in agreement, as he started to count.

"Girl, something ain't right," Mimi said, looking at me.

"Girl, just chill and let the nigga go 'head," I said to her.

"Nah, I'm telling you that this shit ain't right." She lowered her arms and started turning around.

"Turn around!" the dude's voice screamed from farther away.

Mimi ignored his command and turned all the way around. "Bitch, I told you that something was funny. The nigga don't

*even have on no shoes, so how the hell he got a gun?" she
yelled and started walking quickly toward him.*

*"Mimi, girl, chill out before that man shoots you!" I hissed
from behind her.*

*"With what—his fingers?" she asked, running behind him.
I turned around to find him running away, with her in
hot pursuit.* Hell, if he had a gun, then why in the hell is he
running from us? *I thought, taking off after them.*

*We chased him for a solid five minutes but were unable to
catch him.*

*"Bitch, I told you something was funny about that shit. We
got robbed out of our shit by a homeless nigga with no shoes
and no damn gun," she gasped, stopping to catch her breath.*

*"Shit, how the hell we were supposed to know that?" I
broke out laughing.*

*"Why the hell you laughing?" she asked, looking at me
crazy.*

*"Because we just got robbed by a homeless man," I hollered,
laughing some more. She looked at me for a minute before
she joined me.*

*"Bitch, that shit ain't funny. Kaylin gave me that stuff when
we first started going together."*

"Well, it's gone now."

*"Come on, let's get out of here before we get robbed again,"
she said, laughing once more.*

I laughed to myself as I sat there, remembering that day.
It was funny as hell to get robbed by a homeless man with
no gun. Needless to say, a couple of weeks later, we were
both licensed to carry, and trust me, we carried our guns
everywhere we went.

I grabbed my phone to call Mark so that I could see
what was taking them so long, but then I noticed that my
phone was about to go dead. I looked for my car charger, but
I couldn't find it. Then I remembered that it might be in the
glove compartment. Taking my keys out of the ignition, I
unlocked the compartment box. When I looked in the glove

compartment, I didn't see my charger, but I did run across the phone that Mimi gave me.

I'll just use this one for right now, I thought as I grabbed the phone. I was so thankful when I saw that it had a full battery.

Taking out my phone, I copied Mark's number into the spare phone and hit the SEND button. I was about to put the phone to my ear when someone started knocking on the window. I didn't look up. I figured it was Mark and Jayden standing there, so I just grabbed my keys and turned them in the ignition, rolling down the window.

"Hello," Mark said, answering the phone.

"Why y'all knocking on the window like that?" I asked him.

"What you mean? We're over here by the black car. No one was in it when we got here, so we decided to look through it."

Everything he'd just said fell on deaf ears as I looked up just in time to see the gun sticking through my window.

Dropping the phone, I said, "If you've come to rob me, you're going to be sorry, because I ain't got shit."

"I didn't come here to rob you, bitch," I heard a female voice say.

"Oh, yeah? What did you come here to do then?"

"I came here to seek revenge," she said, then busted me in the face with the gun.

"Look, bitch, if you think I'm scared of you or that I'm going to beg and plead like some soft bitch, then you got the wrong bitch." I spit out a mouthful of blood.

"Good, because I don't want you to be scared. I want you just how you was when y'all hoes jumped me." I immediately knew who she was as soon as I heard that.

"Bitch, first of all, we didn't jump you, and I can't believe you'd pull a ho-ass move like this," I replied, my hand carefully searching for the gun that was somewhere beside me. "How are you going to try to come after me with a gun? Bitch, it was a fistfight. Get over that shit."

"Nah, I ain't gettin' over shit. I've been trying to get in contact with Kaylin for forever now, and it looks like he done got ghost and shit on me," she said, sounding like a lovesick groupie. Hell, if that was me, I wouldn't give a fuck after that.

What chick you know would still want to be with a nigga after he done let you get ya ass whooped. I see Kay done succeeded at slinging his dick game the right way again. First, it was that crazy bitch Jade, and now this looney ho done come at me out-of-pocket.

"So, that's what this shit is all about? Kaylin not answering you?" I asked just as I found the gun, wrapped my hand around it, and gently laid it in my lap.

"Nah, bitch, this is about y'all hoes jumping me."

"Like I said, we didn't jump you. This is about Kaylin, and you know it. Y'all side pieces be killing me with that shit. Y'all know from the jump that a nigga taken, and y'all go falling all in y'all's feelings over his ass. Then y'all be wanting to go postal and shit when the nigga leave ya ass. But you shouldn't fault nobody but yourself, and knowing Kaylin, he told you about Mimi from the get-go. So stop ya bitching, please," I said, busting that ho's bubble.

"Bitch, you got me mistaken with the next bitch."

"Nah, I got just the right bitch," I said, bringing the gun up to her eye level. The bitch's eyes got big as saucers.

Suddenly, I heard gunshots and a child crying in the background. I looked to see if the bitch was still there, but she wasn't.

"Damn," I screamed as I suddenly remembered Kayla was in the backseat of the car. I quickly said a silent prayer, asking God not to let her be hurt because I wouldn't be able to handle that.

"Kayla!" I shouted as I tried to turn around in my seat to calm her down. Excruciating pain in my chest stopped me in my tracks. I felt something damp and cold against my skin, and I looked down at my shirt to see that it was soaked in blood. "Kay . . . baby . . ." I started to drift off. The last thing I remembered was hearing two more shots and someone pulling me out of the car, right before everything went black.

Jade

I can't believe that I teamed up with a bitch like that. I don't know where and how Kaylin picked his little side pieces, but he needed to start doing better. I gave that bitch one little assignment—one simple assignment—and she couldn't do that right. When I first got in contact with her, I thought that she was going to chicken out, but she didn't. She actually was eager to assist me in finding Kaylin and seeking revenge on Mimi and Troy. It was an undercover mission, though, because I lied and told her that I was Kaylin's sister and that Mimi and Troy had did something to my brother since I couldn't find him. I'm sure if I would've told her that I was also one of Kaylin's side pieces, that she wouldn't have helped me. Hell, I wasn't dumb enough to do that when I knew that I needed her help. I couldn't do all of this shit alone. I needed an extra person.

Finding out that Mimi was dead was a plus. Hell, if she wasn't dead, I was going to kill that bitch anyway. From the first moment that I met Kaylin and he told me that he had a woman, I hated her. I didn't even know the bitch, and I wanted her gone. She was always in my way. I could never have Kaylin to myself because of her. Now that's she's dead, the shit should be easy. Now all I gotta do is get that bitch Troy out of the way and find Kaylin.

Getting to Troy could be a task because she has two little bodyguards that are always by her side or right around the corner. Finding Kaylin will be easy. His ass don't know that I downloaded an app on his phone that lets me track his location. I wasn't worried about him right now. I was going to get to him later, because right now, I needed to finish this shit with these bitches first.

***

I wanted that ho Troy bad. She took the only thing that I had tied to Kaylin, and now I wanna take her life. I thought the bitch would've been an easy target, but I should've known better. I guess after we trashed the salon and wrote them letters, we spooked that ho. She went and got her some bodyguards. Hell, even without the bodyguards, she looked like she was able to hold her own. I saw that when she blasted Star twice. She was going to slip up, though. When she does, her ass will be mine. I'm going to just fall back for a minute and let that ho think that Star was acting by herself. The minute she decides to let her guard down is when I'm going to strike.

Since I had to ditch the car and travel on foot, I used that time to come up with a plan. I needed a way to get close to Troy without her niggas being there. I wasn't trying to end up like Star. I just knew that she was dead somewhere by now. Hell, if she wasn't dead when dude threw her in the trunk, I knew they killed her when they took her to her final destination. Either way, I didn't care.

I know y'all think that sounds cold, but, hell, I was going to kill her ass too. They just beat me to the punch and did the job for me. Why would I let her live when we both were after the same man? Shit, I wanted Mimi out of the picture. You think I'd let some other chick come in and be my competition? Hell to the no. I wanted Kaylin for myself, and I wasn't trying to share him. It was bad enough that I had to share him with Mimi when she was here. I ain't in the business of sharing no more.

Pulling out my phone, I decided to call Kaylin's phone. I know his ass wasn't still mad about what went down weeks ago. If he was, he needed to get over that shit because we were going to be together forever. *I must be tripping. Did the recording just say that the number has been disconnected?* I thought that I had misdialed, so I dialed the number again. Sure as hell, I got the same recording.

"I know this nigga ain't changed his number like a little bitch," I said, heated. "That's okay, I know how to find yo' ass." I went on the Internet to the site that let me find my iPhone, entered in his information, and waited for the app to tell me where he was. I almost threw my phone down when that thing came back with an error message.

"This shit must be wrong," I said, typing in the information again. When I got the same error message again, I nearly knocked over a trash can, that's how mad I was. "This nigga think he can play me. What he needs to know is that I can't be played. I'm the one who does the playing. Now I gotta put off handling that bitch Troy to find his ass!" I ranted.

I'm sure all the people that passed me by thought that I was some type of crazy person, but I'm not crazy. I tried telling that to my parents when they took me to see a shrink, but, no, they ain't want to listen to me. They insisted that I see that white bitch. That's why I had to toe tag they asses. I couldn't just sit on a couch all day and vent about my feelings. That wasn't for me. I was always one to do something, you know, take action. Which is why after I find Kaylin, I will handle Troy.

I was so busy talking to myself that I didn't realize I had made it to the gas station. Walking into the store, I asked the dude behind the counter to use the phone. He talked a lot of shit, but he still let me use it. He's lucky I ain't feel like fussing with his foreign ass, or else I would've gave him a piece of my mind. Instead, I simply called a cab, rolled my eyes, and threw his phone at him.

As I was leaving, he said some smart-ass shit in his native language. I just flipped his ass the bird and went outside to wait for my cab. Going to jail was not on my agenda. The only thing on my mind at this moment was finding Kaylin's ass.

Mimi

I can't say I'm happy to be here sitting in this hospital bed, but I'm happy to be alive and well. Well, I'm not actually well. In fact, I'm banged up pretty damn bad, but the fact that I'm still breathing works for me. So, yeah, you could say I'm thankful as hell right now.

I've only been up a few hours, but I feel like I can move a fucking mountain right now. Well, that's what I thought before I called myself getting out of the bed and busted my ass on that hard-ass hospital floor earlier. It took two nurses to get my ass off that floor, and I was shocked because my ass is skinny as fuck right now. I mean, I was never a big girl, but at least I had a little meat on my bones. Right now, I feel like a skeleton. I guess being in a medically induced coma for two weeks will do that to you.

The first person I wanted to call this morning was Kaylin, but for some strange reason, his phone was disconnected. I thought I was tripping when I called and heard the recording, but sure enough, when I called the second and third time, the same recording claimed that the number was disconnected or no longer in service. "What the fuck?" I said, looking at the phone in disbelief. "What the fuck is this nigga up to?"

I wanted and needed to hear his voice badly. I also wanted to find out why his ass wasn't here in this hospital room waiting for me to wake up. Oh, and where the hell are my kids and Troy? Where's my best friend? I can't believe she's not here with me right now. Something must be wrong, because I know that Troy would've been the first person I saw when I woke up. Instead, I'm looking at an empty room and four white walls.

Pushing the call button for the nurse, I waited patiently for them to send someone in the room. I made sure to keep my ass still this time, because I wasn't trying to have a repeat of last time. I didn't need these people detaining my ass again. I wanted to get my ass outta here as soon as possible so I could see what the hell was going on and where the hell everyone was at.

I was just about to use the phone when someone came walking through the door. Looking over by the door, I saw this short, little, eyeglass-wearing nurse enter. She was dressed in blue scrubs and wearing braids. She looked like she was in her forties, but whatever her age was—she wore it well.

"Hi, my name is Margie, and I'm going to be your nurse this morning." She held a medication tray in her hand.

"Hello," I replied. "How long have I been in here?"

"Hmm, let me see," she said, picking up my chart. "Well, it looks like you've been here about two weeks."

"Can you tell me what happened to me? How did I get here?"

"I'll get the doctor in here, and he'll be able to tell you everything, but in the meantime, do you need anything? Are you having any pain? Would you like something to eat or drink?"

"I could use something for the pain, but can I ask you something else?"

"Yes, ma'am."

"Please call me Mimi. Has anyone been by to see me these past two weeks?"

"Uhhh, not that I know of. The only one who been by to check on you is a detective," she said, nodding.

"Are you sure that no one's been by to see me?" I asked again for clarification.

"Yes, Mimi, I'm sure," she replied, nodding again.

"You wouldn't happen to have a name and number for the detective, would you?" Shit, if no one had any answers, he should have some.

"Hold on a minute and I'll go and see if he left it at the nurse's station."

"Okay, thank you, Margie." She was being so nice, and I thanked God for that. Some nurses wouldn't work one extra second to help you. They'd brush you off as if you didn't mean shit.

"I'm going to have to sit you up to check your bandages," she said, moving toward the head of the hospital bed.

"Oh, okay," I mumbled as I tried to sit up. Instantly, I felt a sharp pain and grimaced, leaning back on the pillows.

"Oh, no, I'll raise the bed up. That way, all you're going to have to do is lean forward a little bit," she reassured me.

"Okay."

First, she checked my vital signs, then when she was done, she raised the head of the bed slowly and threw on a fresh pair of gloves.

"Lean forward just a little bit. I'll help you." Margie reached over and held my shoulder, making sure that I didn't lean too far. I held on to her forearm, while she checked my bandages. "They're seeping a bit, so I'm going to get the doctor in here to take a quick peek and see what he wants me to do."

"Oh, okay. How many times was I shot?"

"You were shot a total of four times. You were lucky, though. You were within inches of your life. They thought you were dead until the coroner came and felt a faint pulse. You even flatlined a time or two on your way here, but they managed to get you back," Margie said, choking up and shaking her head. "Ain't God good? You were touched by an angel, honey."

I sat back and thought about what she had said, but the question that kept bouncing around in my mind was, *Who the hell shot me four times and left me for dead?* To my knowledge, I didn't have any beef with anyone down here, so I was clueless as to who would want me dead.

I was just about to about to ask her if she knew anything about what had happened to me when a man dressed in a red button-down, True Religion jeans, and some white Js came strolling through the door. I knew for a fact he wasn't a doctor, because he didn't have on a white coat. I also knew that he wasn't someone I was familiar with, so the burning question I needed to be answered was, *"Who the hell is he?"*

As if he was reading my mind or something, he said, "I'm Detective Webber, and I'm the lead detective that's working on your case."

With a confused look on my face, I simply blinked and said, "Okay."

I watched him as he stood there waiting for the nurse to finish what she was doing. I silently chuckled to myself thinking,

*His ass know he was good and wrong for that shit. He too
damn old to try to be dressing so young.* I don't know why,
but I hated the police. I never dealt with the law. I always took
matters into my own hands. People always told me to never
trust them boys in blue because they were full of shit.

"Okay, Mimi, I'm done. I just have to go and get the doctor
to take a look at your back and make sure that everything is
okay." Margie helped me lie back down on the bed, making
sure that I was comfortable. "In the meantime, I want you
to relax and not stress yourself out. Remember, if you need
anything, just push the call button and ask for Nurse Margie."

"Okay, thank you, Margie, I will."

"I'll be back to check on you within the hour."

"Okay, thanks again."

"Good afternoon, Detective," she nodded as she walked by
him.

"Afternoon, ma'am," he replied. He waited until she was
gone before he came closer to my hospital bed. Pulling up a
chair, he took a seat.

"Hello, Miss Washington, like I said earlier, I'm
Detective Webber," he said, putting on his glasses and
took out his pen and paper. "I came to see if you remember what happened to you two weeks ago when you were
shot. Do you remember anything?"

"Umm, uhh, I . . . I . . . I've been in here for two weeks?" I
asked, baffled.

"Yes, ma'am. I'm here to see if you remember anything
about that night so that we can catch the person who did this
to you."

I sat there silently as I scrolled through my memory bank
to see if I could remember anything, but nothing stood out.
The last thing I remembered was that I was sitting at home,
waiting on Kaylin to come. Kaylin had been spending a lot of
time away from home, and I'd decided that I was putting my
foot down that night. I was tired of his ass always being gone,
but—wait a minute—Margie and the detective said that I've
been in here for two weeks. *Who the fuck shot me? Where
are my kids? And, why the fuck have I been in here for two
weeks and no one has checked on me?*

Focusing my attention back on Detective Webber, I mumbled, "I'm sorry, but I can't seem to remember anything." I was being honest, because I really don't remember anything, and if I did, then I wasn't going to tell him. I was just going to let Kaylin handle whomever it was that shot me.

"Umm, do you know where my kids and my fiancé are? The nurse told me that no one has been by to see me since I've been here, except you. Did you all tell them not to come here?"

"Ma'am, the reason they haven't been here is because we can't locate them."

"You can't locate them? Were they shot too? Did they die?" I asked in a panic, trying to sit up. *What if whoever had shot me kidnapped them, or worse, killed them? Why aren't they able to find them?* The questions flowed through my mind faster than I could process them.

Everything that came out of his mouth was a blur. I heard him, but I didn't hear him at all. I was too busy trying to figure out where my family was.

"No, it's not like that. It seems that Mr. Williams was actually the one who shot you. He also killed Mr. Tyreek Carter, and then ran off with your kids."

"No, that can't be right. Why would Kaylin shoot me, and then run off with the kids?" I asked, confused. "That doesn't make any sense."

"Well, according to your sister Troy, you were planning on leaving him because you found out that he was cheating on you," he said, dropping another bomb on me. This shit was getting harder and harder to bear by the second. *When and how did I find out that Kaylin was cheating on me?* Again, I went into my memory bank, but I still can't remember anything.

"Ma'am, I know that this is a hard pill to swallow, and it's going to take some time for you to process it all. With the statements from your sister and other daughter, coupled with the evidence we have, rest assured that this will be an open-and-shut case once we catch him."

I was still stuck on the fact that he said Kaylin was the one who shot me. I couldn't get anything else to register right away. "Hold up—repeat that again. I think I heard you wrong just now."

"Umm, as I said, the facts are there. Mr. Williams shot you and Mr. Carter, and then took your kids," he summarized, clarifying what I thought I heard the first time.

I was flustered. This just couldn't be true. I refuse to believe that Kaylin would do something that low down and dirty to me, after all that we've been through. We had history, and history was supposed to mean something in life.

"Ma'am, I assure you that I have statements from both your sister Troy and your daughter, Kayla," he continued.

"Hold up, didn't you just say that Kaylin took my kids?" I asked, confused. "So how could my daughter give you a statement? Besides, her name is Kailay, not Kayla."

"Ms. Washington—"

"Call me Amina, please," I interrupted him.

"Okay, Amina. Like I said, Mr. Williams took your other kids. Your daughter Kayla is—"

"I told you that my daughter's name is Kailay, not Kayla! Now, while you over there telling me that Kaylin took my kids, how 'bout telling me what y'all over there doing to get them back?" I said. I was playing along with his game, up to a certain point, but fuck, I didn't have time for this shit right now.

"Ms. Washington, we're doing everything that we can to find them and bring them back."

"I told you to call me Amina, and you couldn't possibly be doing everything that you can, because you're sitting here with me, trying to sell me some bullshit-ass story about Kaylin shooting me and whatnot."

Sitting back in his chair, he wiped his face with his hand and just stared at me. I stared back, wondering who the hell he thought he was fooling.

"Ms. Washington, please listen to what I'm trying to tell you."

"No, I'm not about to listen to anything else you got to say unless you're telling me where Kaylin and my kids are!"

"Ma'am, like I said—" A sudden knock on the door interrupted his statement.

A tall, bald-headed, light-skinned man wearing a white coat walked through the door. I assumed this was my doctor.

"Good afternoon, Ms. Washington, I'm Doctor McKenley. I've been your doctor since you've been here."

"Afternoon, Doctor McKenley," I replied, still looking at the detective.

"Afternoon, Detective, is everything all right?" he asked, looking at me and then to Detective Webber.

"Afternoon, Doc," Webber said, rising up from his chair and reaching out his hand for a handshake. They shook hands, and he said, "Everything is fine. Ms. Washington is just having a hard time remembering what happened the night she was shot."

"Well, that's to be expected. Most coma patients sometimes suffer from temporary memory loss," Dr. McKenley explained.

"Okay, so how long do you think her memory will be gone?"

"I really can't tell you that. Everyone is different. Some people get their memory back within days, others within weeks, and some never recover it. There's no telling when her memory will come back, that's *if* it comes back at all."

I sat there halfway listening to what the doctor said. I was too busy thinking about what Detective Webber had said earlier about Kaylin shooting Tyreek and me, and then taking my kids, I desperately needed to remember what happened that day.

"So there's really no guarantee that my memory will come back?" I asked Dr. McKenley, my voice laced with fear.

"Right now, I'm not sure. You've been through a lot these past couple of weeks. You were shot four times, lost a lot of blood, and we gave you a blood transfusion. Not to mention that when you fell, you sustained severe head trauma. I know this may not be what you want to hear right now, and I'm sorry, but we just don't know what's going to happen. We're just going to have to wait and see," he said honestly.

I looked at both men as they looked at me with sympathy. I was both hurt and shocked. I couldn't believe that Kaylin had shot me, left me for dead, and disappeared with the kids without a second thought. What had happened to cause him to shoot me and leave me lying there to die? Thinking about all of this was making my head and my heart hurt.

"Uhh, how soon can I be discharged, Doctor?" I didn't have time to be sitting in this hospital. I needed answers, and I needed them now.

"I really can't say . . . a week or two maybe. It all depends on how quickly your body heals enough for you to safely—"

"Miss, you can't go anywhere. No one knows that you are alive, and we'd like to keep it that way until Mr. Williams is caught," Detective Webber interjected.

"You mean to tell me that *no one* knows I'm alive?" I asked, dumbfounded.

"Only the police and the staff here at the hospital know."

"Does Troy know?" I could feel my eyes getting watery.

"No, she doesn't, and I would like to keep it like that for the time being."

I sat there stuck. No wonder no one's here. They don't even know that I'm alive. I don't know what came over me, but the next thing I knew, I was shaking and sweating profusely.

"Ma'am," I heard someone say. The voice sounded far away, but I could barely make out what they were saying because I was in a daze. One minute I was calm, and the next minute, I was yanking and pulling on any and everything. I felt a stabbing pain in my back, but before it could fully register, I was trying to get out of the hospital bed.

"Get me some help," Dr. McKenley yelled at Webber, who took off immediately, but I was already too far gone. Any and everything that was in my path was knocked down and kicked over. I was in a rage, and I couldn't help myself. Finally, the doctor was able to grab ahold of me.

"Let go of me!" I screamed at the top of my lungs. Tears burned my eyes as I struggled to see. "Let me go!"

In five seconds, the room was filled with nurses trying to restrain me to the hospital bed. I tried to put up a fight, but one person against an army can only do so much. Eventually, they strapped me to the bed, still kicking and screaming, when I felt a pinch in my arm. Slowly, I stopped putting up a fight as my eyelids got heavy. I tried to fight it, but whatever they injected into me was winning the battle. My vision blurred as I looked at all the people it took to take down my little ass, and then I was off into oblivion.